THE DECOY

By

Chester Stern

Prologue

France, 5th June 2000

Colonel Gaston Le Tallec was irritated. He was more than irritated. He was angry. He was furious. But for the moment he would not allow his fury to show. His dignity was worth more than that. He would seethe inside for a while.

The veteran gendarmerie chief had seen it all during a 40-year career – murder, rape, robbery, fraud – and he was not accustomed to having his professional judgement called into question.

Bad enough that he should be summoned miles from his comfortable office to oversee a routine incident that his staff was more than capable of dealing with. But then to have his considered opinion ridiculed and be told what to think by an arrogant young upstart from Paris who was not even a policeman. That was too much.

It had begun with a wisp of white smoke spiralling skyward from a clearing in remote woodland near the village of La Cavalerie on the Larzac plateau in the South of France. No one paid any attention. Small fires were routine in rural farming areas.

But it was early evening and as the sun set behind the hills a local farmer, Albert Dufour, heard what he thought was an explosion coming from the forest that bordered his land. He set out to investigate.

He could see the smoke from the farmhouse but it took him almost an hour to reach the seat of the fire. Across the bumpy terrain his progress was slow even though he rode his most powerful tractor. Eventually he broke away from the potholed farm track and made his way up hill for almost a mile, over a field where his cows were grazing, towards the forest where he had first spotted the smoke. The woodland was dense but the farmer quickly noticed a gap in the vegetation where branches on younger saplings had been torn off and the undergrowth had been freshly pressed down. Something sizeable had broken through the trees to make a path. And, judging from the bruised state of the leaves, the incursion had been recent.

Dufour pushed on into the wood. It was now dusk and the trees shut out what little daylight remained so that he had to use the powerful headlights on the tractor to guide him. Soon he came upon a clearing. A grisly scene met his horrified gaze. The bark on the trees surrounding the clearing was burnt black and still crackling with tiny embers. The ground was baked dry and scorched. And in the centre of the clearing stood a car. At least it looked as though it had once been a car. Now it was just a pile of grotesquely twisted metal still hot to the touch. Molten in places. There were four wheels but the tyres had been incinerated to ash. The windows had been cracked and blown out by the heat. What remained was blackened with soot.

In the driver's seat was a body. Not so much a corpse as a skeleton with its knees drawn up in the foetal position and the right arm stretched out in a gesture of supplication. Where there was flesh remaining it had been baked to a crisp. Jet black. Flaky. And with a shiny texture like PVC. The head was missing.

The farmer took a torch from the tractor toolbox and peered through the car window. In the foot well of the passenger's side lay a crazily grinning skull with strips of ashen flesh waving eerily in the warm updraft of the rapidly cooling

4

convection. Alongside it was a scorched jerry can with the cap missing.

Two soldiers on patrol along the perimeter road of a nearby army firing range had also seen the fire and heard the explosion. They had made a telephone call to the local Gendarmerie. But summoning help from the *Brigade des Sapeurs-Pompiers* or the *Service d'Aide Medicale d'Urgence* was futile. It was all too late. The fire was out and the driver had been far beyond medical aid for a long time.

And now, eighteen hours on, the clearing had been transformed. Tape strung between the trees marked it out as a crime scene. A battery of portable floodlights illuminated the gloom of the dense forest. Four men and a girl dressed in white body suits with hoods over their heads and wearing surgical gloves were crawling over the remnants of the car – taking measurements and occasionally removing fragments of paint, metal or glass which they carefully placed in sealed plastic bags. Another man in a fluorescent yellow jerkin was taking photographs, mostly at his colleagues' direction, of the car and other areas of the clearing. On the crude pathway through which the car had smashed its way into the forest a dozen uniformed gendarmes were on their hands and knees picking through the vegetation searching for clues.

Colonel Le Tallec looked on dispassionately, his grizzled features contorted into a smirk of disdain. He was 57 years old and had come up the hard way. A boy soldier at seventeen. Cracking heads and dodging rocks during the Paris student riots of 1968. Service with the Foreign Legion. Decorated for bravery under fire in Algeria. Platoon commander of a strike unit in the elite GIGN counter-terrorist force. Slow progress through the ranks of the Gendarmerie Nationale with postings all over France and in her overseas protectorates. Now he was enjoying a pre-retirement sinecure as officer in command of the Montpellier Legion.

Ordinarily a suspicious fire in the countryside would have been of no consequence to Le Tallec. He might have glanced at the report from his detective unit when it passed through his In-tray. He might have made a telephoned inquiry as to progress of the investigation but he certainly would not have attended the scene.

Yet here he was on the specific instructions of the General commanding the Mediterranean District who had telephoned him personally from headquarters in Lyon. For some unknown reason The Minister of Defence himself was apparently deeply interested in the causes of this particular conflagration and much exercised over the identity of the unknown victim.

In ordering Le Tallec to take immediate command of the investigation his General had also warned the Colonel to expect a visitor from Paris – a visitor who would demand, and was to be given, the fullest possible co-operation.

And here he was. A clean-shaven, unsmiling young man, with a ruddy complexion, rimless spectacles, highly polished shoes and wearing a gabardine raincoat.

He walked up to Le Tallec, mumbled an almost indecipherable name and briefly flashed a card, which bore his photograph and the legend *'DST – Direction de la Surveillance du Territoire'*. He did not offer a handshake.

Colonel Le Tallec sighed. A child pretending to be a spy and he didn't even have the imagination to turn up the collar of his raincoat.

'I will inform the magistrate at Millau to complete his report on this suicide as quickly as possible and we need not waste the time of your men a moment longer than is necessary Colonel', said the young man. 'Have a copy of the report forwarded to my office and we can wrap this up without delay'.

The Colonel threw his shoulders back and stiffened his spine in the mannerism he always adopted when giving orders to his troops.

'Excuse me, Monsieur'. He almost spat the words. 'This is a criminal investigation under my control and the magistrate will be informed when we have fully completed our inquiries. If you would care to leave your details with my aide de camp I will send you a copy of the relevant papers in due course. And did I hear you offer the opinion that this is a case of suicide?'

If he noticed Le Tallec's dismissive attitude or the contempt in the older man's eyes the young man did not show it. He spoke calmly in a flat, cold, voice.

'This *is* a case of suicide, Monsieur', he said.

'We do not even know the identity of the victim yet', retorted the colonel.

'I know who he is', replied the agent.

Le Tallec gestured towards the bent and scorched number plate hanging off the back of the car. 'Of course we know who the registered owner of the car is', he said, tersely. 'We know that it was a Mercedes. But we don't yet know who the body is'.

'I know who he is', insisted the DST man, 'and I know why he killed himself'.

'With all due respect', said Le Tallec, in a tone which implied no respect at all, 'it might be a woman. We will not be certain of anything until all the DNA tests have been done at the laboratory in Marseille'.

'That won't be necessary', said the young man. 'It is a clear case of suicide. We know the reason and we know the identity of the victim'.

'Listen' said Le Tallec, feigning patience, 'what makes you so sure that this is suicide?'

'The empty can in the car', said the agent confidently. 'He drove up here, poured petrol over himself and torched the car'.

'A long way off the beaten track, to kill yourself', said Le Tallec.

'He didn't want to be seen or found too quickly', came the instant reply.

'He could have achieved that without driving several miles over rough terrain and crashing into a forest', retorted the Colonel, 'and in any case that small receptacle' – he deliberately chose the formal evidential word – 'that receptacle, would not have contained sufficient petrol to cause a massive fireball like this'.

'There would have been petrol in the tank too', said the young man.

Le Tallec shook his head. 'Even if the tank was full it would still not be enough to cause destruction on this scale. Have you considered the possibility that this might be murder?', he asked with a hint of sarcasm.

'No chance', said the young man.

The colonel looked at him and paused portentously. 'Monsieur', he said gravely, 'all the car doors are locked. Where is the car key? It is not on the body and it is nowhere to be found inside the vehicle. And what about the small hole on the left side of the cranium?'

The young man took a deep breath and fixed Le Tallec with an icy stare. There was a long silence then he said: 'Monsieur, by the powers vested in me as an agent of the Republic of France I am telling you that this is a case of suicide. There are no alternatives. Do I make myself clear?'

The two men stood, face-to-face, their eyes locked in an unblinking glare, for all of 30 seconds. Then, without a word, Colonel Le Tallec turned on his heel and marched away.

PART ONE

"There are powers at work..."

Chapter One

London, 8th September 1981

It was just a little thing, really. Mundane. The kind of unremarkable episode which must be repeated a million times or more in households around the globe every single day – a hungry young woman raids the family kitchen in search of a glass of milk and the wherewithal to make herself a sandwich.

But, prosaic though it was, this was an incident with far-reaching, almost historic, consequences. It was to set in motion a chain of events which would alter the face of the British monarchy forever and shape the destiny of the young woman involved for the remainder of her life.

For the kitchen where it took place was no ordinary kitchen. It was the kitchen of Buckingham Palace. And the young woman in question was Her Royal Highness, Diana, the Princess of Wales, newly wed wife of the heir to the throne.

A footman saw her first. He was lounging in the corner of the larder kitchen, with his feet up on a table reading a copy of the New Musical Express, when a figure skipped lightly past him. He glanced up, glanced back at his magazine, and then started up, doing a double take as he did so.

The princess was barefoot and wearing a plain white T-shirt which hung loosely over a pair of tailored jeans. Her hair was wet after a swim in the Palace's indoor pool. She was making tiny shuffling dance steps and her head nodded back and forth and rocked from side to side.

The footman noticed a thin strip of silver metal passing across the top of the princess's head. It was attached to two black sponge rubber spheres clamped over her ears. A wire leading from the right ear disappeared under her T-shirt at the hip.

13

The footman, who loved music and gadgetry, was impressed.
The princess obviously had the latest must-have accessory –
the brand new Sony Walkman WM1 personal stereo player –
clipped to her waistband.

He leapt to his feet, buttoned up his scarlet and gilt tunic to the
neck, drew on his white gloves and began to follow.

The princess stopped. She was oblivious to the footman
behind her but clearly unsure as to what to do next.

The footman was non-plussed. He could not tap her on the
shoulder. Servants were not allowed to touch Royalty. He
cleared his throat.

'May I help you, Ma'am?', he inquired. There was no
response. He tried again a little louder. 'Is there something I
can do for you Your Royal Highness?' Still no response.

The princess turned around to face him and jumped.

'Oh my God', she yelled. 'I didn't see you there. You startled
me'.

'I am very sorry Ma'am', said the footman contritely. 'Can I
help you? Is there anything you need?'

'Sorry? What?', screamed the princess. The music in her ears
was drowning out all other sounds and she obviously had no
idea that she was speaking very loudly.

At the sound of her raised voice several of the cooks and
pastry chefs looked up from what they were doing. There was
a nervous silence broken only by an occasional whisper. Their
colleagues nudged those members of staff who had not noticed
the presence of the unexpected visitor. Some of the older ones
looked as though they had seen a ghost. Members of the
Royal Family were rarely seen in the kitchens. Most of the
kitchen staff could not remember the last occasion. It was a
wonder to them that anyone could find their way from the

Royal apartments, through the labyrinthine maze of rooms, which made up the Royal kitchens in the southwest corner of the Palace, without a guide, or a map.

The princess pushed the headphones back off her head so that they hung around her neck.

'Sorry, what did you say?', she asked the footman.

'Is there anything I can do for you Ma'am? Is there anything you need?'

'Yes. Where is the fridge?', she asked.

'Which particular refrigerator do you need, Ma'am?', he said. 'Fish, poultry, game, dairy products?'

'Dairy products I suppose', said the princess. 'I just wanted a glass of milk'.

'Certainly Ma'am', said the footman. 'I can arrange that for you. Do you want full cream milk, or skimmed or semi-skimmed?'

'Oh, just as it comes. It doesn't matter', said the princess. 'Which fridge is it?'

'That one', said the footman pointing to a refrigerator on the end of a bank of six sparkling white appliances. 'I will get you a glass'.

'I can manage, thanks', said the princess, opening the refrigerator door and removing a bottle of milk.

'Please allow me', said the footman, plaintively.

'Oh don't be so silly', she replied. 'I'm not helpless. Now where are the glasses kept? No, don't bother, this will do'.

She picked up an empty glass standing on a stainless steel kitchen trolley, strode to a sink nearby, and rinsed it out before pouring the milk into it and taking a sip.

'Now, where is the bread?', she asked.

Suddenly there was a bustle and commotion among the kitchen staff. They had all apparently come to their senses and found their voices at the same time. Everyone was anxious to be of service.

A loud clearing of the throat cut through the clamour and silenced everyone once more. They all turned to see the portly figure of the Royal Chef standing above them on the steps, which led down into the central kitchen. This was his domain. His personal fiefdom. And interlopers of any kind, Royal or not, were not welcome.

'Your Royal Highness', he said without a hint of warmth in his voice, I am told that you would like something to eat and drink. If you will kindly leave your instructions with my deputy, Mr Brown, we will see to it that you are served without delay'. He gestured toward a small man, wearing a chef's uniform, who bowed politely.

'Oh no, I don't need to trouble you. You must all be very busy', replied the princess. 'I just wanted to make myself a sandwich but I can't find the bread'.

'Do you wish brown bread or white bread?', inquired the Royal Chef.

'Oh, brown I guess', she replied.

'And what filling would you care for, smoked salmon or, perhaps pate de foie gras? Your husband is very partial to foie gras sandwiches'.

'No, just cheese will be fine', she said.

'Very well. Camembert? Stilton? Brie? Dolce latté? Gloucester?'

'Oh, er, Cheddar will be just fine. But, really, do let me find it and I'll be happy to make my own'.

'I'm very sorry Ma'am but I cannot allow that', replied the Royal Chef pompously. 'My staff are at your service at any hour. It is our responsibility to provide you with whatever you might need in the form of food or drink. Indeed it is our pleasure'.

It did not sound like a pleasure.

'One more thing. Would you like the crusts cut off or left on?'

'On is fine', said the princess.

'In that case, where will you be and I will have your sandwich and your glass of milk brought to you directly', said the Royal Chef.

'I'll be in the drawing room of the Prince of Wales's apartment', replied the princess as she put the headphones back over her ears and stalked out of the kitchen.

Ten minutes later there was a timid tap on the Drawing Room door.

'Come in', called the princess. The footman who had first dealt with her entered bearing a silver salver, which he placed on a coffee table at her right elbow.

On a small china plate bearing her husband's badge as heir to the throne – the triple ostrich feathers – lay a brown bread sandwich which had been neatly cut into eight segments. Alongside it was a crisp piece of lettuce and two freshly cut slices of tomato. The princess was amused to note that her milk had been decanted into a cut-glass tumbler which was wrapped in a stiffly-starched linen napkin so that her fingers

17

would not get cold while drinking nor would she leave fingerprints on the glass.

'That is very sweet of you. Thank you', she said. 'What is your name?'

'Graham, Ma'am', replied the footman.

'Do you like music, Graham?', asked the princess.

'Oh yes, Ma'am', he said.

'What kind?'

'All sorts really. Mainly rock'.

'Like who?', she asked.

'Well I dunno. I like Pink Floyd'.

The princess brightened. 'Oh yes, I love them', she said. 'I've got their last two albums "Animals" and "The Wall". Have you heard any of that stuff?'

'No', replied the footman, 'I haven't Ma'am'.

'Well I'll lend them to you if you like', she said with a dazzling smile.

The footman was flummoxed. He was not sure what the correct response to this offer should be.

'Thank you, Ma'am', he said. 'Will there be anything else?'

'No thanks, Graham, I'm fine', she said. 'By the way I'm Diana. You can call me that when no one else is around. Okay?'

'Your Royal Highness', he said, bowing stiffly from the waist as he backed out of the door.

18

And so an innocent exchange between the 20-year-old Princess of Wales and members of the Royal Household staff came to an end as unremarkably as it had begun fifteen minutes earlier.

But within an hour the Royal Chef had reported the incident to the Master of the Household and by the end of the day a full written report was on the desk of the Lord Chamberlain himself. By the following morning the incident was the main topic of conversation between footmen, butlers, cooks, and serving maids across the entire below stairs world of the Royal palaces from Sandringham to Windsor and Kensington to Balmoral.

No one could recall a member of the Royal Family being so casual, friendly, and above all, normal. It was a disturbing development.

* * * * * *

London, 5th October 1981

In Edwardian times the serene, sophisticated, enclave of Bloomsbury, which lies just a stone's throw to the northeast of London's bustling commercial West End, gave its name to a phenomenally talented group of artists, writers and thinkers – the so-called Bloomsbury Set.

But by the nineteen-sixties, when the Cold War between the West and the Soviet Union was at its height, Bloomsbury had also become home to a rather more esoteric organisation.

Not that the locals would have been any the wiser. They would have been totally ignorant of the fact that an anonymous, unprepossessing concrete tower block at number 40 Gower Street was the headquarters of Britain's Security Service, MI5.

Thomas Crampton had worked in that building, on and off, for almost ten years. This morning he found himself making his way up in the lift to the sixth floor after a polite inquiry as to whether he could spare the Director-General a few moments.

Thomas thought the Director-General's office very unimpressive considering the importance of the role its occupant played in British affairs of state.

It was drab, almost Spartan, and furnished in the functional style which was common throughout the Civil Service. An olive green carpet covered the floor from wall to wall and a glass-fronted bookcase occupied much of one side of the room. It was made from wood which had been stained dark brown to mimic mahogany as, too, was the large square-framed desk angled across the corner of the room. The black leatherette inlaid top to the desk gave the secret away but at least the IN and OUT trays were wooden unlike the plastic ones in Thomas's office. On the wall behind the desk hung the standard Government Issue portrait of The Queen wearing a tiara at the time of her Coronation in 1953. She looked much younger than her twenty-six years.

'Ah, Crampton, come in', said Sir Granville Sleight, the current Director-General. 'So good of you to come. Do please, sit down'. He gestured towards a square brown wooden chair with a seat upholstered in black and grey tweed.

'There is a little task I wondered whether you might consider taking on for me.'

Nothing to consider, thought Thomas, *this is an order*. 'Of course, sir', he said.

'Good', said Sir Granville. 'Now look. I've had a number of interesting discussions with Richard Arbuckle over recent weeks'. He pronounced the surname 'Arb-yew-kell'.

Thomas knew that Sir Richard Arbuckle was the Lord Chamberlain, head of the Royal Household and guardian of all things to do with the Monarchy. He had always been amused by the eccentric pronunciation of his surname, which, he assumed, Sir Richard had affected in order to distance himself from the vulgarity of being associated with the American silent film comedian, "Fatty" Arbuckle.

'He has been receiving a number of very disturbing reports recently concerning the conduct of Her Royal Highness the Princess of Wales', went on Sir Granville. 'There is an alarming ignorance of protocol, indeed a wilful disregard for the proper procedures and behaviour and many instances of entirely inappropriate fraternisation with members of the staff. She is displaying an independence of spirit which, if left unchecked, might have serious long-term consequences for this country'. He bent his head forward and gazed balefully over his half-moon spectacles at Thomas.

Thomas said nothing. He was not entirely sure where the conversation was leading.

'The Princess is, of course, the consort of the future King', said the Director-General, leaning back in his chair. 'One day she will be Queen and have a vital role to play at the head of affairs of State. But she is essentially a commoner. Until recently she was a commoner and all her friends and associates are still commoners. They may be having an adverse influence on her. Sir Richard has asked if we could use our good offices to address the situation'.

Still Thomas did not see the point. He was a studious man with a fine intellect and impeccable connections to the British ruling class. His family had been landowners in Wiltshire for generations and his father reached the rank of Brigadier with the Royal Dragoon Guards during the Second World War. Educated at Marlborough and Baliol College, Oxford, he was an ardent patriot and committed Royalist. Was he being asked to spy on the friends of the wife of Prince Charles? He nodded and kept silent.

21

'Are you familiar with the work of Professor Dettweiler in the United States?', asked Sir Granville.

'No, sir. I don't believe I am', replied Thomas.

'No. Well there is no reason why you should be', said the Director-General. 'Since the 1960's Dettweiler and his colleagues at the University of Dallas, Texas, have been studying the subliminal effects of popular music on the psyche of a nation. They have published several significant papers on the subject.

'It is a science which was developed after the War by the Russians. It works on a similar principle to the conditional reflexes of Pavlov's dogs. The theory is that primitive, repetitious, rhythms in music act on the brain of the listener breaking down the rational responses and replacing them with emotional ones. In this state the listener becomes highly suggestible and the constant repetition of certain key phrases in songs can produce a change in the behavioural pattern of the individual'.

Sir Granville was aware that he was delivering a lecture and, with a captive audience of one seated in front of him, he warmed to his task.

'Primitive civilizations were fully cognizant of the effects of repetitive drum beats on the subconscious mind, for instance, and employed them in religious and pagan rituals to establish mass mind control over their subjects.

'Approximately ten years ago, shortly after Dettweiler alerted the world to the inherent dangers of this science, the Central Intelligence Agency identified a major operation by the Soviets to infiltrate the American popular music industry and exert an influence for evil over American society.

'There is evidence that the Communists deliberately flooded the market with songs, the words of which promoted sexual promiscuity, the use of drugs, and a disregard for all forms of authority. If you can break down the moral fibre of a whole generation of a nation's youth you can influence the direction which that society takes in a number of different ways. It is a very dangerous threat indeed'.

The Director-General paused and Thomas felt the need to say something.

'Are we facing such a threat in Britain, sir?', he inquired.

'Indubitably', said Sir Granville. 'Morrison in F2 has produced a very interesting report "Subversion in Contemporary Music" which I recommend you withdraw from Registry. It makes disturbing reading'.

Thomas himself had served in F Branch, the Anti-Subversion section, but at the time had been employed in monitoring the movements of suspected members of the Communist Party of Great Britain. He had never come across Morrison.

He nodded gravely. Ever since his childhood he'd had a highly developed sense of moral duty. He had a puritan streak. It was what had drawn him to MI5. He interpreted the Security Service's motto: "In Defence of the Realm" as entrusting him with an obligation to protect the set of values, ideas, and social mores which had served his family and others like them so well for generations. He was certainly a member of the stiff upper lip brigade. Johnny Foreigner was a nuisance and not to be trusted.

'Now, you may be wondering what all this has got to do with Her Royal Highness', said the Director-General.

Thomas was so absorbed that he had momentarily forgotten the original subject of his briefing. He nodded curtly.

Sir Granville tapped a file, which lay in front of him on the desk.

'One of the matters which most concerns the Palace is the Princess's interest in popular music. I am told that she spends most of her waking hours listening to it. Indeed, it is almost an obsession.

'Arbuckle has provided me with a list of her most favoured works which I have had analysed by Morrison. I will just give you some idea of the tenor of this material'.

He opened the file and began to shuffle through the papers.

'Ah yes, here we are', he said at last. 'One of HRH's most frequently played songs is performed by an individual calling themselves Toyah. It is entitled "I want to be free" and is full of rebellious sentiments. For instance…'. He picked up a piece of paper and began to read.

'*Tear down the wallpaper, turf out the cat; Tear up the carpet and get rid of that. Blow up the TV, blow up the car…*'.

Sir Granville paused and glanced knowingly over his glasses at Thomas.

'*Without these things you don't know where you are*', he read. '*Pull down the abattoirs and all that's obscene*'…well you get the drift. I believe these words are termed lyrics though Lord knows why. There's nothing bloody lyrical about that kind of thing.

'And as for the chorus which is typically repeated many times, just listen to this: '*I'm gonna…*', he shuddered and began again. '*I'm going to turn this world inside out; I'm going to turn suburbia upside down; going to pull my hair, scream and shout; going to crawl through the alleyways being very loud*'. Practically an incitement to riot.

'The Princess of Wales is a role model who is expected to set an example to the youth of this country and if she is poisoning her mind with this seditious filth on a regular basis God alone knows where it will all end'.

Sir Granville shook his head sadly, sighed, and looked distractedly out of the window. When his gaze returned to Thomas his mood was businesslike and efficient.

'This is a highly sensitive issue', he said at last. 'It requires very delicate handling so I propose that, for the time being, we do nothing but monitor the situation closely. I want you, Crampton, to open a docket on the subject and keep a discreet note of anything you might feel significant within the bigger long-term picture. We will need detailed notes on everyone Her Royal Highness associates with regularly outside the immediate confines of the Royal Family. By that I don't mean casual acquaintances or individuals she may meet in the course of her Royal duties. I mean her personal friends or individuals who provide her with any professional services on a regular basis. In particular, if she should show any inclination to establish a relationship with anyone engaged in the popular music or entertainment business or, Heaven forefend, any leftward leaning politicians, I would expect a form of positive vetting to be carried out on that individual or individuals'.

Thomas nodded. The Director General continued:

'Initially we will not need a classification any higher than "Confidential" but I would expect things to be conducted on a strictly need to know basis. You may employ the services of any branch or the specific skills of any colleague provided that you obtain my personal clearance. When it comes to vetting, the Metropolitan Police Special Branch will, as usual, be the appropriate agency to use. You may liaise directly with Sir Richard without referring to me. He has your name and is expecting an approach. Is all of that quite clear?'

'Yes sir, quite clear', said Thomas, 'I will get on with it straight away. Do you wish me to register the docket under any particular operational name at this stage?'

'Yes. I thought "Ephesus" might be appropriate, don't you agree?', replied Sir Granville with a telling grin.

'Absolutely', replied Thomas returning the Director-General's smile. 'Operation Ephesus. I'll do it immediately'.

I wouldn't have had the old man down as a classical or biblical scholar, he thought to himself as he left the office and headed back to his desk. *Diana, the Great Goddess of the Ephesians. Yes, of course, Ephesus was the perfect name for this operation.*

Chapter Two

Belfast, 12th September 1982

Christopher had always found the Ulster accent intrusive. To his mind it compared unfavourably with the softer, more lilting, brogue of the Southern Irish. There was a hardness. An extra edge. And a peculiar acoustic resonance, which made the voice of an Ulsterman or Ulsterwoman distinctly audible at a distance of more than half a mile on a clear day across open country. To Christopher's ear it was a most unattractive sound.

And here it was again. Multiplied. The babble of voices in the bar was incoherent and yet rising above it there was that all-pervading irritating whine.

Christopher decided that he didn't much like the Northern Irish. He couldn't put his finger on it. It wasn't their religious bigotry. It wasn't their polarised politics. And it certainly wasn't their tendency to murder and maim each other in the most brutal and bloody way imaginable. After all that was why he was here.

There had been that boy at Cambridge. Eamonn somebody or other. Son of a wealthy Protestant from Coleraine. He was a decent enough sort of chap.

Christopher's musings were abruptly cut short. A short stocky man with bushy eyebrows and a neatly clipped moustache had turned away from the bar and was walking towards him. Beneath the table his left hand silently undid the zip on the bum bag around his waist and his fingers felt for the Glock semi-automatic pistol.

'Scuse me', said the stranger, 'have yooze got a light, Mister?'. Christopher tossed a pack of matches across the table at him and watched as he lit a scrawny roll-up and turned

27

way, instinctively noting, as his instructors at "The Fort" had drilled into him, that the man's eyes were a pale amber colour.

Seated with his back to the whitewashed wall and facing the heavy wooden door, he had a good view of the entire bar, now smoke-filled, and packed with a cosmopolitan mix of old and young, the affluent and the not so well-heeled. The maritime paraphernalia on the walls gave it away as a dockside pub enjoying a naval heritage tucked away, as it was, in the Sailorstown neighbourhood of old Belfast.

'Hi, may I join you?'. This time there was no mistaking the accent. An American. Christopher looked up. The man was in his late twenties with jet black hair swept back in an ostentatious ponytail and was wearing large wrap-around sunglasses despite the dingy light in the bar. Without a word Christopher shifted to his left and the newcomer put his backpack on the bench seat between them before sitting down.

'Howya doin?', inquired the American. 'My name's Greg. Greg Krushelnycky'. He pronounced his surname 'Crucial-knit-ski' and the inflection in his voice went up as he spoke making it sound like a question. Almost as if he were asking 'surely you've heard of Greg Krushelnycky?' Christopher did not respond but reluctantly shook the American's proffered hand. He picked up his pint of Guinness and returned to reading *The Belfast Telegraph* in the hope that an air of studied indifference would dissuade his new companion from attempting further conversation.

'This place is awesome, isn't it?' said Greg. 'Did you know that prisoners who were going to be transported to Australia in the last century were locked up here in this little Rotterdam Bar before they were shipped out? I read that in the guidebook'.

Christopher said nothing.

'Your first time in Belfast?', asked Greg. 'No, I work here', grunted Christopher, wondering why American tourists were always so remorselessly friendly and so incorrigibly inquisitive.

'What a great city', said Greg, 'and the women are so babe-licious'.

Under different circumstances the sheer crassitude of that remark would have offended Christopher's patrician sensibilities and cause him to wince but he was no longer listening. His gaze was fixed on the door where a large man stood surveying the room. He was unshaven and wore a blue woollen beanie hat pulled down over his ears and a dark donkey jacket. As his gaze passed the alcove where Christopher sat he closed both eyes tightly in a double blink. It was an almost imperceptible gesture. To the casual observer it might have been a nervous tick.

He moved towards the bar and a younger man entered immediately behind him. He was blond with piercingly blue eyes. He had the look of a Scandinavian. His clothing was fashionable - grey cowboy boots under tailored jeans and a grey leather bomber jacket.

He smiled warmly at his big companion. Leaning forward, Christopher heard him ask: 'What'll yer have yerself?' in a gentle accent which was neither Scandinavian nor local. The boy came from south of the Irish border.

'Excuse me, but I need to get back to work', said Christopher as he knocked back the dregs of his Guinness and stood up. Greg was not insulted. 'Sure, no problem, it was nice meeting you', he grinned.

Rolling up his copy of *The Belfast Telegraph*, Christopher leant across the bar and handed it to the barman. Gently brushing the shoulder of the young blond man as he did so, he turned and briskly marched out into the street. In the corner of the room two burly men with shaven heads glanced at one another. One got up and followed.

He was just in time to spot the departing figure of Christopher striding down Pilot Street towards the Clarendon Dock. Turning right the man hurried to the corner of Short Street where a battered Ford Cortina, with two men in it, was parked. He tapped on the driver's window and when it was wound down simply whispered: 'Target's on the plot. Don'll pick him up when he moves'.

With that he withdrew into a darkened alleyway and all that could be seen was the occasional glow from his cigarette end.

An hour later the young blond man and his muscular companion finished their drinks and left The Rotterdam bar. They did not notice that the shaven-headed watcher fell in behind them. The larger man muttered a curt farewell and set off in the same direction that Christopher had taken earlier.

The young man paused as if to get his bearings and then strolled casually up Pilot Street towards the city. As he drew level with the Cortina he was grabbed from behind. His arms were pinned to his sides. A gloved hand was clamped over his mouth and the muzzle of a revolver was thrust roughly into his neck just below his right ear. With another deft movement his own .38 Smith and Wesson revolver was whipped from his waistband.

He turned his head to look at his assailants but the dim orange light from the sodium street lamps cast strange shadows on their faces. Then he noticed that the car engine was running. He heard a gruff whisper in unmistakeably Geordie tones. 'Shut up. Get in the car and you'll be champion, pal'. A hand on the top of his head thrust him downwards and he was hurled onto the back seat of the Cortina.

The doors slammed shut and the car began to move. No squealing tyres. No wheel spin just a smooth takeaway. Checking the rear-view mirror, wing mirrors and side windows all four men in the car barked a single word in staccato succession: 'Clear', 'Clear', 'Clear', 'Clear. The abduction had gone unnoticed.

Within a minute the car had reached the M1 motorway and was picking up speed as it headed south.

'What the fock are you fockin' swaddler bastards doing with me?', yelled the captive. He spat the words out with venom. Without turning, the man in the front passenger seat responded calmly: 'We're not Protestants. We're taking you to see someone who wants to ask you a few questions. Now be quiet and you'll be fine'.

He spoke with a heavy Glaswegian accent. A Geordie and a Scot? The young abductee was both puzzled and alarmed. He fell silent then suddenly began to plead. 'I've nothing to do with the IRA, swear to God', he sobbed.

'Tell that to the RUC when we get there', came the swift reply.

The RUC? The police? The young man said nothing but his breathing was shallow and he was shivering. He didn't like the way the driver and the front seat passenger seemed to be regularly checking a grid reference on their map. He saw the sign for Lurgan as they turned off the motorway and reckoned they must be somewhere on the Lurgan to Dromore road.

The car slowed and turned down a track running alongside a wooded area. The driver stopped the car. After a few seconds a red light flashed three times from the hedgerow thirty yards ahead.

'Get out of the car and walk towards that light', said the Geordie.

'I'm not going fockin nowhere', said the young man. His voice was trembling.

'It's the RUC guy who needs to talk to you. Just do it now or you'll be in trouble', came the reply as he was bundled out of the car.

31

Once again he shivered then began to walk in the direction from which the red light had come. He had taken just two steps when there was a 'thump, thump' sound. To the men wearing camouflage in the hedgerow it was the unmistakeable sound of a Browning 9mm pistol with a silencer being discharged - the Hereford assassin's double-tap. Four men emerged swiftly from the shadows, picked up the lifeless body, and carried it into the forest guided by a miner's lamp strapped to the head of the front man. After about a quarter of a mile they came to a freshly dug trench. Unceremoniously they tossed the body in and threw his revolver in after him. By dawn the trench would be filled in and a row of young conifers would have been be planted.

In the Operations Room at the British Army's Northern Ireland headquarters in Lisburn it was a quiet night. Two young soldiers sat facing a double bank of TV screens on which there appeared to be precious little activity. In one section the screens were linked to cameras covering the gates and perimeter areas of the vast Ministry of Defence complex itself. Other screens beamed back pictures from key points across the Province which might turn into flashpoints requiring military intervention at any moment – cameras inside the prisons which held terrorist suspects or at sensitive border crossings, for instance. Radio traffic also seemed unusually light with routine communications between patrols in the trouble spots of Belfast and Londonderry and the occasional request for a vehicle or Criminal Record Office check coming in from soldiers on duty at roadside checkpoints. Only the radio channel linked to RUC headquarters at Knock was busy with a constant stream of police jargon detailing the kind of incidents which keep the forces of law and order busy the world over – traffic accidents, pub brawls, burglaries, muggings, suspects on premises.

At the far end of the console sat Christopher. He was chain smoking and his eyes never left a twinkling display of ever-changing lights on a small panel in front of him. It was a radio channel scanner. The yellow numbers on the screen denoted radio channels, which might be operative at any one time. The scanner scrolled repeatedly through the numbers and froze momentarily when it found one of the channels in use. It moved swiftly on if the operator did not react quickly by cutting in.

Christopher was watching for activity on Channel 8, his own dedicated channel for the evening. Suddenly there it was. The number 8 appeared on his screen and remained.

There was a burst of static from the small speaker to his right then an urgent voice. 'Charlie Bravo. Charlie Bravo to Foxtrot Niner X-Ray One. Receiving? Over'.

Christopher pressed the red "open carrier" button on the console and leaned into the microphone. He could not be bothered to use his own call sign. It was his personal MI5 identity code – F9X/1. It was far too clumsy. He should have insisted on something pithy, short and sweet, like the police or the army call signs.

'Receiving. Go ahead', he said.

Another burst of static then the disembodied voice simply said: 'Nemesis, repeat, Nemesis'.

There it was. Clear as a bell. The agreed codeword.

Christopher wanted to be sure. He needed absolute confirmation. 'Charlie Bravo', he said, 'you broke up. Say again'.

With a hint of irritation and an air of exaggerated patience the voice began to spell. 'Charlie Bravo, Foxtrot Niner X-Ray One, I repeat - November, Echo, Mike, Echo, Sierra, India, Sierra – Nemesis. Do you copy?'

Christopher opened the carrier. 'Received. Out', he said and slumped back in his chair.

He took a long drag on his cigarette and wondered how long it would be before the disappearance of one of the IRA's most influential young lieutenants would be noted. And, without a body, who would be blamed? The Loyalist gangs, no doubt, but would that suit the Machiavellian purposes of his political masters? No. Better that the Nationalist community be led to believe that the IRA leadership was fragmenting and diluting their Republican zeal with brutal infighting. He would need a word with *The Belfast Telegraph*'s security correspondent in the morning. It was time for a leak from "sources close to the IRA high command".

But for now one of Ireland's most cold-blooded and ruthless murderers would kill no more. The courts would not be troubled with a costly trial and the prison service would have one less prisoner to deal with. Rough justice was a good thing.

The officers' mess at Lisburn, with its harsh strip lighting and garish regimental coats of arms festooning the walls, was never a very inviting place but tonight Christopher felt the need of a drink.

The bar was empty but for two young men in military fatigues playing pool.

'Whiskey, please. Irish. Bushmills', said Christopher to the uniformed orderly.

'I would have figured you for a Scotch man', said a familiar voice from behind him. 'Still, when in Rome, I guess…'

Christopher turned.

Remember me?', asked the interloper. 'Greg Krushelnycky?'

* * * * * *

Monte Carlo, 18th September 1982

Monaco police headquarters is housed in a most imposing-looking building.

Built from a mixture of yellow sandstone blocks and white granite it hints at Byzantine architecture while nodding in the direction of more traditional Gothic style. From street level, twin staircases flanked by ornate stone balustrades curve left and right to meet beneath a pillared portico over the heavy wooden doors. Above, and to either side of the entrance, stained-glass windows point upwards to a small castle battlement feature beneath the red tiled roof.

When he first set eyes on the building's curved frontage Pierre Charron thought he must have come to the wrong address. No police station he had ever seen looked like that. It should have been a church. Perhaps it had been, once upon a time.

Now he sat quietly in the corner of a large open-plan room on the first floor at the rear of the building. It was a hot day – Riviera-style – with the sun blazing out of a flawless azure sky and, in the absence of air-conditioning, all the windows in the room were wide open to take advantage of a light breeze off the sea.

But there were very few sounds coming from the street below. The usual hustle and bustle of the world's favourite playground had been stilled for a day. Monaco was in mourning.

Her Serene Highness, Princess Grace of Monaco, was dead at the absurdly young age of fifty-two. A wave of intense grief had washed over the tiny principality and there was a palpably deep sense of shock among the Monegasque people as they gathered in solemn groups on every street corner.

She had been the living epitome of every little girl's dream. Her's was a real fairy story come true. Grace Kelly, the kid from Philadelphia, who grew up to become a movie star only to fall in love with a handsome prince who whisked her away to his glittering palace on a mountainside to reign over the richest country in the world.

Now the dream was over. The fairy-story had ended in tragedy.

Pierre Charron looked around him.

The room, which was normally used for conferences and lectures, had been temporarily converted into an operational incident suite. This was unprecedented because police inquiries of any kind were always based in the police station nearest to the scene of the incident being investigated – never at headquarters.

But this was different. The Royal wife of the Head of State had been killed. And there were those who believed her death to have been suspicious.

Five days earlier Princess Grace had been driving home with her 17-year-old daughter, Stephanie, from the royal retreat at Roc Agel in France when she apparently lost control of the car on a winding mountain road at Cap d'Ail. The vehicle plunged down a 45-foot embankment somersaulting three times before bursting into flames.

Initial reports suggested that, although the Princess had suffered a broken thigh, rib and collarbone, she was in good condition. But within 24 hours the Royal Palace was forced to announce that Grace had failed to regain consciousness and her life-support machine had been switched off because she was irreparably brain damaged. She died peacefully with her family at the bedside.

The rumours, claim and counterclaim began immediately. Conspiracy theorists were having a field day. The car's brakes had been tampered with…the Princess had been poisoned…it was a Mafia hit because Grace had attempted to shut down their illegal gaming operations in the Monte Carlo Casino...she was a member of a secret sect and was taking part in a bizarre suicide ritual.

Although the apparent accident had taken place just outside the borders of Monaco, the victim's husband, Prince Rainier, insisted that his own police force, the *Surete Publique*, investigate. In order to spare the family's feelings at such a sensitive time the French government agreed a compromise whereby a team of forensic experts and crash investigators from Paris would work alongside local detectives in the principality's police headquarters.

Within this diplomatically delicate arrangement Pierre Charron had to tread warily. He had no particular locus in the investigation. He wasn't even a policeman. He was there on sufferance and the shirt-sleeved men and women, busily making telephone calls and writing up statements all around him, knew it. Even the French contingent was suspicious of him. He was an outsider. An interloper whose role was to poke and pry. As far as the detectives were concerned he was a spy in the camp.

Actually he *was* a spy – an operative of the *Direction de la Surveillance du Territoire*, France's internal intelligence agency – but his bosses in Paris simply wanted him to keep an eye on progress in the crash investigation and report back any developments which might indicate a political dimension to the case.

It was routine stuff. The kind of job you would give to the junior member of staff just to get him out of the office. And in a sense Pierre was the junior. Newly recruited to the DST but already showing sings of genuine aptitude.

His uncle Phillipe had worked for French intelligence after the war and Pierre's mother always thought it would bring honour to the family for her son to follow in her brother's footsteps. Pierre wanted to be a lawyer and pursued his dream all the way through school and university. He graduated from the

37

Sorbonne Law School with a first class degree but, after months of trying and failing to find a law firm to take him on, he reluctantly gave way to his mother's insistence and applied to join the DST. The English he had learned during the year exchange at Bristol University in England clinched it for him.

Initial training had been a breeze. He was a natural and privately being talked of as a future star in the espionage game. But he would have to work his apprenticeship first. He was only young after all. Just twenty-six.

Pierre pulled a Styrofoam cup from the bottom of a stack lying on the windowsill and poured himself a slug of tepid, muddy-looking, coffee from the machine, which seemed to be permanently gurgling and hissing steam in the corner of the room.

He strolled over to the operations boards – two whiteboards propped on rickety easels against the far wall. One was covered with more than twenty black and white photographs attached haphazardly to the surface with drawing pins. The mangled wreckage of Princess Grace's Rover 3500 saloon had been pictured from every conceivable angle both inside and out. There were also pictures looking back up the road towards the direction from which the ill-fated vehicle had come and close-ups of the point at which the car had left the carriageway.

Charron noted that there were no visible skid marks on the road surface.

He made a tour of the office picking up copies of three documents he wanted to read from trays on the desks of detectives who had dealt with the actions which most interested him. He sat down and began to read.

The first document was a report written by two automotive engineers who had flown in from England to examine the wrecked car. They were employed by British Leyland, the manufacturers of the Rover. Pierre could not understand most of the technical jargon but one passage jumped out at him. Despite the age of the car, which was ten years old, it was in perfect working order and the brakes were functioning perfectly, they wrote.

Pierre scratched his head. If the brakes were working why no skid marks? He had seen a statement from a witness who was driving behind the Rover at the time of the accident and reported that it zigzagged backwards and forwards for quite a distance before veering off the road. The Princess had obviously been fighting to control the vehicle. So why had she not tried to use the brakes?

Next he turned to the autopsy report. Again much of the medical terminology was beyond his grasp but he understood that the victim had suffered a brain haemorrhage and noted the pathologist's opinion that she might have suffered a stroke while at the wheel.

That would make sense, he thought. She has a stroke, loses consciousness, and loses control of the vehicle so that her steering goes all over the place and she is too comatose to hit the brakes.

The statement taken from Princess Stephanie made very interesting reading.

'Mummy kept saying: "I can't stop, the brakes won't work. I can't stop"', the young princess told her interviewers. 'Mummy was in a complete panic. She kept screaming about the brakes. I slammed the gearstick into the "Park" position and hauled on the handbrake as hard as I could. Then I leaned over to Mummy's side and put my hands over her foot and pushed down on the brake pedal but I just couldn't stop the car', she said.

Pierre sucked his pen.

Princess Grace could not have been comatose if she was capable of telling her daughter that the brakes weren't working. And her foot was on the brake pedal. The handbrake, the automatic gearbox system and the main brakes had been used in an attempt to stop the car yet all three attempts had failed and there were no skid marks on the road. The engineers, however, were insisting that the brakes were in perfect working order. Curious. Very curious indeed.

This is a mystery that will run and run, thought Pierre. They'll be writing books and making movies about the strange death of Princess Grace in a car crash that never was for many years to come.

He looked up. A reverential silence had fallen on the room. The funeral of the Princess was being relayed live to a television audience of millions around the world.

Charron glanced at the small black and white television set propped on a desk next to the coffee machine. The moving sound of Samuel Barber's "Adagio for Strings" came echoing mournfully from the Cathedral of St Nicholas. The tortured features of Prince Rainier came into sharp focus – a broken man inconsolable in his grief.

Outside, in the Place de St Nicholas, photographer Jean-Jacques Iversen looked anxiously at his watch. The mass was dragging on and in his business time was money. Somewhere in the world it was edition time every hour of every day.

He was perched on a tiny folding stool leaning on the wrought iron balustrade of a small balcony which jutted out from the second floor of one of the pink terraced houses which line the side of the square. He could have taken up a position on the steps of the Palais de Justice directly opposite the entrance to the cathedral or he could have taken his chances with the jostling throng of snappers balanced on portable ladders or standing on camera boxes in the square below him.

But Jean-Jacques Iversen liked to be different. He always thought laterally. If he could take a picture, which would stand out from the crowd he could get one over on his rivals, when it came to catching the eye of demanding picture editors.

The day the tragic news of Princess Grace's death broke he had come to Monaco for a reconnaissance. Her funeral was a potential goldmine for photographers. Not only would kings, presidents and prime ministers attend but also many of the Hollywood stars with whom she had worked would be bound to turn up.

Standing in front of a row of houses which ran down one side of the square Iversen noted that they all afforded a view directly up the Rue du Tribunal down which the funeral possession would come en route from the Royal Palace. They also gave an angled side view of the front entrance to the cathedral and the steps down which the mourners and celebrity guests would leave. To his disappointment, however, he spotted that the entrance to the church would be obscured by several large palm trees from all the houses…except for one.

A fee of 20,000 francs for the use of the balcony for the day was easily negotiated with the house owner and Iversen was sitting pretty.

He was a big man. Bulky rather than muscular. In his younger day he had been a paratrooper and his commando training was often put to good use in the physically demanding, knockabout world of professional news photography. His opponents knew him as a pugnacious competitor who could be ruthless in pursuit of a picture. Yet beneath his thinning hair there was a round, jolly, open face and a ready smile which stood him in good stead when it came to charming his subjects into posing for the camera.

Today Iversen was using two cameras and half a dozen lenses – shooting in black and white for the newspapers and colour for the magazines. He wore a khaki canvas jerkin covered with pouches and pockets of varying sizes containing all the paraphernalia of his trade – rolls of film, a light meter, pens and barley water sweets to keep the energy levels up during the long boring hours of watching and waiting.

He worked for the international photographic agency *Parfaite Image* and his office in Paris had arranged with the local English-language newspaper, *The Monaco Times,* to share their darkroom and photo-transmitting facilities for the day.

He had found a local teenager who, for a modest payment, was willing to act as a runner conveying exposed film to the newspaper office for a colleague to develop and wire the pictures to Paris and thence around the world.

Iversen leant back, sighed, and checked his watch again. His first set of pictures would be on their way by now. He was pleased with them. He had captured the procession head on. The coffin flanked by the Carabiniers du Prince in their white uniforms with red plumes fluttering atop their white helmets. The women with their black lace veils mingling with black-capped priests in the cortege. And the silver-haired Prince Rainier, bedecked with medals, walking, head bowed, behind his wife's casket with a white handkerchief clamped almost permanently over his mouth and nose. Iversen was particularly pleased with one close-up, which showed a single tear trickling down His Royal Highness's cheek. The pictures should sell well. Especially the colour ones.

The music from inside the church, which was being relayed via loudspeaker to the crowds in the square, had stopped and been replaced by a dirge of prayers. It surely could not be long now.

There was movement at the door of the church. The service was over and a lengthy organ recital was being broadcast. The first mourners would soon emerge into the sunlight.

Iversen changed lenses on the Nikon to give himself a more powerful magnification and propped it on the rail in front of him. He knew the picture he wanted. The Brit. Diana. The new kid on the block. Her Royal Highness, the Princess of Wales.

The 21-year-old princess had just produced the son and heir for which Prince Charles had taken her to wife fifteen months earlier, and now she was representing Her Majesty Queen Elizabeth, alone at a foreign State occasion for the very first time in her Royal career. She had begged for the assignment because she was determined to pay her last respects to the woman she had come to rely on as a kindred spirit.

Although a generation apart, the parallels between Grace and Diana were striking. Both beautiful blonde commoners who married Royal princes much older than themselves.

The poignancy of the moment had not escaped the courtiers at Buckingham Palace who recommended that the Queen accede to Diana's request.

Iversen knew that the story would be in the newspapers the next day. The baton had been handed over. The fairytale lived on. He must get a picture which would symbolise the moment.

In his mind's eye he could see the pictures of the first meeting between the two women just eighteen months earlier. Famous pictures. Princess Grace had been in London giving a poetry reading at the Goldsmith's Hall – an event at which the newly engaged Diana Spencer was to be guest of honour. She was only nineteen and still naive when it came to understanding the effect her looks could have on the world's media. She chose an extremely décolleté black strapless evening gown and the sight of the buxom young blonde struggling out of her car in that dress sent the paparazzi into a frenzy.

Iversen could still picture the look of embarrassment on her face. And what was quickly becoming known to photographers as her trademark look – head bowed, big eyes peeping upwards demurely from beneath a blonde fringe and a coy smile playing about her lips.

And here it was again. The Princess blinking as she emerged from the sombre half-light of the church. She paused to allow some of the dignitaries in front of her to clear the steps. She looked elegant and poised beyond her years, wearing a long black coat, black gloves, and a black hat with a tiny brim from beneath which her large, limpid, eyes gazed sadly at the scene before her.

With a deft flick Iversen sharpened the focus and began to fire off a burst of frames.

Diana turned towards him and momentarily her head was framed by the arch of the chancel and the national flag of Monaco – the Grimaldi family ensign – draped across the coffin, which appeared across her chest like a caption.

The two words of the family motto: "Deo Juvante", stood out beneath the coat of arms.

It would have made the defining picture, thought Iversen, but with the depth of field involved it was impossible to keep both the words and the face in focus.

He knew the English translation of the Latin motto. It meant "With the help of God". *'You're going to need it, ma cherie'*, he said to himself. *'You're certainly going to need it'*.

Chapter Three

Murlough Bay, Northern Ireland, 13th November 1983

It was a most unusual night for November. Unusual, at least, for the North Antrim coast this late in the year. Cold. Very cold. But clear.

There was no wind to speak of and a gentle swell had replaced the normally boisterous waves in the North Channel of the Irish Sea. A full moon shone silvery down from a cloudless sky leaving a shimmering pathway across the surface of the inky black water.

The only sound was the hiss and gurgle of the sea lapping to and fro against the loose scree at the foot of the cliffs. Somewhere in the distance a dog barked. It had reached that slow hour too early to be called morning and too late to be called night. The birds were stirring but the dawn chorus was still a long way off.

The men had worked tirelessly for almost three hours. A score of them. Saying little or nothing to one another as they worked side-by-side heaving the boxes up the beach chain-gang style. They could have done without the moon focussing an ethereal spotlight on their nefarious activities but there was no one about. The landing place had been chosen for its remoteness.

This was the Derry Brigade of the Provisional Irish Republican Army on manoeuvres and tonight's work was of particular importance to what they liked to call: "The Armed Struggle".

Riding at anchor half a mile offshore lay the trawler *Columbine*. She had set sail across the Atlantic nine days earlier with a deadly cargo on board – a present from customers in the Irish bars and clubs of New York, Boston, and Philadelphia to their freedom-fighting cousins in a homeland most of them had never seen.

Inside the heavy boxes were enough arms and munitions to equip a small mercenary army – five surface-to-air guided missiles, fifty automatic rifles, twenty machine guns, twelve sniper rifles, grenades, night-sights, flak jackets and scores of rounds of ammunition. NORAID – the organisation that the American government was seeking to proscribe because of its overt funding of terrorism, had paid for the entire cache.

IRA commanders had long ago marked out Murlough Bay as the perfect spot for a hidden arms dump. It was a lonely area of natural beauty well away from the prying eyes of the law and visited only by bird-watchers and hikers whose interest lay far away from the bloody business of bombing, shooting, and killing. Best of all there were three disused mine shafts at the foot of the cliffs abutting the beach where the munitions could easily be stored. Even if a walker should wander into one of these caverns they would be unlikely to be suspicious of a pile of boxes covered with tarpaulins.

Landing the hardware was a laborious business. Orchestrated by a series of flashed signals from ship to shore, the cargo had been ferried to the beach in a large inflatable dinghy with an outboard motor. The operation entailed many journeys and took a long time but once on land the arms were manhandled into the old coal workings relatively easily.

At sea the NORAID representative who had come ashore from the Columbine with the first consignment was running the operation. He was a tall young man with a ponytail which poked out incongruously from beneath a yellow souwester. He wore a shiny new oilskin – also yellow – and a pair of olive green thigh-length waders.

When he first landed, the IRA men waiting on the beach gazed at him open-mouthed for a moment as the low light from their hurricane lamps reflected back at them from the surface of his lurid yellow garb. But the startled expression on their faces soon turned to amusement and an acceptance that this was just another example of American eccentricity.

An older man with a weather-beaten face, wearing a roll-neck sweater and a flat cloth cap was obviously in command of the IRA unit. He did not say much but the men clearly deferred to him as they went about their business.

When the last box had been brought ashore and the men were standing in a semi-circle around the entrance to the mine the American took his leave.

'Gentlemen it has been a privilege and an honour', he said. 'Good luck and God bless Ireland'.

He turned to walk towards the dinghy drawn up on the beach. As he did so the entire scene was transformed in an instant.

The area in front of the mine entrance was suddenly illuminated by shafts of brilliant light from a battery of portable floodlights strategically placed on the cliffs above. From the darkness the voice of a man with a distinctive Strabane accent boomed through a loudhailer: 'Police, police. This is the RUC. You are under arrest. Put down your weapons and stand still. Put your hands behind your head and you will not be hurt. I repeat. Stand still where you are with both hands behind your head'.

As he spoke the beach came alive with the sounds of men running across the shingle, scrambling over rocks, sliding through the shale – dozens of men charging out of the darkness and swarming towards the light. They wore the bottle green uniforms of the Royal Ulster Constabulary with flat peaked caps and black flak jackets. Each man carried a Heckler and Koch sub-machine gun or an assault rifle. They formed a circle around the startled IRA volunteers. Some dropped to one knee or crouched behind rocks to cover their colleagues as they raced on into the pool of light, throwing

47

their captives to the ground and roughly handcuffing them as they did so.

Amid the shouting, chaos and confusion the American stood transfixed. The scene before him was surreal. He decided it looked like a movie set. That was it. He had stumbled across a movie being made on location.

A second announcement from the man with the megaphone snapped him out of his reverie. 'Stand still, stand still, stand still. Keep your hands up where the officers can see them'.

The American looked around him. He was alone in the dark. In their haste to close in on the mineshaft the police had all run past him and were now busily engaged in the arrest operation some fifty yards away.

He turned. To his left a steep ravine cut through the cliff and up towards a plateau woodland above. He began to run. The crunching of his waders on the shingle sounded deafening to him but there was so much shouting going on to his right that no one heard him.

When he reached the ravine it proved to be wider than he had imagined with a path rising gently in front of him. In the moonlight he could just make out the shape of a copse – more bushes than trees – about three hundred yards ahead at the top of the slope. The waders were slowing him down but he kept his head down and pumped his arms to keep himself going.

He paused once to catch his breath and heard footsteps running up the path behind him. As he drew nearer to the shelter of the copse he looked behind at his pursuer who seemed to be gaining. He was relieved to see that the man was wearing a flat cap. It was the IRA commander also making his escape.

They both reached the copse at the same time and threw themselves bodily behind the shelter of a large gorse bush.

For a long while the two men lay side-by-side panting, their faces pressed against the icy stone-hard ground, their lungs heaving against their ribs. They tried to keep silent but the gulps and groans which their exertions force from them startled a herd of feral goats and sent the animals braying and skittering away through the woods.

The American – the younger and fitter of the two – was the first to recover. He stood up and peered through the foliage in the direction from which they had come. He could see lights flickering around the shoreline but could hear no sound.

Eventually his companion stood too and came up behind him.

'You fockin' bastard', he said, in a growl that was barely above a whisper.

The American turned. His eyes were growing accustomed to the gloom but the moonlight had failed to penetrate beneath the trees so he could only make out a bulky shape looming over him.

'You fockin' wee shite', repeated the man in a voice filled with venom.

'What the…', the American tried to interject but the Ulsterman was now in full flow.

'Not one of my people is a squealer. Not one single man. I'd trust them all with my life. So it had to be you, you bastard. I never wanted an Amerrrigan on this job. I knew there was something wrong. I didn't like it from the start'.

A twig snapped in the undergrowth. The IRA commander was too preoccupied to hear it but the American turned involuntarily towards the sound. In that moment he felt the muzzle of a pistol at his neck.

You're a fockin' Briddish spy, so you are', said his assailant, pushing downward on his shoulder, 'say your prayers mister'.

49

The American knelt with his hands clasped in his lap and closed his eyes. The pistol was pressed against his spinal chord at the junction of the neck and skull. *A Mauser broomhandle* he guessed by the shape and feel. *What were the IRA doing with such old-fashioned weaponry? Strange the things that go through a man's head at the point of death*, he thought.

He felt, rather than heard, the safety catch released. And then, another voice.

'Don't do that old man. It's quite against the law and could get you into awful trouble'. The accent was Oxbridge. Cultured. Familiar.

'Let the gun drop. Now. To the ground. Step back and put your hands where I can see them'. The instructions were given calmly but firmly. The American turned. He could just make out a tall figure behind the IRA commander with knees slightly bent, arms outstretched and hands clasped together in the classic marksman's pose taught to Special Forces the world over.

Two policemen, still panting, emerged from the shadows and handcuffed the Ulsterman's wrists together behind his back. They led him away in silence.

He had nothing more to say. His fury was spent. He had vented his anger against the American who now found himself staring into the beam of a powerful orch.

'Mr Krushelnycky, I believe', said his saviour, turning the torch to illuminate his own face. 'Remember me? Christopher?'

'Hey, how'ya doin' Chris?', said Greg Krushelnycky. 'Thanks a lot, Bub. I owe ya'.

'What the hell did you think you were playing at?', snapped Christopher. 'You were bloody lucky I saw you go'.

'I figured that if I escaped and was known by those guys to have gotten away it would keep the cover real for another time', said Greg.

'You're a bloody fool', said Christopher. 'How long have you worked in this Province? You know these people don't trust foreigners easily. You have to earn their trust by getting alongside them and sharing with them. And that means being detained along with them on operations like this'.

Christopher knew that now was neither the time nor the place for such a lecture but he was too angry to stop himself.

He was shouting now.

'If you, the outsider, were the only one to get away in terrain that was unfamiliar to you while they were all arrested. And then you popped up again on another arms shipment operation; your cover would be completely blown.

'We would have arranged for you to escape from custody later on, you knew that. You almost got yourself killed and now you can never work undercover in Northern Ireland or on any Irish counter terrorism operation ever again'.

Greg could not see Christopher's face but he could sense the animosity. He remained silent.

'Get yourself back to base, have a bath, and get the hell out of my country', spat Christopher as he turned away.

'Oh, and get rid of that ridiculous outfit. You look like some more-money-than-sense Wall Street trader on a weekend sailing trip out of the Hamptons'.

Chapter Four

Paris, 5th February 1985

Christopher's career was in transition.

He was about to become the guinea pig in a unique experiment.

In Whitehall they called it 'cross-fertilization' but the old hands in the espionage game were convinced it would all end in tears.

No one in history had ever been transferred from the Security Service to the Secret Intelligence Service. MI5 acted domestically against subversive elements in defence of the realm. MI6 spied on foreigners overseas.

For the purist, the two disciplines could not be transposed.

Christopher was not a natural for the spying business. He had not been one for Cowboys and Indians as a small boy. No fascination with guns and fast cars. He was a studious child with an aptitude for science, which was seized upon by the eccentric and somewhat irresponsible chemistry teacher at the Yorkshire boarding school he was packed off to at the age of eleven. By the time he took his A Levels and won a place at Cambridge University, Christopher's destiny was marked out. He was going to be an engineer.

But two hitherto unknown aspects of his character, which would alter the direction of his future career, began to emerge during Christopher's three years as a student at Gonville and Caius College.

He had never made friends easily as a boy. He preferred his own company and concluded that he was naturally shy. But he was quick-witted and imaginative and when plunged into the hurly-burly of student life, with its attendant need to impress the opposite sex, he soon discovered that he was a gregarious creature. He was good at networking and by the time he left university had a contacts book which every one of his wannabe journalist contemporaries would have killed for.

He also discovered that he was a gifted linguist. A girl with long black hair and gipsy eyes and the enchanting name of Giselle was responsible. Her father was a diplomat whose most lengthy posting had been in French Guyana and his daughter had grown up bi-lingual. Christopher was smitten from the first time he saw Giselle and took a crash course in French to impress her. He found the tapes and booklets supplied by the Berlitz Language School so easy to assimilate that he moved on to learn rudimentary German, Spanish and even dabbled in Russian. It became a hobby.

He graduated with a first class honours degree in aeronautical engineering but by then his horizons had shifted. There was a yearning for adventure, which he had never before acknowledged, beginning to stir deep within his soul.

Nonetheless the approach from the MI5 talent spotter was a delightful surprise.

For decades the British security services have maintained a clandestine recruiting operation at Oxford and Cambridge and several other leading universities by retaining a network of tutors whose job it is to pick out potential secret agents from among the most talented students and discreetly lure them into the service of Her Majesty.

Christopher was flattered when, during one of the end of term garden parties, a senior law tutor gently inquired if he might consider government service as a career path. He knew instantly what was meant. Everyone knew the talent spotters existed. It was occasionally a matter for discussion among the undergraduates. Based on nothing more than what he had read in the newspapers Christopher had an image in his mind of the ideal candidate. It would surely be an arts student. One of the more louche, decadent types with family connections to the aristocracy and a plummy line in name-dropping. A scientist or an engineer would not make the right material for a spy.

But when the offer came Christopher took it up immediately. Everything about the job suited his personality.

The training he found almost laughable. Role-playing through a series of espionage scenarios, which might have come straight from the pages of a very poor spy novel. Then commando training - learning tracking and survival techniques while living in rough terrain and handling a variety of weapons – the stuff of small boys' dreams. Despite, or perhaps because of, a rather repressed upbringing, Christopher loved it all.

The studious scientist in him relished the endless hours of boring paperwork which drove his colleagues to distraction. Sitting at a desk analysing newspaper articles, speeches, and political documents while matching them with surveillance reports from agents in the field was utterly fascinating to him.

And when the time came for him to take his learning into the operational sphere his gregarious nature and language skills soon marked him out as an agent with star quality – at least to those who took note of these things. The undercover work he did recruiting and running informers within the Irish Republican movement in Northern Ireland was quite exceptional.

And so it was that Christopher became the first man chosen to cross the divide between the two fiercely competitive arms of Britain's spying network.

There seemed no obvious reason for carrying out such an experiment. The Security Service, MI5, was heavily engaged in support of police efforts to defeat the miners' strike, which was crippling the country. With its commitments in Ulster the service was clearly overstretched but the Director-General took a triumphalist view of his agents' dubious successes and wasted no opportunity to tease his opposite number at MI6, claiming to head the superior of the two organisations. So, when the Foreign Secretary, irritated by what he saw as a failure of intelligence gathering in the Middle East, asked the Home Secretary for MI5 assistance, a plan was hatched, to the chagrin of the Secret Intelligence Service. Christopher was on his way to MI6 – the first, it was hoped, of many such transfers between the services.

He was posted to the Western European Controllerate - UKB - and initially attached to the French section based in Paris.

His posting happened to coincide with a minor intelligence-gathering breakthrough for his former colleagues at MI5.

They had infiltrated the environmental protest group Greenpeace and produced a sailing schedule for the group's ship Rainbow Warrior which showed that the vessel was due in the South Pacific within months to mount a campaign of disruption against a series of nuclear tests which the French government planned to carry out on the tiny island of Maruroa atoll.

The information was of no direct interest to the British government but senior officers at MI5 reasoned that it might be useful to the French and could help bring about a thaw in the somewhat frosty relations, which had long existed between themselves and their opposite numbers in Paris. Someone had the bright idea that entrusting the intelligence to Christopher to deliver would have the dual effect of giving their man a good introduction to his new posting while at the same time securing bragging rights over their rivals in MI6.

The SIS head of station in Paris – known in the organisation by the acronym H/PAR - was a Welshman called Eddie Bartlett who held the rank of First Secretary at the British Embassy and the official job of Commercial Attache. A secret telex from London alerted Bartlett to the fact that Christopher came bearing gifts for the French so he had arranged a meeting for his new charge with the liaison officer for the

DST – *Direction de la Surveillance du Territoire* - the host nation's domestic intelligence service.

The meeting was scheduled for five o'clock at Le Petit a Cheval. Christopher knew of the place as a Mecca for tourists visiting the picturesque Marais district of the French capital. He looked it up in the guidebook and instantly approved of his host's choice. To the casual observer it would appear the natural venue for two businessmen to have a social drink or meal together while anyone attempting to eavesdrop a conversation would be thwarted by the babble of voices in such a bustling atmosphere.

Christopher arrived early and took up a position on the outside of the horseshoe-shaped bar where he could see everyone who entered yet would not have anyone within earshot behind him. Even without a description he spotted Pierre Charron as he approached from the street. It was in the eyes as he scanned all corners of the room while lingering over opening and shutting the door. Christopher guessed that Charron would have watched his own arrival from a discreet vantage point and, sure enough, the Frenchman made straight towards him with his hand outstretched in greeting.

'So nice to meet you', he said. 'My name is Pierre, Pierre Charron. Welcome to Paris. I hope I did not keep you waiting'. His English was impeccable, his French accent almost undetectable.

'No, no I've not been here long', replied Christopher, thank you for sparing the time to meet me'.

They ordered drinks and, for a while, engaged in small talk. Charron was younger than Christopher had imagined. Darkly good-looking in a classic Gallic way. He wore a wedding ring and a well-cut navy blue suit with a mauve silk tie. Probably in his late twenties. Liaison between the DST and the secret services of France's ally countries was the first major responsibility he had been given since joining the agency. He was determined to be up to the task.

When conversation eventually turned to the matter in hand Christopher passed on just those essential facts he had committed to memory and promised to convey full details of the Rainbow Warrior's Pacific schedule via secure courier the following day if his French counterpart was sufficiently interested.

'The essential dates are as follows', said Christopher. 'They arrive at Rongelap in the Marshall Islands on the seventeenth of May to begin an evacuation of all the inhabitants to Mejatto Island. The operation is scheduled to last ten days. From there they go to Vanuatu for a fisheries protest in June then back to New Zealand arriving in Auckland on or about the seventh of July. They will then re-provision and take on new staff and crew, sailing about five days later for a blockade of Maruroa Atoll where they will attempt to disrupt or even prevent your nuclear testing programme.'

He paused. 'These matters are of no concern to HMG but…'

Charron cut in. 'HMG?'

'…so sorry, Her Majesty's Government', said Christopher apparently embarrassed. 'Just our jargon. Kind of shorthand I'm afraid. Sorry. Anyway my people believe it may be of some interest to your people. So in the interests of friendship and mutual co-operation and all that…'.

Pierre Charron smiled an enigmatic smile. He was diplomacy itself. His tone was polite, his demeanour non-patronising.

'My government is extremely grateful', he said. 'Your assistance is much appreciated. Actually we do have an asset in place and we are monitoring the situation but, at present, there is no indication that these eco-warriors, as they call themselves I believe, will cause any undue problems'.

He swilled the ice around the bottom of his glass.

'Since you have been so kind as to express an interest in this issue', he went on gravely, 'I have been authorised to ask for a favour'.

Christopher raised an eyebrow but said nothing.

'There is a potential difficulty arising in the region, in our colony of New Caledonia. The native population is trying to achieve independence from France against the wishes of the European settlers. The DGSE have an operation planned, using New Zealand as a staging post, to infiltrate some of the pro-independence groups and disrupt their gunrunning activities.

'Naturally our people will be operating under deep cover so we may need a little logistical help in arranging flights for certain personnel originating out of United Kingdom airports and for operational reasons, to which I am not privy, we may need to acquire certain items of nautical equipment from British suppliers'.

Christopher knew that the DST was the French equivalent of MI5 while the DGSE – *Direction Generale de la Surveillance Exterieur* – equated to MI6.

'I will take advice and get back to you tomorrow', he said.

'I will await your call. It has been nice meeting you. We must meet for lunch soon so that we can get to know each other better', said Charron, shaking hands and leaving without paying the bill.

* * * * * *

Paris, 1st March 1985

Christopher studied the business card once more. It certainly looked authentic. The logo in the top right-hand corner depicted the familiar crossed swords symbol of CDI – Cimeterre Defense Industrie, France's third largest arms manufacturer.

There was something slightly incongruous about the name, though. Marielle Norstrund. French first name, Scandinavian surname. And the title. Director of Corporate Affairs.

He turned the card over and glanced at the telephone number scrawled on the back – a private number he had called just a few hours earlier.

Madame, or was it Mademoiselle, Norstrund had answered in the kind of deep, husky, seductive voice which reminded Christopher of Marlene Dietrich - but without the sophistication or the hint of mischief.

She had suggested a meeting at the Caveau de la Huchette jazz club and here he was, bang on time, but without a clue what she looked like. She would find him, she had said.

Christopher was not at all sure about this assignation. It was the first operational assignment his Head of Station, Eddie Bartlett, had given him since his posting to Paris.

Marielle Norstrund was a 'walk-in' as MI6 termed informants who literally walked in off the streets to offer information uninvited. Most of these people were a complete waste of time. Usually Walter Mitty types living in their own fantasy world of intrigue, they either wanted money, craved attention, or needed urgent psychiatric help – or all three.

Marielle was not strictly a 'walk-in', in that sense, since she had approached the British Embassy seeking a meeting with the Commercial Attache about a proposed business

59

relationship between her company and the British Government.

Eddie Bartlett, whose cover role was that of Commercial Attache, knew that he was not the proper channel through which to conduct such transactions but he suspected that Ms Norstrund had another agenda. After many years in the business he had a nose for these things. He prided himself on it. The clue, for him, lay in the fact that she had left a business card but insisted that she be contacted on her private telephone number, not at her office.

The Caveau de la Huchette, a stone's throw from the Sorbonne University campus, was packed with the usual youthful clientele – a mixture of students and tourists. It was Christopher's first visit and as he descended the spiral staircase into the subterranean cavern he pondered on Marielle's choice of venue. As the location for a business meeting it was hopeless – too dark, too noisy, too crowded. As the location for a clandestine meeting at which secret information was to be exchanged, however, it was perfect. There could be no eavesdropping here. Christopher wondered what was really on Marielle's mind.

He moved from room to room looking around him. No one looked in his direction. He bought a Martini soda and found a seat at a table in the corner of the largest room.

In front of him a few people were dancing. A large woman caught his attention. She had her back to him and was dancing with a small child in her arms. She wore a clingy floral dress. Her hips were broad. *German*, thought Christopher, *probably a Brunhilde*. Her shoulders, too, were broad and muscular. *Breaststroke swimmer*, thought Christopher. Her hair was plaited in a pigtail, which ran the full length of her back to the base of her spine. It was so pale it was almost white. In his mind's eye Christopher recalled the album cover of his father's favourite long-playing record – a collection of songs by the sixties folk duo Nina and Frederick. This woman's hair was exactly the same as Nina's.

She turned around and momentarily caught Christopher's eye. Immediately she turned away and carried the child – a small boy – to a table on the far side of the room and handed him to another woman. Then she turned back and made her way towards Christopher's table. She was large. Over six feet tall and buxom with a glowing tan which had not come from the sun.

'Monsieur Christophe?', she inquired. She was leaning forward and yelling to make herself heard over the music.

'Yes', said Christopher. 'How did you...?'

'Your shoes, they are English, non?', she said.

Christopher looked down at his heavy brown brogues and nodded. 'May I get you a drink?', he asked.

'No, no, thank you, I have one', said the woman. 'One moment. I will join you.'

She turned and walked over to the table where the woman and the small boy were sitting and when she returned she was carrying a gin and tonic in one hand and a large leather handbag in the other.

She sat down, leaned across the table, and planted a kiss on Christopher's cheek. 'Hello, I am Marielle', she said. 'Nice to meet you'.

Well, thought Christopher, *this woman is either barking mad or she has been very well trained in this business. She chooses to meet in a noisy crowded place, with a child in tow, and if anyone was watching our first introduction just then they would have thought we were either old friends or I was a casual pick-up. Impressive.*

He took a closer look at Marielle. She was certainly a bulky woman but everything was in proportion. Indeed, she had an excellent figure. Her face, close up, was most attractive, too. She had high Slavonic cheekbones, pale blue eyes and invitingly full lips. She was leaning in to him and he could smell her perfume. He had no idea what it was but it smelled expensive.

'It is lovely to meet you, Christophe', she said. 'I hope we can do some very good business'. She smiled. Her teeth were dazzlingly white and perfectly aligned. *Good dentist*, thought Christopher, *I bet he doesn't come cheap*. He took a sip of his drink.

'Go on', he said.

'My company has recently developed a new weapons guided missile system for anti-tank missiles', said Marielle. 'It meets perfectly the requirements of the British but we understand that your Army wants to buy an American product. We can produce the system at almost half the cost of the American version. Would you like me to show you?' She fished in her handbag and produced a thick glossy brochure.

'No, just wait a second, Marielle', said Christopher. 'Take a step back. Here's the thing. I do not wish to be rude but I don't know you from Adam. I have been able to check out the company you say you represent but all I have is a business card to say who you are and suggest a connection with CDI. I cannot prove that you have the right to negotiate on behalf of that company and I, certainly, am not empowered to negotiate on behalf of Her Majesty's Government. I am a member of the diplomatic service. I am not a defence or armaments expert'.

Marielle began to pout like a spoilt child.

'If you are indeed involved in this business', went on Christopher, 'you will know that such transactions are conducted on a government-to-government basis. There are all kinds of European community rules to be obeyed. Your company will need permission from the appropriate French ministry to approach the British Ministry of Defence, then you will need an export licence and most important of all you will need an End User Certificate from the British end'.

Marielle brightened.

'No problem', she beamed. 'I have it'.

She pulled a piece of paper from her handbag and passed it across the table. Christopher withdrew a pair of reading glasses from his inside pocket. He didn't need them but he carried them as a device to give himself thinking time.

The first thing he noticed was the Ministry of Defence crest and the Whitehall address at the top of the sheet. Beneath the address was the legend 'Defence Procurement Secretariat'. There was a lengthy reference number and a date, which Christopher mentally calculated, was about three weeks ago. The document was headed 'End User Certificate' and stated simply: 'This is to certify that the following items purchased from Cimeterre Defense Industrie, Paris, France are for the sole use of Her Majesty's Armed Forces and no other purpose'. It went on to list several items of electronic hardware under the title of Weapons Guidance Systems. There was an official-looking stamp and a signature above the title 'Assistant Secretary, Defence.'

A forgery, of course, thought Christopher, but a very convincing one. What on earth was Marielle playing at? This pretence of wanting to do business with Britain was a ruse. She wanted to prove that she had inside knowledge of the illegal arms trade and access to someone who could make it happen. But why? What was in it for her? And why come to the British?

'I have the export licence from our Department of Trade, if you would like to see it', said Marielle.

I'll bet you have, thought Christopher. 'No that will not be necessary', he said. 'Look, Marielle, what is this all about? You have got me here to prove something. But you know that

I cannot take anything forward between your company and my government. So how can I help you?'

'There are very bad things happening', she said. 'Weapons are going to places they should not go. People are making money they should not make. The world would not approve if they knew, but they do not know'.

'But why come to us?', asked Christopher. 'If you have evidence of wrongdoing why not go to the police, or the DST or even the newspapers? Why all this secrecy…the personal visit to our embassy, the home telephone number, the meeting in a jazz club?'

Marielle shook her head. 'Nathalie Cagoule', she said, look what happened to her'.

'Who?', asked Christopher. 'I'm sorry I don't follow'.

'Find out about Nathalie Cagoule', said Marielle, 'and I will explain it all next time. It was nice meeting you, Christophe. I must rejoin my sister and my little nephew now. Au revoir'.

She got up and walked way.

Next time? I don't think so, thought Christopher.

Chapter Five

Aldershot, England, 16th April 1986

Sandra Donne always made her husband wear a dressing gown around the flat. It was maroon towelling. She had bought it for him for Christmas the year they married.

Kevin thought it ridiculous. She didn't make him wear pyjamas in bed. He wore boxer shorts or Y-fronts. But lately he had found a use for the dressing gown. It had pockets.

He felt in the pocket for the bottle. There was about two inches of vodka left. He unscrewed the cap and poured it into his bowl of cornflakes. The milk looked grey and watery. He took a spoonful of cornflakes but quickly spat it out. He picked up the bowl and put it to his lips, tipped it up, and slurped back the liquid. He sat back in his chair at the kitchen table and wiped his mouth with the back of his hand. He looked at the pulped cornflakes remaining in the bowl. Solids. He decided he couldn't face them without a drink.

He walked across the tiny landing to the bathroom and pulled aside a hardboard panel which was loosely clipped to the side of the bath with a strip of plastic cowling. He lay down on his stomach and pulled another bottle of vodka from beneath the bathtub.

She'll never find my hiding place, he thought as he stood up and looked at himself in the mirrored front of the shaving cabinet. His eyes were bloodshot. His chin was covered in stubble. Two, three, four days' growth? Who knew? Who cared? He poked out his tongue. It was covered in thick white slime.

I am an alcoholic, he thought.

'I'm an alcoholic, holic, holic. I'm an alcoholic. Taran taran tara!', he sang to himself as he shuffled back into the kitchen.

He looked at the digital clock on the cooker. Nine forty-five in the morning.

Whoops! Late for work, again.

He'd had the dreams once more. The awful dreams that drove him from the army – the only job he loved. The shooting. The killing. The execution. He put his hands over his ears but in his head he could hear the thump, thump of the rounds passing through the silencer and the thud of the bodies hitting the ground…the ground…the ground…the ground.

Kevin had been twenty-four years old and a corporal in the elite Special Air Service when he was sent to Northern Ireland on a secret mission to kill strangers for Queen and country.

The Queen didn't know he was there going about her business. The Prime Minister didn't know – or didn't want to know. The police certainly didn't know. Only a handful of top brass in Whitehall and at Army Intelligence headquarters in Lisburn knew that he and his three SAS comrades had a licence to kill.

The targets were all active figures in the Irish Republican Army terrorist movement. Each one was identified and condemned to death without trial by some faceless individual in MI5 who would, in turn, have been acting on the word of a paid informer. Lisburn would then pass on his picture and where he could be found and he would simply disappear…forever. Abducted, taken to a remote spot, shot, and his body buried in a distant forest.

Kevin and the other members of the unit – Geordie Phil, Brummie Colin, and their Scottish sergeant, Don – always took it in turns to pull the trigger. None of them liked the job. They had joined the army to fight proper wars. They had joined the SAS to undertake daring missions against terrorists and insurgents – to pit their physical skills and mental strengths, under the most extreme conditions, against clever and resourceful enemies. They were disciplined men who obeyed orders. But summary execution of strangers who couldn't fight back and would never face a trial of any sort left a bad taste in the mouth.

Kevin shivered and winced. He had been the triggerman the night they snatched the young blond guy from outside the Rotterdam Bar in Sailorstown.

The boy reminded Kevin of his own brother. Who was he? What had he done? He looked too young to be any kind of a threat to the security of the United Kingdom. Suppose the MI5 guy had got it wrong. Suppose the informant was acting out of spite. It didn't bear thinking about.

He lit a cigarette, unscrewed the bottle top, and took a gulp of vodka.

His hands were shaking. No point in going to work today. It wasn't much of a job anyway. Stacking shelves in a supermarket. Not for one of Her Majesty's fighting men. Not for one of the elite – a badged member of The Firm. It was the fourth job he'd had in less than two years since his medical discharge.

Sandra was at work. The kids were at her mother's. Little Shane, and the baby, Tara. Sandra worked on the checkout at the same supermarket that Kevin was about to walk away from.

The dole was a more honourable way to get your money, he thought. It came from the government and the government owed him. He'd fought for his country. It was in their name that he'd carried out all those...murders.

He sniffed and wiped a tear from his cheek.

Leaving Ireland had been easy. Leaving the army was harder. But there was Sandra. Sweet, understanding Sandra. There had always been Sandra.

She had beautiful wavy rich brown hair, which tumbled down her back to her waist and sparkling black eyes, inherited from her Maltese mother. They met at a dance in the Hussars barracks at Tidworth, before Kevin ever applied to join the SAS, and soon became inseparable.

Even when he was posted to Northern Ireland they corresponded and talked occasionally on the telephone. Sandra was waiting when he came home a broken man. She never asked what he had been doing. She never asked why he had left the army. She just held him. And kissed him. And comforted him when he woke screaming in the middle of the night.

They were married. They had the children. But Kevin's personal hell would not go away. His only solace was in the bottle. It would not be long; he knew it, before he would have to leave Sandra. For her sake. And the kids'.

He pulled on a pair of jeans and a T-shirt. By the time he had shambled his way to "The Crimea Inn" in Crimea Road it would be opening time.

And it was. He sat in a corner and nursed a pint of Guinness, from time to time surreptitiously pouring a slug of vodka into it from the bottle in his pocket.

He wondered what might have happened if any members of the Royal Ulster Constabulary, the police, had ever stopped him and his colleagues while they were about their dirty business in Northern Ireland. He did not have to wonder long. He knew. They would have had to kill the policemen too.

Because, if they had ever been arrested, everyone from the Prime Minister down would have denied their very existence let alone the fact that they were carrying out specific government policy. It would have been unthinkable for anyone to acknowledge that an SAS hit squad was killing IRA men on direct orders from Whitehall.

'Hey dozy, what are you having?' It was the voice of Billy Manders, Kevin's regular drinking partner. He, too, had been in the SAS but was invalided out after a heavy parachute landing in Aden, which shattered the lower part of his left leg.

'I'm alright thanks, Bill', said Kevin.

'Yeah, right. The usual for my dozy friend please landlord', said Billy as he sat down on a bench seat next to Kevin.

'I'm an alcoholic', said Kevin with a directness which startled his companion.

Billy looked at him momentarily and then said: 'No you're not Kev. You're just a pisshead'.

'No, no, I really am an alcoholic', repeated Kevin with urgency in his voice.

Billy was reassuring.

'Alcoholics drink in secret not in public like you', he said. 'They hide drink and they never get pissed. At least not falling down drunk like you'.

'I hide drink all over the house', said Kevin. 'Look, I've even got a bottle of vodka in my pocket now. And I never show it when I'm pissed.

'Did you know that when we were in The Firm we were members of King Arthur's Knights?', he asked suddenly.

Billy shook his head.

'Yep, the regiment's winged sword is Excalibur…so we were knights in shining armour'. He began to chuckle and broke into a wheezing cough.

He had not noticed the slurring as he tried to pronounce the words "Excalibur" and "shining".

But Billy had.

'Listen', said Billy, leaning forward with genuine concern for his friend in his eyes. 'Maybe you do have a problem'.

He put his hand on top of Kevin's.

'The time to get it sorted is now, before it destroys you. There is a fantastic clinic at Andover. They do a lot of work with guys like us, drying out and rehabilitation and all that kinda shit.

'You need to go to your doctor and get him to refer you. Do it now. Today. Do you want me to come with you? I will if you like'.

'No. I'm fine. I can do it myself. You're right. I'm going now…while the…iron is…hot', said Kevin.

He got up and staggered through the door.

'Dozy pisshead', muttered Billy to himself as he took another sip of his drink.

* * * * * *

London 17th June 1986

Peter Gray fingered the immaculately tied Windsor knot on his expensive silk tie and frowned. He shifted the weight from his left foot to his right as if to shift the burden of responsibility, which he felt bearing down on him. Beneath his bespoke Savile Row suit he sensed the shoulder holster digging into his armpit and mentally rehearsed a quick draw of his Smith & Wesson revolver. At six feet four inches tall he cut an imposing figure standing on the pavement in Beauchamp Place outside London's fashionable San Lorenzo restaurant.

He bent down and opened the rear door of a black limousine as a lissom young blonde clattered down the steps squealing girlish goodbyes to her luncheon companions. Peter paid her no attention. His eyes were scanning up and down the pavement and checking the movements of passersby on the opposite side of the street.

Once his charge was safely seated he closed her door and jumped into the front passenger seat as the car drew smoothly away into the afternoon traffic.

Just two months earlier Peter had reached what he considered to be the pinnacle of his Metropolitan Police career so far. On promotion to the rank of Inspector he had been selected for the elite Royalty Protection branch and posted to Buckingham Palace. As one of the new boys he had not been assigned to protect a specific member of the Royal Family. Instead he was attached to a pool of men required to stand-in whenever one of the regular protection officers was on leave or unwell.

Today he was covering for the Princess of Wales's bodyguard whose wife had been taken ill with appendicitis. He had not worked with Diana before and approached the assignment with keen anticipation. Her butler had briefed him that the Princess was entertaining two old friends – a man and a woman – to lunch at her favourite restaurant.

Peter could see no particular security problems in the excursion. The Royal chauffeur was familiar with the best routes between Kensington Palace and the restaurant and the staff at San Lorenzo always gave Diana a table which afforded a degree of privacy. Her bodyguard, he was advised, was always given a single table in direct line of sight of the

71

Princess with no obstructions between himself and her should he need to move swiftly to her side.

And so it proved. The detective drank a glass of fizzy water and toyed with a salad while he watched the three friends chatting animatedly.

The Princess was wearing a light summer dress with long sleeves loosely buttoned at the wrists. At one point she raised her left hand and ran it casually through her hair. Momentarily her sleeve slipped down a couple of inches and Peter, who was sitting directly to her right, noticed two angry parallel lines running across her left wrist. He waited until she repeated the gesture a few minutes later and decided that the marks looked like knife cuts. One of them appeared to have been fairly deep but both looked as though they were scars in the process of healing.

Diana was eating very quickly. She was bolting her food. As soon as she had finished her main course she got up to go to the ladies restroom.

Peter's training told him that he should follow and stand guard outside the door. Had he been the Princess's regular protection officer he would have known that such a move was unnecessary. There was only one way in and out of the restroom area and it could be clearly seen from where he was.

But in his ignorance Peter got up and followed obediently. He stopped in the lobby outside a door marked 'Ladies' and folded his arms in the time-honoured pose of the bodyguard. He glanced at his watch and then heard retching. He looked towards the door. The sound was unmistakeable. Someone was vomiting. There were only two doors between him and Diana. No one else had gone in or come out. There was no doubt. He was listening to Her Royal Highness the Princess of Wales throwing up.

A sense of helplessness and anguish swept over Peter. He knew exactly what this meant.

His younger sister, Moira, was in a psychiatric clinic battling against chronic depression. He had shared the pain and despair of his ageing parents as they watched their beautiful, vivacious, daughter decline into a gaunt shell of neurosis and self-loathing. The first clues the family had had of Moira's distress came with the diagnosis that she was suffering from the eating disorder Bulimia. She was losing weight alarmingly yet apparently eating normally. But the telltale sign was her tendency to bolt her food and then rush to the lavatory where she would make herself sick. Then followed the self-harming episodes and the suicide attempts made by slashing her wrists. It was a cry for help, the doctors said, and she could die if she were not treated and treated quickly.

Peter was in turmoil. The wife of the heir to the throne and mother of the future king was a suicidal Bulimic. He was sure of it. He had the proof. And now he came to think of it she looked painfully thin. But who else knew? It was characteristic of this illness that the subject was able to fool those around them and keep their condition secret, sometimes until it was too late to receive treatment.

Peter's duty was to protect Diana from physical harm but it was not his duty to protect her from herself. He knew that the cardinal rule of being a Royalty Protection officer was to keep your principal's private life strictly confidential. Anything you learned about their personal habits and behaviour you must keep to yourself.

Images of Moira flashed through his mind as they drove in silence back to Kensington Palace. He had sensed something was wrong with his sister but had told no one until her illness was finally diagnosed. He could not rid himself of the guilt.

'Are you alright, Peter?', inquired a soft voice from the back seat. 'You look awfully worried about something'.

Peter started. 'No, no I'm fine thanks, Ma'am', he replied. Then after a pause he asked: 'Did you enjoy your lunch Ma'am?'

'Oh yes, thank you', said the Princess. 'It was absolutely delicious. I could do with a second helping'.

Peter's mind was made up. No matter what the personal cost to his career he had to tell someone. He would make a confidential report to his Commander. It would probably find its way to Scotland Yard and others would have the responsibility of deciding what to do. He had heard all the gossip below stairs. He knew that there were those within Royal circles who were already labelling the young princess mad. He guessed there were those who wanted her given psychiatric treatment. This would play right into their hands. But at least his conscience would be clear. He might have failed Moira but he would not fail Diana.

Chapter Six

Paris, 11th November 1986

'Monsieur, you will have another pastis, non? If you will, I will have another Martini. Let me get them'.

The voice was warm and friendly. The manner charming and persuasive.

For the first time in his life Henri Paul felt…valued.

'Yes. That would be nice. Thank you. And then I must get back to work', he said.

His companion smiled and motioned for a waiter. They were seated in one of the wooden alcoves on the ground floor in Harry's Bar. Close together so that they could hear one another above the babble of tourist voices.

The previous evening they had met, apparently by chance, when Henri Paul popped in to the bar for a quick whisky on his way home from his new job at The Ritz. A man, whom he now knew as Jacques, had politely inquired if the bar stool next to him was occupied and had promptly engaged him in conversation.

Jacques was anxious to talk about himself and revealed that he worked for the government in a department which employed private pilots on a part-time charter basis to fly civil servants around the country. Even though the pilots only worked part-time the pay was extremely generous.

Jacques seemed astonished to learn that Henri was himself a qualified pilot and keen flyer. They agreed to meet the following day to talk about the possibility of some freelance work.

When the waiter brought their drinks Jacques pulled out a packet of cigarettes and offered one to his companion. They both lit up.

'I have made some inquiries since we met last night, Henri...may I call you Henri?', said Jacques, 'and I think I am in a position to offer you some work. Well-paid work. Very important work'.

Henri Paul nodded expectantly.

'Your flying record is very good. You have held a private pilot's license for, let me see, just over ten years and you are instruments rated. One year's service in the air force at Rochefort base. Enlisted as a lieutenant in the reserves. What a pity your eyesight prevented you from flying for the air force'.

Well, thought Paul, *he must be working for the government. He's had access to all my official records.*

'Born in Lorient, Brittany. Baccalaureate in mathematics and science at the Lyon St Louis, prizes in classical piano'.

Jacques was reciting from memory now.

'Hang on, what's this got to do with...how did you know that?', asked a bemused Paul.

'You are a patriot, Henri. We know that', purred Jacques.

'We? Who's this we? I...'

Jacques put his hand on Paul's arm.

'Will you do something for your country? Will you do something for France? It is not very much but it will be very helpful', he said.

Henri Paul threw back his Ricard in one gulp and took a drag on his cigarette.

'What?', he asked with more than a hint of suspicion in his voice.

Jacques's charm was switched on again.

'For the past six years you have been a sales representative at Emeraude Marine...

Paul interrupted: 'How did you?.....'

'I understand that you have recently taken up employment as a security officer at The Ritz. We need to have some information about one of the long-term guests in the hotel'.

'I thought you were going to give me a flying job', said Paul a little plaintively.

'Yes, I am sure that can be arranged if you are able to help in the way I am asking. This is a more important task at this time', said Jacques firmly.

'Well, what do I have to do?', asked Paul.

'I need you to report the movements of this individual in detail', said Jacques. 'Every appointment he has in the hotel, who he meets, and where he goes when he leaves the hotel'.

'How will I do that?'

'Guests invariably leave the names of people they are due to meet with the reception desk or the bar or restaurant staff', said Jacques. 'And they invariably tell the concierge where they are going when they order a taxi. And in any case I am sure you have the facility to monitor telephone calls to and from individual rooms and suites'.

'I don't know', said Paul. 'I don't think my employers would like this. There is such a thing as protecting the privacy of guests'.

Your employers need never know', said Jacques. 'It is your job, is it not, to keep a close eye on everyone and everything in the hotel. For you to keep an eye on one single guest for a while would not appear abnormal to anyone. And besides, your employers are not French. They have no desire to protect the Republic'.

Henri Paul's mind was racing. Protect the Republic? This guy was pulling his leg. This was like something from a cheap spy novel.

'And what's in it for me?', he asked.

Jacques reached into his inside pocket and withdrew a white manila envelope. He put it on the table in front of Paul.

'Ten thousand francs, in cash', he said without lifting his hand from the envelope. 'If things go well, the next time we meet you can give me details of your bank and we can discuss having a regular retainer paid directly into your account'.

Henri Paul's gaze shifted from the envelope to Jacques's eyes and back again. He took another drag on his cigarette. Eventually he spoke.

'Okay. I'll do it. But just this once. Who is this guy?'

Jacques reached into his pocket once more and produced a black and white photograph showing a balding man with a dark, bushy, moustache, wearing a dinner jacket and grinning at the camera. The picture had obviously been taken at a banquet of some sort.

'His name is Hosni Maartensson. He's half Iranian half Dutch', said Jacques.

'Yeah I've seen him around the hotel', said Paul. 'What has he done?'

'Nothing' said Jacques, 'he is an enemy of France. You are doing good for your country. Okay?'

'Okay', said Paul pocketing the envelope. 'Now I must be going my lunch break is over'.

'Just before you go take this', said Jacques handing his companion a business card. 'You can contact me at any hour through this number and I will expect regular reports anyway. Call me tomorrow and let me know how you are getting on'.

Henri Paul glanced at the card. It read "Compagnie de Recherche Beton, Jacques Fontaine, sales executive"

Concrete Research Company. Very good. He left the bar chuckling to himself. He was in a bad spy novel. He was sure of it.

* * * * * *

Elysee Palace, Paris, France 20th June 1987

Maurice de Champvieux was an odious creature.

Short and squat. Not quite five feet four inches tall with his boots on. His stocky frame carried an excess of fat – nearly seventeen stone. His white, hair flowed over his shoulders unkempt, lank, and matted at the ends where it curled upward in an almost feminine affectation. His sweaty complexion had the appearance of putty and his once handsome grey eyes were bloodshot and red-rimmed from lack of sleep and an over indulgence in his favourite tipple – the rare French brandy, Haut Armagnac Chateau de Neguebouc. His irregular teeth were nicotine-stained and his breath stank permanently with a mixed aroma of garlic and the large Cuban cigars, which he chain-smoked. On the small finger of his chubby right hand he wore a white gold ring with a single ruby inset – the last relic of a long-forgotten romance, which had blossomed and died one steamy summer long ago in far off Sri Lanka. Lately he had taken to wearing kaftans for comfort but his colour scheme never varied from shades of grey and his footwear of choice was open-toed sandals.

Maurice was every inch a French eccentric. The very embodiment of a decadent bohemian. He would have been entirely at ease prowling the bars and café's of the Left Bank - a caricature posing provocatively for the cameras of tourists eager to capture an image to confirm the popular concept of a Parisian artist for the folks back home.

Absolutely no one, except those in the know, would have this man down as the head of French Intelligence. Yet that is precisely what he was. The *Directeur* of the *Direction de la Surveillance du Territoire* – the fabled DST.

Despite his bizarre appearance Maurice was a genuine aristocrat. Scion of the 8th Baron de Champvieux he could trace his ancestors back to the Battle of Agincourt and was the last member of the family to be born in the ancient and spectacular Chateau de Champvieux nestling in the forested foothills of the Mont d'Or just to the north-west of Lyons.

The family left the castle and estate soon after Maurice was born at the end of the First World War and moved to Lyons where his father, who had given up his baronial title, was practising as a lawyer. After an unremarkable schooling the young de Champvieux, who was precociously bright, went to study mediaeval history at the Sorbonne in Paris where he fell under the influence of the legendary economics professor Marc Bloch.

In 1939 Maurice was drafted into the French army, much to his disgust because fighting offended against his dilettante leanings and sensitive nature. But the war was to throw him on to a path, which would take him ultimately to a pivotal position at the heart of French government. Captured and wounded early on he escaped and made his way to Vichy where he took a job as a clerk in the collaborationist government of Marshal Petain. There he shared an office with a young Francois Mitterrand, who was also an escapee from the Germans, and the two became firm friends. When Mitterrand quit to set up his own cadre of resistance fighters in 1943 Maurice went too.

They parted after liberation but Mitterrand's vision for a post-war France standing free and proud at the heart of a modern Europe had captured Maurice's imagination and he quickly embarked on a career in the *Corps Diplomatique*. At some point during his first tour of duty in Indochina he was recruited into the DGSE – the French secret service - and became an overseas agent while serving as press attaché at the embassy in Saigon.

After that it had been a steady climb up the intelligence ladder with postings at home and abroad while acquiring a reputation for ruthlessness and attention to detail. It was this combination of ebullience and aggression along with his general appearance, which earned him the nickname *'Le Sanglier'* – The Wild Boar – within the service. No one was surprised when Mitterrand appointed him his spy-in-chief on election to the Presidency in 1981.

Today Maurice was on a secret mission. He was the only man who could see the President without an appointment and often took advantage of his special position to call in on his old friend for a chat on the pretence of delivering an intelligence briefing. But today he had been summoned and was perplexed by the urgency implicit in the suddenness of the call.

Maurice always drove himself. His staff could not work out whether it was part of his cover or a general desire for anonymity or simply his disdain for formality and the ostentatious trappings of power. But whatever it was he drove himself in an old, battered, Citroen 2CV - grey, of course. His only concession to personal security was a Beretta pistol, which he kept in the ever-expanding waistband of the trousers he wore beneath his kaftan.

The short journey from DST headquarters in Rue Nelaton across the Bir Hakeim bridge to the Rue du Faubourg St Honore took a matter of minutes and soon he was turning in to the Elysee Palace through the archway beneath the grey stone portico. The two sentries, accustomed to saluting as official limousines passed, paid him no attention and the duty inspector waved him through the security check beneath the inner arch.

Maurice drove to a discreet corner of the courtyard where he parked and let himself in through a side door. Making his way down an anonymous corridor he soon found himself in the grand vestibule where he nodded to the frock-coated usher and made his way up the carpeted granite stairs beneath the enormous chandelier. Turning left he opened the ornate doors, which led into the *Salon des Ordonnonces* where the ADC of the day rose from his desk and crossed the room without a word. He knocked briefly on the double doors with the gilt handles, which opened into the President's private study and, opening the left one, announced, 'Le Directeur, Monsieur le President'.

As soon as the door closed behind him Maurice sensed that the President was in no mood for pleasantries.

Mitterrand did not rise from behind the desk to greet him as usual. Instead he gestured to the padded leather armchair which was drawn up to face the front of his desk. Maurice sauntered over and sat down. As he did so he noticed a green-coloured DST file on the President's desk. Rapidly reading upside down he deciphered the word 'Confidentiel' – the lowest classification given to DST dossiers – and a name, 'Carina'.

Only Maurice could authorise the removal of such a file from the DST headquarters. No one else could, no one, that is, apart from the President himself. Maurice did not stop to ponder how the papers could have reached the Elysee Palace without his knowledge. He was running a rapid mental inventory of all he knew about the name 'Carina'.

Born Katerina Borisova in Kiev. Discovered by French film director when winning Miss Ukraine competition aged 20. Brought to Paris for massively successful pop singing career. Adopts stage-name Carina. Becomes international movie star. One failed marriage. Many lovers, two of whom commit suicide. And a major public scandal involving the disclosure of a long-running affair with...Francois Mitterrand.

The President was glowering. He leant across the desk and thrust a letter into Maurice's hand. It was typed on the headed notepaper of a Paris law firm well known for aggressive and tenacious litigation. It was headed "Strictly Private and Confidential: For the personal attention of addressee only".

Maurice scanned the contents rapidly. Several phrases caught his eye. *...irrevocable damage to her career...severe financial hardship...hitherto undisclosed details of physical abuse and unnatural practices known only to the President and to my client...distasteful and politically damaging in current climate...substantial settlement...mutually agreed terms.*

'It's blackmail', growled Mitterrand thumping the desk with his fist. 'I will not be blackmailed by some cheap Ukrainian tart'.

Maurice was irritated. He had become resigned to the fact the President saw him as his personal face-saver. If Mitterrand was in a scrape, if he stood to be politically damaged or privately embarrassed by accusations or revelations of any kind, his foes would have to be neutralised. And that invariably meant abusing his friendship with Maurice by blatantly enlisting the secret services' expertise at playing dirty tricks.

'Just ignore it, Monsieur President', he said, 'the details of your friendship with the lady became public five years ago and everyone has forgotten it. The newspapers tried to make it a scandal then but it has done you no harm. In fact', he added with a chuckle, 'most people were very envious and saw you as a bit of a hero'.

'This is different', snapped Mitterrand.

'How can it be?', asked Maurice with a leering grin. 'What did you get up to that was so disgusting, eh? These things happen. We all do it from time to time. You are a busy man. You need your leisure activities. N'cest-ce pas?'.

Maurice always adopted a jocular, comradely, boys-will-be-boys approach when dealing with Mitterrand's many sexual indiscretions though they both knew that his own homosexual fantasies were played out nightly in the gay bars and nightclubs of Pigalle where the habitués knew him as Denis and thought he was a director of porn movies.

'This is not a joke', barked the President. 'I repeat, it is serious. The dignity of the office of President could be damaged and the standing of France in the world could be affected. I need you to deal with her'.

Maurice was familiar with the tactic. The President was making a thin pretence that the issue was one which could impact on State security and thus fall under his aegis.

He sighed. 'Leave it to me Monsieur President', he said. 'She will be compromised…a scandal…from which her reputation will never recover'.

'No, no, no', shouted Mitterrand, his face reddening with anger. 'She will simply create a counter-scandal involving me. She must be stopped. I will leave it to you. Do whatever you have to do but make sure she cannot damage me any further. Do you understand?'

'Yes', replied Maurice, 'absolutely. I think this is a job for "L'Appeau".

"L'Appeau"?, The Decoy?, asked the President, perplexed. Then suddenly recognition. 'Ah yes, the Decoy. That is the man with the special skills you told me about once before. Are you sure he can keep her quiet?'

'Definitely', said Maurice. 'She will know him professionally and she will trust him'.

As he spoke he looked steadily into the eyes of the President who, just two weeks later, would stand, head bowed in dignified grief, at the graveside of his former lover and tell her army of desolate fans that his blackmailer was: 'France's beautiful broken songbird who could no longer bear the burden of life'.

Chapter Seven

Tidworth, England, 17th May 1989

It was a windy day. But otherwise dry. And there was an extra frisson of excitement in the air.

The troops on parade at Aliwal Barracks in the military town of Tidworth, Hampshire, were all turned out in their number one uniforms. This was the headquarters of the 13th/18th Kings Royal Hussars and today they were expecting a visit from their Colonel-in-Chief.

The Hussars had a proud history dating back to the Crimean campaign and beyond. They were the cavalry regiment which featured in the ill-fated Charge of the Light Brigade.

The reason for the heightened sense of anticipation was the fact that theirs was no ordinary Colonel-in-Chief. They were to be inspected by none other than Her Royal Highness, the Princess Diana of Wales.

Kevin Donne stood in a corner of the parade ground well away from the temporary stands where the families and friends of the troopers were gathering for the spectacle.

He didn't really want to be there. The square-bashing and ceremonial of army life were a thing of the past for him. These occasions brought back memories. Unhappy ones.

Former members of the regiment were routinely invited to passing out parades and special inspections of this kind. Most of the veterans used it as an excuse to get together for a beer or two with old comrades and an opportunity to swap war stories. They looked forward to it.

Three weeks ago while wandering down Oxford Street in London, Kevin had bumped into an old chum, Ted Williams.

The pair had joined the army together on the same day. Williams was an ebullient Welshman who enthusiastically invited Kevin to the Tidworth parade and simply would not take no for an answer.

'It'll be a chance for you to meet some of the guys again', he said, and then we can all have a drink, a proper drink, together afterwards in The Ram'.

Kevin was far from sure about the advisability of this. He would dearly love to see some of his old friends again but he was recovering from drug and alcohol dependency and was making good progress. He did not want to put himself in the way of temptation and a possible relapse.

In fact he had already met Diana. Almost a year earlier she had visited the drug rehabilitation centre in Andover where Kevin was being treated. She had shaken his hand and wished him well. She seemed very sympathetic.

And now here he was, against his better judgement, waiting to see her again. He took a drag on his cigarette and remembered the first time he had come across Diana.

It was not long after her marriage. She and her husband were visiting the SAS headquarters in Hereford and took part in an anti-terrorist training exercise. A group of 'terrorists' played by SAS soldiers had seized a mock embassy and the Royal couple joined the units sent to storm the building. Prince Charles flew one of the helicopters carrying troops into the attack and his wife drove a Range Rover with one of the ground assault parties.

When her group reached the scene of the siege the Princess unwisely ignored advice and jumped out of the vehicle just as a flash grenade detonated near her, singeing her hair and covering her in flames, sparks and smoke.

Kevin, who had just finished his SAS training and was awaiting an active service posting, was the first soldier to reach her. He beat out the flames with his gloved hands but the badly shaken princess had to have her hair cut short as a result. The following day the world's press waxed lyrical about Diana's stunning new hairdo.

Kevin smiled to himself as he recalled the incident.

'Parade. Parade 'shun', bawled the Regimental Sergeant Major. 'Royal salute. Preeesent…arms!'

There were three loud clattering crashes as fifty hands slapped against rifle butts and fifty booted feet stamped to the ground in unison. The band began to play as a shiny black limousine with the Royal Standard fluttering at the prow of its bonnet cruised to a stop in front of the saluting base. Two officers in summer uniforms with swagger sticks tucked under their arms snapped to attention and banged their right hands, palm outwards, against the braided peaks of their caps.

Her Royal Highness stepped elegantly from the car and shook hands with the officers before taking her seat on the rostrum between them. From where he stood Kevin could just see that she was wearing a long white jacket and a white pleated skirt.

During the next twenty minutes or so the band, dressed in the Hussars' traditional black plumed busbys and heavily braided jerkins, played a medley of military tunes while the troopers executed a series of complicated marching manoeuvres, each one of which was greeted by ecstatic cheering from the public stands.

When it was all over, the Princess, escorted by the two officers, walked up and down the lines of the band and the troopers, occasionally stopping for a brief word or two with the men on parade. Then she headed for the public stands where flag-waving schoolchildren stood expectantly waiting for a chance to glimpse her at close hand.

At the far end of the first public enclosure stood a group of about thirty former Hussars dressed in an untidy assortment of civilian clothes. Kevin stood at the front with his hands loosely clasped in front of him. The whole scene was a matter of indifference to him but he could not escape an innate sense of loyalty to the Crown and he retained a modicum of respect for royalty.

A few yards away a tiny girl in a pink dress presented a posy of marigolds to Diana who squatted down on her haunches to chat briefly with the toddler. She stood up, handed the flowers to her lady-in-waiting and looked straight at Kevin who involuntarily came to attention.

The Princess strode towards him. 'Hello', she said warmly, extending her hand. 'How are you?'

'Fine thanks Mam', said Kevin. 'How are you?' He took her hand and bowed stiffly from the waist.

'Oh, yes, I'm very well. Thank you', she replied. Her brow furrowed briefly and she looked him straight in the eye. 'Haven't we met somewhere before?'

'Yes Mam. Last year. The rehab clinic. Andover?'

The police plain-clothes protection officer at her side shot him a wary glance.

She smiled a radiant smile. Her teeth were perfect. Her skin was perfect. Her hair was perfect. *She was absolutely gorgeous*, thought Kevin.

'Of course', she said. 'How's it going? Are you okay now?'

'Absolutely mam', said Kevin. 'Right as rain. Completely cured'.

'Oh I'm so glad. That's brilliant', she said. 'They do a wonderful job those clinics don't they?'

She smiled again.

She fancies me, thought Kevin. His face began to feel warm.
He was blushing. *This is ridiculous*, he thought. *I'm a
roughty toughty soldier. Pretty women don't embarrass me.
Even Royal ones.*

'We also met a long time ago. In Hereford', he said.

Now he had the Royal detective's full attention.

Diana looked at him inquiringly.

'The hair incident, Mam?'

'Oh my God, how funny was that?', she said. She started to
laugh. A sweet innocent girlish giggle. It sounded like a peel
of tinkling bells to Kevin.

'Well it's lovely to see you again', she said. 'Good Luck'.
And she moved on down the line. Kevin gazed after her. In
that moment he had found himself an obsession.

And Diana had found herself a stalker.

* * * * * *

Paris, 13th October 1989

The message left on Christopher's voicemail was from the
Commercial Attaché's secretary at the British Embassy…and
it was cryptic.

A woman with a deep husky voice had called on the dedicated
line which was reserved for the exclusive use of informants.
She wanted Christopher to contact her urgently. She said it
was about Nathalie Cagoule. Christopher would know who
she was, she said.

Christopher scratched his head and tried to remember. Nathalie Cagoule. Nathalie Cagoule? The name rang a bell.

Suddenly it came to him. The crazy woman with the phoney End User Certificate who claimed to have information on the illegal arms trade. Marielle somebody or other. She had mentioned Nathalie Cagoule and promised more information the next time they met. How long had it been? Three, four years?

At the time, he recalled, he had asked the secretary to run a check on the name Nathalie Cagoule in the French national newspaper cuttings library. Her inquiries revealed that Nathalie had been the victim of an, as yet, unsolved murder on the Paris Metro some years before. Christopher remembered asking the embassy's security officer to make further inquiries with his contacts in the French police but he could not recall the results of those inquiries.

He sighed. He would have to make one of his rare visits to the office.

Christopher didn't have an office as such. The Paris station of MI6 was based, as in most parts of the world, in the British embassy. The head of station was given the diplomatic service rank of First Secretary and operated under the cover of Commercial Attaché.

If Christopher ever did visit the office it was usually to see the Commercial Attaché's secretary who would pass on any messages or documentation thought too sensitive to be entrusted to the post or e-mail. She had access to material passed on from London via the diplomatic bag and transcripts of scrambled radio messages.

He called the secretary and asked her to get out the file on Marielle Whatsername and to put the kettle on.

An hour later he had arrived at the Embassy and was sitting with his feet on the Commercial Attaché's desk, sipping a mug of instant coffee, and reading a file marked "Marielle Norstrund". He ignored his own report on the bizarre meeting with the mysterious Ms Norstrund. The report of the security officer was much more interesting. It revealed that the murder of Nathalie Cagoule had been referred to the DCRG – *Direction Centrale des Reseignements-Generaux* – the political police who dealt with matters of national security and subversion, because the dead woman had been a secretary working in the French Ministry of Finance at the time of her killing. The investigation had apparently been dropped and the file closed soon after the DCRG took it over.

Christopher found Marielle's business card in the folder and rang the telephone number on the back. She answered after the first ring and quickly agreed to a meeting at a small café, which Christopher knew on The Left Bank.

When she arrived Christopher was already there. He had forgotten what an imposing figure she was and once again was taken by her striking appearance. She was wearing a charcoal grey trouser suit over a black woollen roll neck sweater and wrap around sunglasses even though it was an overcast autumn day. Her platinum blonde hair was piled dramatically on the top of her head.

They ordered coffee and Marielle seemed much more businesslike than on their first encounter.

'You know about Nathalie Cagoule?', she snapped, without preamble.

'Yes', replied Christopher. 'You promised to tell me about her and what connection she had to you the next time we met. But it has been four years so why the urgency now?'

'They killed her because she knew too much and they thought she was going to talk to you', said Marielle.

'To *me*?', said Christopher, puzzled.

'No. The British', said Marielle. 'She was the private secretary of the Minister of Finance and she knew exactly what was going on'.

'What was going on?', asked Christopher, but Marielle ignored the question.

'She was also the lover of the main man – the man who was protecting someone very high and very important. So they killed her'.

'Look, Marielle, you are talking in riddles', said Christopher. 'Who are *they*, for a start?'

'The conspirators. The people who are doing this', she said. 'I keep telling you'.

'No. You are telling me nothing', said Christopher. 'You are assuming I know what you are talking about. Just let me ask a few questions and keep the answers simple. Okay?'

Marielle nodded.

'You are the Director of Corporate Affairs for Cimeterre Defense Industrie, right? So what does your job entail?'

'It is a form of public relations, really', said Marielle. 'I am a political lobbyist. I keep relations between my company and the government smooth. I try to make a case with ministers for our company to be preferred to our rivals when it comes to placing contracts'.

'I see', said Christopher, 'but the last time we met you indicated that you knew of corruption involving the French arms trade. You demonstrated that you could produce forged documents and the like. What was all that about?'

'My company is supplying arms and munitions to Iraq against all the United Nations embargoes', said Marielle. 'We obtain false export licences and forged End User Certificates from Jordan. The hardware is shipped to Jordan and transhipped on to Iraq. We are not the only French company which is doing this'.

'But that is not corruption, that is the French government flouting international law and going behind the backs of the United Nations community', said Christopher. 'Why the need for forged documentation?'

'Because it is not the French government', said Marielle. 'It is being done by a cabal of powerful men, going right to the very top, who are being paid massive bonuses by the Iraqis, under the counter, as you say in English'.

'And these people had Nathalie Cagoule killed because she was about to blow the whistle?', said Christopher. 'But why would she tell the British?'

'Because her mother was Scottish and she knew that Great Britain has a place on the United Nations Security Council. Just going to the French police would be no good. It would be covered up very quickly'.

'It is all very interesting', said Christopher, 'but why are you telling me now?'

'The war between Iran and Iraq is over so the embargo has lapsed. But the corruption is still going on and Saddam is secretly re-arming, with French weapons, in a massive way', said Marielle, shaking her head sadly. 'The same cabal is still involved and the same people are still making huge profits. It is blood money.

'They carry out the negotiations with Saddam's man in secret meetings, mostly held at The Ritz', she went on. 'I know the DST have a paid agent at the hotel so they must know exactly what is going on but nobody tries to stop it. I suspect the

DST, or at least some important people in that organisation, are in on it all'.

'You mentioned the main man earlier', said Christopher, 'who is he?'

'I cannot tell you that', said Marielle, 'because he is still the main man'.

'But how do you know he is the main man and why can't you tell me who he is?', said Christopher impatiently.

'Because he was Nathalie's lover', said Marielle. She paused dramatically. 'We shared him, actually. He is still my lover. It is good for business, non? I will tell you next time'.

She pushed her chair back and stood up.

'No, no. Not that again. Tell me now', yelled Christopher after her as she hailed a taxi on the opposite side of the street.

Why are you doing this? What is your real motivation? Why take the risk?, he said to himself as he motioned to the waiter for the bill.

Chapter Eight

Sandringham, England, Christmas Day 1989

It was cold in the way that only Norfolk could get cold. Not bitter. Not biting. Just bone-achingly cold.

But the people waiting outside the church of St Mary Magdalene on the Queen's Sandringham estate did not feel the cold. They were warmed by anticipation.

The Royal Family always spent Christmas at Sandringham and they always attended Christmas morning service at the tiny sixteenth century chapel. Over the years it had become a tradition that the workers on the estate, together with their families, gathered outside the church to offer Her Majesty yuletide greetings as she left for the short walk back to the main house for her Christmas lunch.

As worldwide interest in the British Royal Family grew this charming feudal ritual had been taken over by the demands of the modern media so that today there were three television camera crews, a dozen or more photographers and a host of reporters gathered outside the church.

They were corralled behind a length of plastic tape strung between two metal staves, which were borrowed from the pigpen on the Royal farm and had been crudely rammed into the soft earth to one side of the lych gate through which the Royal Family would depart.

On the other side of the gate about a hundred people, mostly families, were similarly contained. By the looks of them they were not estate workers. They were middle class, middle aged, middle England.

At the back of this crowd stood Kevin Donne, hands in his pockets, deep in thought.

I must stand out like a sore thumb in this lot, he thought. *Young bloke on his own. Scruffily dressed. Got to be a terrorist. They must suss me. Good job I'm not tooled up.*

'You alright there, sir?'

Kevin jumped.

It was a large policeman with ruddy cheeks and a friendly grin. He spoke slowly with a warm Norfolk burr in his voice.

'Nice day for it, isn't it?', said the constable. 'Shouldn't be long now. Why don't you stand at the end of the line over here, sir, you'll get a better view'.

Kevin thanked him.

'No trouble', he said, 'you have a happy Christmas now won't you'.

He wouldn't know a terrorist if he knocked his stupid pointy helmet off with an Uzi sub-machine gun, thought Kevin.

He'd driven up from London that morning. It meant an early start but Kevin had nothing better to do on Christmas Day. It was two years since the divorce. Sandra couldn't handle his drinking and his depression. He didn't blame her. She and the kids were at her mother's. He'd see them that evening. They were still friends, now that he was clean and putting his life back together. He had a job, driving a van for a mail order company. He even had presents in the car – a Barbie doll for Tara, Action Man for Shane, and a lacy black negligee for Sandra.

There was a murmur in the crowd. Kevin looked up. The Queen was walking down the path towards the lych gate. Her family followed in a solemn procession. As they reached the gate they all paused so that the crowd could see them and the press could get their pictures. Princess Diana seemed preoccupied with her two young sons who jostled and nudged each other as they gambolled along the path in front of her.

She doesn't know I'm here or she'd acknowledge me, thought Kevin. *Come on your Royal Highness, over here, look up, give me a smile.*

Diana looked up, smiled and waved absently at the crowd. She was not looking at Kevin. He raised himself on to his toes and craned forward concentrating on her face. Willing her to look at him.

Then he noticed, just behind Diana's shoulder, another face looking at him. It was her police bodyguard. The same man who had been at her side at Tidworth. Their eyes locked. The detective did not blink. He kept staring at Kevin until the Royal party moved off.

Okay mate. So you've clocked me. Big deal, thought Kevin as he made for his car.

Back at Sandringham House Diana was feeling sad and lonely.

She picked up her mobile telephone and called an old friend. A boyfriend.

* * * * * *

London, 31st December 1989

The two men sat staring at each other for fully thirty seconds before either of them spoke. They both struck identical poses – leaning back in their swivel chairs with their hands clasped behind their heads. Both had a large set of padded earphones positioned loosely around their necks.

Lighting in the windowless room was dim. It was heavily carpeted and acoustic tiles lined the ceiling and two walls

98

giving the soundproofed feel of a recording studio. The other two walls were occupied, floor to ceiling, by banks of metal, glass-fronted cabinets – twenty-two in all. Through the glass doors of each cabinet could be seen large spools of recording tape – each about the size of a dinner plate. There were six such spools in each cabinet. Virtually every spool was rotating but too slowly to be detected by the naked eye. Rows of tiny green, red, and yellow lights flickered on and off below each spool indicating which of the sixteen tracks on each tape was actually recording.

Eventually the older man let out a low whistle and said: 'Bloody hell, what have we got here?' He spoke slowly as though struggling to come to terms with what he had just heard.

'It's dynamite. Gold dust', said his companion, cheerfully mixing metaphors in his excitement.

'It's not quite that good', replied the first man, 'but it is certainly very revelatory, very damaging, I would say'.

'What did he call her? Squodge or Squodgy wasn't it? What the hell does that mean?', asked the younger man.

'It was Squidgy, I think', said the other man. 'I assume that is some form of private nickname, a term of endearment agreed between the pair of them. That might be a little embarrassing but it is the other stuff which is dynamite, as you put it. We need to run it all again so that we can identify the best bits'.

He turned to a control panel in front of him and pressed a button. There was a whirring sound, which turned into a high-pitched whine as the spool on recording machine number eight rewound. It clicked silently to a halt after a matter of seconds – pre-set to find the beginning of the desired recording.

The first man depressed another button marked "Speaker" and hit the play button. The voice of a young man with an aristocratic accent came through loud and clear. The recording had apparently cut in to a telephone conversation.

'And so, darling, what other lows today?', inquired the young man.

The voice, which replied, was instantly recognisable as belonging to one of the best-known young women in Britain. Virtually any member of the public passing through the room at that moment would have realised that they were listening to the voice of Princess Diana, the wife of the heir to the throne and mother of the future king.

'I was very bad at lunch and I nearly started blubbing', she could be heard saying. 'I just felt very sad and empty and I thought: bloody hell, after all I've done for this fucking family'.

Both men looked at each other. The older man winced, the younger grimaced.

For the next forty-eight minutes they listened in silence, occasionally scribbling comments on pads in front of them and regularly noting down numbers from the digital spool counter so that they could quickly locate key passages in the dialogue at a later date.

The conversation was banal, gossipy, almost childish. But it was couched in deeply affectionate terms. Even the most innocent of observers could not have failed to recognise that the couple were lovers.

Clearly they were blissfully unaware that their most intimate secrets were being listened to and recorded. Secure in the mistaken belief that they were engaged in a private telephone conversation, their chatter included indiscreet observations about other members of the Royal Family and strongly hinted that all was not well in the Prince of Wales's marriage. They talked about clairvoyance and a prediction that Prince Charles would never succeed to the throne.

At one point the conversation degenerated to a pornographic level as the couple exchanged graphic verbal descriptions of their lovemaking. The eavesdroppers shifted uncomfortably in their seats during this passage and refrained from making notes.

Then suddenly the woman could be heard saying: 'I don't want to get pregnant'.

The listeners stiffened and began to scribble again.

'Darling, that's not going to happen', came her lover's confident reply. 'Don't think like that, darling, you won't get pregnant'.

'I watched Eastenders today', said the woman. 'One of the main characters had a baby. They thought it was by her husband; it was by another man'. There was a note of alarm in her voice.

'Kiss me, please', said the man. 'Do you know what I am going to be imagining I'm doing tonight at about 12 o'clock? Just holding you close to me. It'll have to be delayed action for about 48 hours'.

Eventually the conversation drew to a close and recording shut itself down.

'Right. Okay. What have we here? Let me see', said the older man, checking his notes. 'Evidence of adultery, a possibility of pregnancy outside the marriage, disloyalty to the Royal Family, a belief that her husband will never be king, a reliance on television soap operas as guidance for life, evidence of a belief in alternative faiths and spirit world mumbo jumbo. Oh Diana, you naughty girl. What a mess'.

His companion cut in: 'What now?', he asked.

Outside the building New Year's Eve revellers were already beginning to throng the streets around London's Berkeley Square as they made their way towards Trafalgar Square for the traditional end of year celebrations. Apart from a handful of middle-ranking officers, doing holiday overtime duty, the two men were the only staff working in MI5's technical base in Bolton Street, Mayfair.

'I wonder what old Crampo will make of it, we'll have to run it by him', said the first man.

'What Tommy Crampton? What's it got to do with him?, asked his colleague. 'He's Director of K Branch, Counter-Espionage. He's not our line manager'.

'Ah, but he's the Diana expert', said the other man.

'So what?'

'Well the D-G tasked him to keep a close eye on the loony bitch almost within hours of her wedding, by all accounts, and he's made it into a labour of love over the years. He's definitely I/C Diana. All decisions relating to her go through him', said the older man. 'I'm going to see Quinn. Give him a verbal report. You change the spool and bag and label this one up. I shan't be long.' He hurried out of the room.

Fifteen minutes later he returned.

'Okay. Quinn has had a word with Crampo at home and here's what's going to happen', he said. 'We've got to get this over to Technical Support right away. They will clean it up, get all the crackle off it so that it can be heard more easily, and edit out the boring bits. Then they will re-record a clean version and we're going to put it out so that it can be picked up on the regular radio ham networks. That should ensure that it gets into the public domain – as if by accident'.

'Oh dear, I do hope none of this falls into the hands of the newspapers. That would be just too, too, awful for darling Squidge', grinned the younger man.

'Yes. Especially the telephone sex, particularly all that masturbation stuff. Most unseemly', replied his colleague. 'If any newspaper has the balls to publish that, it is hardly likely to go down too well over the Great British Breakfast'.

'Well it is extremely explicit', agreed the younger man. 'I doubt whether even the most lurid of our despicable rags will have the stomach for it. They want to sell papers not disgust their readers totally. But where will we put it out?'

'Well we know where she is – Sandringham', said his companion. 'But we'll get a stronger signal if we put it out on a local frequency. That way it will be more likely to be picked up and appear to be an intercepted mobile telephone conversation to any radio ham listening in. We know that Mr Squidgy is using his mobile while sitting in a lay-by somewhere in Oxfordshire because he said so. So Quinn's feeling is that we should use our Bracknell transmitter – the strongest in that area which is alive with radio hams all busily listening to the airwaves'.

'How long before we can get it out?, asked the younger man.

'Two or three days', came the reply.

'But there are references to New Year's Eve on there', said his companion, that will give the game away'.

'The explicit references can be edited out and the others can be explained as referring to other days', said his older colleague. 'Let's get this done and get out of here before midnight strikes. I'm dying for a beer'.

The younger man raised a plastic coffee cup in a mock toast.

'I'll drink to that', he said, adding, with a sarcastic sneer: 'Happy New Year, Squidge'.

Chapter Nine

Nevers, France, May 1st 1993

May Day dawned bright and clear in the picturesque town of Nevers.

Just the kind of day to gladden the heart of Pierre Beregovoy.

This was his town. These were his people. And the annual celebration of the Labour movement had always been his favourite date on the calendar.

'Bere', as he was affectionately known throughout France, was a workingman through and through – a trade union stalwart - and the most famous son of this tight-knit little community nestling in the Loire valley 150 miles south of Paris.

He had been a political animal since the latter stages of the Second World War when, as a 16-year-old metalworker employed by SNCF, the national railways, he had been recruited into the French Resistance. For the past 24 years he had led France's Socialist Party and been Mayor of Nevers for a decade.

But today there was a darkness in the soul of Pierre Beregovoy. A heaviness in his heart and a deep sense of foreboding.

A light breeze ruffled the tricoleur on the flagpole jutting from the austere façade of the Town Hall where he stood on the steps amid a phalanx of self-important municipal officials.

It had all been so different just twelve months earlier. Then he had stood in triumph at this very spot. The newly appointed Prime Minister of France acknowledging the cheers of the crowd and inwardly revelling in the culmination of a lifetime of public service.

Now he looked out on the colourful scene through unseeing eyes.

The procession was led as usual by a small herd of ceremonial cows with flowers woven into their tails and the traditional halter of thirteen bells around the neck of the leader.

Pierre Beregovoy was oblivious to its tinkling melody.

The marching band parped, tooted, blared and thumped a rousing tune. Excited children squealed with delight and their parents happily sang along.

But in his morose reverie Beregovoy might just as well have been watching television with the sound turned off.

His premiership had survived strikes by farmers, doctors, nurses, and car workers – but not the ballot box. To his profound shock and dismay the French people had resoundingly rejected him and his party at the General Election just two months earlier and his self-esteem had not recovered. He shuddered as he recalled the cold disdain in the voice of his lifelong friend Francois Mitterrand when the President telephoned to express his deep disappointment at the outcome.

And to add to his misery the clouds of scandal were beginning to gather over the head of this chubby, bespectacled, little man so frequently mocked for his bumbling persona. An official investigation had been launched into a 1-million franc interest-free loan he had been given by another of Mitterrand's closest allies, Roger-Patrice Pelat, to buy a flat. He would soon have to face the inquisitors and the press over the issue and he could not escape the feeling that the President was keen to wash his hands of him.

'Bere. Look this way. Over here'. The cry came from a gaggle of photographers jostling one another at the foot of the steps.

A friendly face was grinning at him and waving from among the pack of gleaming lenses and popping flashguns. It was Jean-Jacques Iversen, semi-official photographer to the court of Mitterrand, and always a companionable man.

Beregovoy allowed himself a rueful smile. He recalled, with affection, happier times in the company of the jovial ex-commando who had become one of Europe's most celebrated paparazzi. Iversen had been his official photographer and he often dropped in to the wealthy lensman's large, rambling, farmhouse at nearby Charenton-du-Cher to swap anecdotes or debate politics with friends over a convivial lunch or a bottle of fine wine.

Iversen's cheery greeting jolted Bere's memory. The two of them had an appointment later that day. He had agreed, just hours earlier, to pose for a series of informal May Day pictures in his home town so that a portfolio could be put together which would act as an historical full-stop at the end of his premiership – the successful politician at ease with himself riding off into the sunset satisfied with a job well done. And who said the camera never lied? Beregovoy grimaced at the thought.

He turned and strode towards his car. Most of the trappings of office had been stripped from him but he still warranted an official car. The motorcycle outriders had gone, of course, and there were no bodyguards but his driver was a former soldier and there was a Smith & Wesson Model 19 .357 magnum revolver in the glove compartment just in case.

His head was bowed as he walked so that he did not see the old woman when she stepped from the pavement into his path.

'Monsieur. Good Luck. You would like to buy some good luck?', she asked in a cracked voice.

Beregovoy looked up, distracted. She was waving a small bouquet of Lily of the Valley towards him. Its pungent fragrance momentarily teased his nostrils. Such 'muguets' are a feature of May Day in France – the only day of the year when you can sell these flowers without a licence.

'No. Get out of my way', he snapped as he brushed past the startled crone.

Pierre Beregovoy was a deeply superstitious man and immediately regretted his hastiness. Instinctively he knew that if ever he needed some good fortune it was now. But the moment had passed. He had rejected the offer. It was too late. The die was cast.

The driver was holding the rear passenger door open as his boss approached.

'Where to, Chief?', he inquired.

'Just drive around for a while Tom. I'll let you know when I want you to stop', came the terse reply.

Tomas Cassiers shrugged his muscular shoulders. He had driven Beregovoy for five years and had never seen him as depressed as this. But after years of military discipline as a paratrooper fighting with the French Foreign Legion in Africa he had learned to follow orders and not ask questions.

And so they drove. In silence.

Cassiers' job had taken him to Nevers many times in recent years but he was not a local so he did not really know his way around the sleepy little town. In the absence of any clear instructions from the rear seat he opted to tour the town in a circular route on the basis that sooner or later he would come upon an area close enough to his passenger's chosen destination to trigger a more specific order.

The Boulevard Pierre de Coubertin and the Rue Charles Roy skirt the heart of downtown Nevers forming a natural ring road. By the time Cassiers had cruised slowly around it six times he was getting bored. He looked in the rear-view mirror. Beregovoy's eyes were fixed glassily ahead. Neither man spoke.

Cassiers turned south across the Pont de Loire on the Faubourg de Lyon. In the distance he could see the traffic thundering along the A77 trunk road, which links Paris with Lyons. He notice a sign for Magny-Cours – the Mecca of French motor racing and the source of much pride to Pierre Beregovoy who, along with President Mitterrand, had raised the funding to make it a centre of excellence renowned as such in worldwide motorsports circles.

Should he take the boss there to cheer him up? He glanced in the mirror. Beregovoy was checking his watch. The driver took a detour through the village of Sainte Antoine.

After about an hour of this aimless perambulation Pierre Beregovoy suddenly heaved a massive sigh and began to issue directions for his driver to follow. Tomas Cassiers noticed that he was smiling and seemed more relaxed than he had been all day. But he was still constantly checking his watch.

Their destination soon became clear. They were heading for a local beauty spot much favoured by Pierre Beregovoy as a place for quiet contemplation and renewal of spirit after the hurly-burly of political life.

The hinterland of Nevers is criss-crossed by a network of canals and rivulets feeding off the mighty Loire and one of these 'ruisseaux' wound through wooded countryside overlooked by rolling hills and open fields. It was remote. It was tranquil. It was picturesque.

Cassiers knew that his boss loved nothing better than to stroll along the towpath communing with nature. As a city dweller and a man of action such placid pursuits were not for him but it came with the job so he had patiently endured many an hour on this particular towpath scanning the hills for hidden snipers and listening for signs of unwanted company in the undergrowth while his charge walked, and walked and walked.

As the car approached the picnic spot where they always parked the driver braced himself for another hour or two of tedium.

He leapt out smartly and moved quickly to open the rear door but Beregovoy had beaten him to it.

'You don't need to come with me Tomas', he said.

The driver noted the formal use of his full name. That was unusual. His boss usually called him Tom.

'I am sorry Monsieur but I must be with you at all times. It is my duty', he replied respectfully.

'No, no. I'll be fine on my own. I would prefer to walk alone today. I don't need you. Thank you', said Beregovoy.

'But Monsieur…

'No!' snapped Beregovoy. It was a bark. Almost a bellow. You will not accompany me. That is an order'.

As he spoke he opened the front passenger door, leaned in and flicked open the glove compartment. He pulled out the police-issue Smith and Wesson revolver, expertly broke it open, and spun the cartridge chamber.

To his relief Cassiers noticed that the weapon was fully loaded.

'I will not need you. I have this', said Beregovoy as he slipped the gun into his jacket pocket and made off towards the canal.

As he watched the retreating figure the driver mused over the fact that his boss had not once looked him the eye during their terse exchange. That was uncharacteristic.

A moment of anxiety gripped him but it soon passed. Pierre Beregovoy was no longer a security risk. That was why his full-time bodyguards had been withdrawn. He was yesterday's man. A spent force. Nobody cared about him anymore. And in any case nobody knew they were here. They certainly couldn't have been followed. Not after the tortuous and random drive he had just endured.

No. Nothing to worry about.

Cassiers settled down to wait. Waiting was the unenviable lot of the professional chauffeur. They were good at it. They had no choice. He lit up a Gauloises cigarette, folded his arms and leaned back against the bonnet of the car.

He looked up at the sky. It was early evening but it had been a beautiful spring day and the sun was still shining. He took a long drag on his cigarette and ran his fingers through the wiry grey brush of thinning hair on his head.

In the distance there was a crack. Every sinew in Cassiers' body stiffened. To him the sound was unmistakeable. A gunshot. About a quarter of a mile away, his senses told him.

He spun round to face the direction from which the sound had come. A flock of birds flapped into the air. Even at a distance their alarmed squawking carried to him in the stillness.

He was already sprinting when the second shot came.

He saw the body when he was still some two hundred yards away and by the time he reached it he had raised the alarm on his mobile phone.

His thoughts were racing. A terrorist assassin had murdered the former Prime Minister of France, his boss, on his watch.

He had neglected his duty. He would be blamed for this. The whole nation would blame him Tomas Cassiers for allowing this to happen.

Then he saw the revolver. It was clutched in the chubby right fist of Pierre Beregovoy.

He was lying on his side with his knees drawn up like a babe in the womb. His glasses had been dislodged and ridden up to the top of his head. There was a bloody mess, which looked like a hole about the size of a golf ball behind his right temple, and a trickle of blood came from his mouth. A larger pool of blood was slowly beginning to grow on the stony path beneath his head.

Cassiers bent to help the stricken man. He thought he detected the faintest of pulses. He made another urgent call for help on the mobile.

'Poor guy', he said to himself. 'I should have seen the signs. He just couldn't take it anymore. I guess he thought this was the only way out. But to kill yourself in your sixties? Who'd be a politician?'.

He looked across the canal at the empty hillside bathed in the setting sunlight, embarrassed that under the stress of the situation he had begun talking out loud to himself. There was no one there to hear him.

He looked down again at the dying man. His jacked had fallen open and Cassiers could see that the diary-cum-notebook in which Beregovoy recorded absolutely everything was missing from its usual place.

Strange, he thought. *Perhaps he didn't bring it out with him today.*

A mile away Jean-Jacques Iversen looked up as the helicopter air ambulance clattered overhead. He checked his watch.

Pierre Beregovoy was not going to make his final photo call.

* * * * * *

Paris, France, 2nd May 1993

The pungent aroma of formaldehyde embalming fluid mixed with the stench of death was all-pervasive in the otherwise clinically antiseptic atmosphere of the Paris morgue.

But Professor Thierry Bollack no longer noticed it. The distinctive smell was simply the backdrop to his daily existence.

As a young pathology student he had learned that sucking extra-strong peppermints removed the foul taste left in the mouth by hours spent breathing in the fetid air of a mortuary. And recently, under protest from his wife and family, he had taken to showering after every autopsy session and leaving his working clothes behind in a locker separated from his office apparel.

Thierry Bollack was France's leading forensic pathologist. Graduating in forensic medicine from the Sorbonne medical school in the early sixties, he had gone on to teach at the prestigious Institute of Forensic Science and Criminology at the University of Lausanne in Switzerland and was now Director of *L'Instit Medico-Legal de Paris.*

If a prominent person in French society died, whether the circumstances were suspicious or not, the police would send for Dr Bollack to conduct the post mortem. If a murder had hit the headlines and captured the public imagination Thierry Bollack did the autopsy. If a major terrorist outrage occurred or a death connected to a political scandal was uncovered the first man whose services were required by the government was

113

Professor Bollack. When it came to probing death he was a superstar.

Today was a sad day.

Thierry was the consummate professional. Focussed. Dispassionate. Detached. He had long since forgotten what it was to be emotionally affected by the ugly sight of death. But he knew 'Bere' socially and had become fond of the studious, clumsy little fellow with the owlish glasses and the sheepish grin.

The corpse lying on the stainless steel trolley before him was no different from five others the professor had examined already this morning but he could not escape the thought that just two months earlier this man had held the highest office in the land beneath the President. What a shame that he had chosen to end his life so suddenly and so violently.

'Entry wound located twenty-three millimetres above right ear on the median line. Triangular in nature measuring eight by ten millimetres'.

The professor spoke in his customary flat monotone. His assistant, Claude, a tousle-haired youth in a laboratory coat which was not as white as it should have been, faithfully scribbled the notes on a clipboard file.

'No singeing of the adjacent hair. No evidence of propellant tattooing on the skin surface. Entry hole bevelled on inner surface. Small triangular piece of bone embedded in dura. Rupture of dura and arachnoid consistent with passage of bullet. Bullet track pierces right occipital lobe, left parietal lobe and superior longitudinal sinus.

'Pass me the cranial probe, Claude...'

The youngster handed the pathologist a thin metal rod and watched as he carefully inserted it into the bullet hole and slid it forward, probing for the exit hole on the other side of the skull.

'Exit wound above left eye. Measures twenty-five by twenty millimetres and is fifteen millimetres below entry wound. Damage to eye socket and left eye. Bullet appears to have tumbled on entry causing considerable tissue damage to the brain'.

Bollack glanced across at his assistant to see if the significance of this last statement had made any impact. But if Claude had noticed anything it did not register on his face.

The professor pushed his glasses to the top of his head and peeled off his surgical gloves.

Glancing at the dead man's brain which now rested in a steel bowl with pink liquid in it he said: 'Take the samples for toxicology and histology and then you can clean him up, Claude. And make sure he looks pretty for the world's press tomorrow. But before that give the notes to Beatrice and tell her I need the draft typed up as a matter of urgency.

The young man nodded but said nothing. He hadn't missed it. He knew very well what was troubling the professor.

Three hours later Thierry Bollack sat across the desk from Maurice de Champvieux at DST headquarters.

'You have read my autopsy report on Bere?', he asked

'Yes', said the head of the secret service without looking up. He was playing with a string of beads in his lap.

'This is a very grave matter indeed', said Bollack. I am sorry to have brought you such unpleasant news but under the circumstances I felt it best that you were advised first before the police become involved'.

'No, no. You did absolutely the right thing Thierry, said de Champvieux, 'as usual your judgement was perfectly correct'.

'Well, what will happen now?', asked the professor. 'The funeral is tomorrow, the President will be giving the eulogy and the press will the there in large numbers no doubt'.

Maurice de Champvieux rocked back in his chair and placed the tips of his fingers together in an attitude of prayer.

'You have done your duty, Thierry, and this matter need no longer concern you', he said.

'But my report will have to go to the coroner and to the police', came the reply.

Maurice was becoming irritated. 'Thierry you are a medical man, a scientist; this is not your territory. Leave it alone'.

But Bollack was in no mood to leave things as they stood. 'Are you going to bring the police in on this or not?', he demanded.

Maurice shook his head.

'No? No? The Prime Minister of France…excuse me…the former Prime Minister of France is murdered and you do nothing? You are content to pass it off as suicide?' He was red in the face and had raised his voice to a pitch out of keeping with his normally placid and equable temperament.

'It was suicide', said de Champvieux.

'You either haven't read my report or you haven't understood it if you think that', said Bollack, his lips taught and his jaws tensed.

'He was depressed. He ordered his driver not to accompany him. He took the gun from the car, walked to a remote spot, and shot himself. The gun was still in his hand', retorted Maurice.

'The entry wound is too far back and too high up for him to have comfortably shot himself and there is no sign of the muzzle being held against the head anyway', said the agitated professor. 'The behaviour of the bullet inside the skull and the exit wound can only mean one thing...rifle, from distance, above and behind the target. A sniper'.

He paused and glared across the desk. 'This is a matter of State security. The President will have to be told'.

'It is a matter of State security and State security is my responsibility', said de Champvieux. 'I will make sure that the President is fully aware of the situation but there are extremely delicate issues surrounding this whole affair of which you are unaware and which simply must remain secret. I know that we can rely on your discretion and your loyalty to France. I need hardly remind you of the confidentiality oath which you took when you began working for this department'.

There was an awkward silence then Professor Bollack rose and left the room without a word.

He was just stepping into the lift, deep in thought, when a cheery voice greeted him.

'Doctor Bollack, how are you? I haven't seen you for ages'. It was Pierre Charron.

'I'm just on my way to the canteen for a coffee, can I buy you one? It would be good to have a chat'.

The professor was not in the habit of taking coffee in office canteens but he had been shaken by the events of the past few hours and felt in need of a break. He had always liked agent Charron, too. There was something open, honest and principled about him.

117

'That would be nice', replied Bollack. 'How are Sophie and the children?'

Charron's wife was the daughter of a doctor who had trained with the professor so he knew the family in a casual way.

'Oh, she's fine', said Pierre cheerily. 'She's given up work for a while. Did you know that we've had a third? Another boy'. He pulled out a billfold from his hip pocket and proffered a coloured photograph of a pretty young woman holding a baby in her arms while a scowling small boy and a shy little girl stood either side of her clutching at her skirts for protection.

The professor was in no mood for small talk but he forced himself to make polite noises of appreciation as his companion gushed enthusiastically about his young family.

Bollack had always been fond of Sophie Charron. She was stunningly beautiful with an immaculate figure, long blonde hair tumbling down her back and hazel-grey eyes, which always held an engagingly mysterious look as though she were trying to fathom an impenetrable secret. She had what the French call 'chic' in abundance – the indefinable ability to look good at anytime, anywhere, in anything. Her clothes, jewellery, make-up always understated yet always perfect for the occasion.

She was a lawyer. The pair had met at University and while Pierre failed to follow through with his legal training Sophie's career had blossomed. They were seen as the golden couple – he darkly handsome, she pale and pretty – by their large circle of friends who never questioned why Sophie was so happy to talk about her clients while her husband always changed the subject when anyone asked what his work as a civil servant actually entailed.

'So what brings you to this den of iniquity?', asked Pierre when the pair sat down. 'Don't tell me. You came to tell *Le Sanglier* that Pierre Beregovoy was murdered and did not commit suicide'.

118

Bollack was startled. 'How did you know that?', he asked, a little too quickly to be joking.

'Just kidding', laughed Charron, 'none of my business, I shouldn't have asked why you are here'.

'No, but how did you *know* about Bere?', said Bollack.

'Well it is no secret. It was in the papers that you were doing the autopsy this morning', grinned Pierre, sipping his coffee.

'No, I mean, why did you say murder?' The Professor was tense, leaning forward.

'Oh I was just pulling your leg. Sorry I shouldn't have joked about someone who's just died in such tragic circumstances'.

There was a pregnant pause. Bollack's brow was furrowed. Charron caught the expression in his eyes.

'Wait a minute, I hit the nail on the head, didn't I?', he said.

Bollack nodded. 'He was shot with a sniper rifle – AK-47 I'd say because of the behaviour of the bullet – the characteristic tumbling action in soft tissue. Range about 300 yards from slightly above and behind while he was half turned away'.

'But what about the revolver in his hand?', asked Pierre.

'It did not fire the fatal shot. There is no powder residue or scorching on his hair or skin and he'd have had to be a contortionist to get that kind of bullet track angle through his skull', said the professor.

'Well the driver did hear two shots', said Charron, 'but only one bullet has been discharged from the Smith & Wesson according to the initial police report. They can't explain that one. At first they said Bere had fired a proving shot to make sure the gun worked before killing himself but now they are saying the witness must be mistaken'.

'The explanation could be that the sniper had an accomplice who had lured Bere to a rendezvous. Then after he was dropped by the assassin the accomplice fired one shot from the revolver before putting it in his victim's hand and making his escape', said Bollack.

'This is extremely serious', said Charron. 'The police will have a tricky time piecing this together when the killers have had a 48-hours start. We're obviously going to be pretty busy too...

'I don't think so', said Thierry Bollack bitterly, 'your chief has sworn me to secrecy and told me that there will be no investigation. The world will be led to believe that it was suicide. The President knows the facts and do you know what? I got the impression that *Le Sanglier* knew all about it in advance. I would not be at all surprised if he sanctioned the killing himself. I'll bet Bere has embarrassed the administration, or was about to, and he's had to be done away with'.

Pierre Charron was shocked. He knew that political assassinations took place. They were part and parcel of the shadowy world in which he lived. He had even taken part in the planning stages of one. But such eliminations could always be justified, at least to those involved, on the grounds of preserving the national interest or the international balance of power or even, ironically, peace itself.

But if a good and decent politician had been murdered just to save the face of others that was unacceptable.

Twenty-four hours later Pierre Beregovoy was laid to rest.

At the funeral President Francois Mitterrand was in fighting mood. His friend and ally, a great servant of the Republic, had been driven to take his own life by cowardly critics not worthy to breathe the same air.

'All the explanations in the world do not justify throwing to the dogs a man's honour and, in the end, his life, as his accusers doubly renounced the basic laws of our Republic – those that protect the dignity and liberty of each one of us', he boomed in sonorous tones.

Listening to the service on a radio in his office Pierre Charron raised his eyes to heaven and sighed.

* * * * * *

Paris, France, 4th May 1993

Christopher was in a foul mood. He metaphorically sucked his pencil as he contemplated the right choice of words with which to begin his report for his bosses in London.

He was a man of action, not of words, and although much of his daily routine required him to file detailed intelligence reports – known in the business as CX – he was never comfortable behind a typewriter or, in this case, the keyboard of a computerised word processor.

Christopher was a career spy and, although he didn't see his espionage work as in any way glamorous, he resented the interference of MI6 bureaucrats who, with their constant demands for written memoranda, he felt trivialised his efforts in the field and reduced his status to that of a civil servant.

And today he had a particular reason for resentment. He had just had his weekend ruined for no good, or at least, no obvious, reason.

For weeks he had been looking forward to seeing Giselle. His university sweetheart. The girl who had inspired his love affair with France and the French language.

Christopher had never married, he told himself, because his job would not allow him to. Intelligence service personnel could not have long-term, stable, meaningful relationships with the opposite sex. The only MI6 operatives who were married had met their spouses in the organisation.

Giselle had never married because she didn't want to. Like Christopher she was thirty-seven years old now and still a strikingly good-looking woman. She was a curator of antiquities at the British Museum and her job brought her to Paris to work with her opposite numbers at the Louvre on a regular basis.

Whenever she came to Paris, Giselle stayed with Christopher. She had a spare set of keys to his apartment in case he was away on an assignment.

But with the British May Bank Holiday coinciding with the French May Day holiday this year, the couple had planned to spend a relaxing long weekend together free from the pressures of work for a change. That was until the telephone call on the previous Thursday, which assigned Christopher to a four-day surveillance operation.

Work always came first with him but his frustration and anger grew to fever pitch when he learned that his mission this time was to track the every move of Princess Diana during a secret Paris shopping trip she was taking at short notice ostensibly to help her get over the recent separation from her husband.

He kept asking himself why. *What was the point*? Diana's recent actions had not endeared her to the Royal Family and her public revelations about the state of her marriage and the inadequacies of her husband had infuriated the British Establishment. He knew that. But she was no threat to the State so why was he being deployed? Still, his was not to reason why so he simply did what he was told and followed the lady all around town for four days.

But now, as he came to write his report, Christopher was at a loss. He could not imagine that anything he had seen or heard could be of any intelligence significance whatsoever...unless he was missing a trick somewhere. There was nothing for it. He would have to recount every moment of Diana's visit – every cough and spit – and leave the analysts in London to make what they would of it.

The visit had been intentionally low-key. The Princess wanted to be anonymous. She needed to be able to move around Paris free from the prying eyes of the media or the constant recognition of the public.

She had flown into Le Bourget airport on the Friday and hired a plain Renault Espace people carrier from Hertz to transport herself and her two girlfriends, Hayat Palumbo, wife of the billionaire property developer chairman of the British Arts Council, and Lucia Flecha de Lima, wife of the Brazilian ambassador to London.

The vehicle gave Christopher his biggest advantage because a chauffeur from the British Embassy in Paris had been detailed to drive the party. This man was given a mobile telephone and instructions to keep Christopher abreast of every move the women intended to make.

Their first port of call had been the headquarters of Chanel, Diana's favourite couturier, then on to Dior and several more high class boutiques in the Paris fashion quarter before withdrawing to the private home of a friend in the exclusive area of Neuilly close to the Bois de Boulogne where they were staying for the weekend. Discreet inquiries through security at the stores led Christopher to the calculation that the Princess had spent in the region of ten thousand pounds sterling on clothes. *A little excessive for a marriage breakdown pick-me-up, even for a Royal*, he thought.

The following day Diana kept a lunch date with the French film star Gerard Depardieu at the chic Marius and Janette restaurant off the Champs Elysee.

Christopher had sufficient notice to have the British Embassy book him an adjacent table. It would have been the perfect place to lunch with Giselle had she not cancelled her trip as soon as she knew he would be working for most of the weekend.

She knew what he did for a living, of course. He had never told her. She had never asked. But she herself had been approached by an MI6 recruiter at university and had a pretty good idea which of her contemporaries might have received a similar tap on the shoulder. Her suspicions were aroused when Christopher told her that he was a civil servant with the Ministry of Defence and was being sent to Northern Ireland. As an aeronautical engineer that might just have been a legitimate posting but when he joined the diplomatic service as a commercial officer at the British Embassy in Paris, Giselle guessed immediately what his job entailed. She determined never to ask him the question he could not answer.

In the event Christopher was able to report from the restaurant that the princess and the actor drank white wine and ate lobster and sea bass. He was relaxed and charming. She giggled incessantly like a star-struck teenager. No obvious threat to British interests overseas there, then.

The remainder of the day was taken up with a visit to a comic shop called Album where the princess bought a video, presumably for her two sons Princes William and Harry, and a sightseeing tour of Notre Dame Cathedral and dinner at the Brasserie Balzar.

On Sunday there was an early visit to the Pompidou Centre to take in the Matisse exhibition and a stop for coffee and croissants at a pavement café. Then the princess travelled alone to the secluded Chapelle Notre Dame de la Medaille Miraculeuse to spend an hour praying at the shrine of Saint

Catherine Laboure – a Catholic icon said to radiate healing powers both physical and spiritual.

In the evening the three friends dined at The Ritz hotel. Christopher could not follow them into the Espadon Restaurant so he kept watch in the Bar Vendome where he knew several of the waiters. He learned that the princess had bumped into the Hollywood film director Steven Spielberg and chatted to him for a while and as she left she passed a handwritten note to the concierge obviously meant for a resident of the hotel.

It had long been an irritation to Christopher that he had no proper sources at The Ritz - especially after the remarks Marielle had made concerning the quality of information his French counterparts in the DST were able to get out of their informant in the hotel. More and more visitors to The Ritz were coming under MI6 scrutiny. The lack of an informant was a situation which would have to be addressed soon.

On this occasion, however, it did not matter because a two hundred franc tip secured for Christopher the information that Diana's note was to be delivered to her stepmother, Countess Raine Spencer, who was staying at The Ritz with her new fiancé Comte Jean-Francois de Chambrun.

On the Monday the party flew back to London from Le Bourget.

That was it.

Christopher pushed back his chair, scratched his ear, and gazed at the ceiling. *Where was the intelligence nugget in that? Perhaps the visit to the shrine was what they were looking for. It would not do for the wife of the future king and the mother of his heir to espouse the Catholic faith when her husband and her son would become head of the Church of England and inherit the title 'Defender of the Faith'. It might also be seen as unhealthy for a senior Royal to become involved in mysticism and religious mumbo jumbo.*

Suddenly it dawned on him. His report was not for MI6 at all.
It was going to MI5, he was sure of it. He recalled that, when
he was a member of the Security Service, rumours were rife
that a secret file existed on which all the peccadilloes of the
Princess of Wales were recorded. Tommy Crampton was said
to be the keeper of the file and Christopher knew him to be an
obsessive. Now he was Deputy Director-General it would
have been he who ordered the Princess's Paris adventure to be
monitored.

Christopher took a bet with himself that he was right on this.
But still he could not answer the question: why? All he knew
was that his chances of a romantic weekend with Giselle had
been destroyed and not even by his own organisation.

Sometimes he hated his work.

Chapter Ten

Paris, 19th August 1993

L'Ilot Vache restaurant on the Ile St Louis had become Christopher's favourite watering hole in the whole of Paris. And during his various postings to the French capital over the past seven years he'd had plenty of time to become a connoisseur of good food and fine wine at the British taxpayer's expense.

It wasn't the preponderance of the eponymous cows worked into the décor in every conceivable form which attracted him to this place. It was the food. The ambience was certainly agreeable. But the food was divine.

Today he had chosen escargots to start. They were always served without their shells, which was so much more convenient. His main course was Filet de facon Rossini – perfectly cooked tender filet of beef with a sautéed toast and a slice of foie gras. The whole gastronomic delight was to be washed down with a fine Cote de Beaune. Christopher was definitely in a good mood and he was optimistic about the outcome of his meeting.

He leant across the table and raised his glass in a toast to his guest.

'Pierre, as always, a delight to see you old boy', he said. He loved to affect the manner of the stereotypical upper class English gentleman because, while it might have impressed the Americans, it always irritated the French. Especially because it irritated the French.

Pierre Charron's mask of impeccable charm did not slip for an instant. 'And a delight to see you too…old boy'. He chuckled to cover the sarcasm.

'I hope we can do a little mutually useful business today', said Christopher, 'but first why don't you choose what you would like to eat. I'm afraid that I took the liberty of ordering before you arrived. I hope you don't mind.'

Charron placed his order with the attentive waiter without even glancing at the menu. He, too, dined frequently in the restaurant and had an easy familiarity with the range of cuisine. He was well-enough known in the establishment to be confident that the chef would provide whatever he wanted whether or not it was listed on the menu of the day. He approved Christopher's choice of wine with a curt nod of the head and a knowing smile.

Once the pleasantries were over and the pair had settled into their first course Christopher came straight to the point.

'As I am sure you are fully aware', he began, 'we have recently been paying some attention to one particular aspect of the arms trade between Russia and a country in the Middle East'.

He was being circumspect. They both knew it. His opening statement was not simply designed to flatter his guest. He was right to assume that the French knew all about the current MI6 operation in their capital because of what he was about to say next.

'One of the individuals we have targeted is a frequent visitor to Paris and invariably stays at The Ritz', he said. 'Most of the meetings he has with his various connections are held in the hotel'.

He paused. Pierre Charron dipped a piece of bread in the sauce on his plate and popped it in his mouth. He held Christopher's gaze. He knew what was coming but was determined to hold his ground.

'It has come to our notice that you have an extremely well-placed asset in the hotel', said Christopher. 'The quality of the intelligence you appear to be getting is far superior to ours. This asset could be very useful to us. I was wondering if we could find a formula between us which might allow for the sharing, on an ad hoc one-off basis of course, of this asset?'

Charron said nothing. He glanced casually out of the window.

Christopher tried again. He might have misjudged his friendship with Charron. This was going to be harder than he had anticipated.

'Perhaps we might come to some kind of an accommodation. I could arrange for the French Embassy in London to be given assistance in finding and making use of similar assets in the UK'.

Pierre Charron remained silent for a moment and then he said, somewhat stiffly; 'Frankly, Christopher, I am astonished that you even raise such a matter with me. You must know that I cannot disclose the existence of an agent to you without clearance at the highest level. Even if we did have an asset in place at the Ritz – which I doubt - I would not be authorised to share him or her with you, even on a temporary basis. In view of the rather difficult relationship between your government and mine at present I think it highly unlikely that I would be given such permission. This is a non-starter. Don't even go there.'

'But…', Christopher cut in.

Charron raised his hand. 'This is non-negotiable. I cannot and will not take your request forward to a higher level. Drop it….excuse me'.

His hand went to his right hip and unclipped a mobile telephone. It must have been on silent mode and vibrated to alert him to an incoming call.

He flipped it open. 'Allo', he said, non-committally.

Christopher, who had been studying his French counterpart's face, thought he noticed an involuntary flicker of the eyes in his direction. This was clearly a call Charron would have preferred not to have received in his presence.

The conversation was in French. 'It is not convenient to talk. I am in a meeting....', said Charron. He turned his head away but the caller's voice was loud and clear. Christopher was able to pick up the occasional word or phrase.

He heard the word 'important' and 'he hasn't left his room' and then 'money'. At this he thought he detected a look of irritation on Pierre Charron's face. The caller was obviously asking for money and wanted to meet.

'Another hour at least', said Charron. Christopher thought he heard the caller then suggest a meeting at half past four at 'the usual place'. His lunch guest nodded. 'Oui', he said. 'Bon' and cut off the call with a radiant smile and an apology for the interruption. He changed the subject and spent the remainder of the meal making small talk about fly-fishing - a hobby he had recently taken up and was evidently passionate about.

But Christopher's thoughts were elsewhere. He had been offended by the manner of Charron's snub and a thought was slowly taking shape in his mind. If they wouldn't co-operate he would have to steal the French's asset from under their noses.

He pondered why his companion had been so discomfited by the earlier phone call. Suddenly it came to him. The phrase 'he hasn't left his room' was the clue. By an extraordinary coincidence the very man they had been discussing had burst in on the conversation. It had to be him. The Ritz asset.

Charron would be meeting him at a rendezvous known only to the two of them in less than an hour. If Christopher could somehow eavesdrop on that meeting he would know the identity of the agent whose services he urgently needed to recruit.

He called for the bill and asked the Maitre'd to summon a taxi.

'That was delightful. Thank you so much', said his guest.

'Not at all', replied Christopher, it was lovely to see you again…long overdue. Where are you going now? May I offer you a lift somewhere? We could share my taxi'.

'That's very kind', said Charron, 'but I wouldn't want to take you out of your way'.

Christopher was thinking on his feet. He would have to invent a destination far enough away across the city so that Charron would at least accept his offer for part of the journey. He had not pretended that he was going back to his office, which Christopher knew was on the south of the river so he gambled that the 'usual place' would be north of the Seine.

'Oh it is no trouble at all', said Christopher. 'I have a meeting in Montmartre so I'll be going across town. I can drop you off anywhere you want'.

'In that case, thank you', said Charron, 'I'll let you know when we get somewhere near to where I'm going'.

Neither man spoke much during the journey and as they headed up the Boulevard Beaumarchais Charron suddenly leant forward and ordered the driver to stop.

'This'll be fine for me, Christopher', he said. 'I'll be in touch. We'll meet again soon, non?'

They shook hands and once he was out of the cab Christopher told the driver to wait. He watched out of the rear window as Charron crossed the road and made for the Metro Station. Anticipating his next move Christopher had already checked the fare on the meter and had sufficient cash to cover it and a generous tip in his hand. He thrust it at the driver, leapt out of the taxi and sprinted across the road towards the Metro station.

This was going to be fun, he thought. He had not had much use for 'tradecraft', as tracking people without being spotted was known in his business, ever since he and his fellow MI6 recruits had mounted surveillance and counter-surveillance operations on one another during their induction course. Then his training had taken place under the highly critical eye of an instructor and the action had been played out on the streets of Portsmouth, the sleepy naval town on the Hampshire coast of England. Today he was tailing someone in the bustling heart of one of the world's busiest cities.

Deep down he felt slightly embarrassed. This was schoolboy stuff. Playing at spies. Following an agent of a foreign country in his own capital city.

He trotted down the stairs into the subway booking hall taking in the whole area with one glance. On the far side of the hall he saw a pair of trousers he recognised as Charron's disappearing up the steps. Classic counter-surveillance technique. His benign and charming lunch guest was making sure he was not being followed. Either he did not trust Christopher or he was so nervous about his rendezvous with his contract that he was being over-cautious.

Christopher knew that the next move would be for Charron to double back and re-enter the subway by his first route. If anyone else did the same they would have to be tailing him.

Christopher turned on his heels and scampered back up the steps he had just come down. He would just have time to take cover before Charron re-emerged. He stood directly in line with the Metro entrance gazing into a shop window, which afforded an excellent reflection of people coming and going.

He saw Charron return, stop and check behind him before moving away up the street. Christopher looked after him and was just about to follow when the Frenchman bent down to tie his shoelace and then stepped into a shop doorway apparently intent on looking at a display of women's clothing.

He's good, this boy, thought Christopher, stepping back into the shadows himself. He watched in frustration as Charron hailed a cab and drove away.

He looked at his watch. Five past four. Twenty-five minutes to the meeting.

He hailed a taxi. 'Ritz Hotel, Place Vendome', he said.

By the time he reached the Ritz, Christopher had made a plan. He paid off the taxi and walked through the revolving doors into the main foyer of the hotel. Its grandeur and elegance always impressed him.

He walked straight ahead, past the glass cases filled with jewels and objets d'art to delight the most critical eye, past the Espadon restaurant, past the Hemingway Bar and out of the back door into the Rue Cambon. He crossed the street and took up a position to wait and watch.

If Charron's contact were indeed a member of the Ritz staff he or she would most likely be at work. Otherwise, why the need for an urgent meeting in the mid afternoon? If he or she was a staff member and on duty they would be more likely to leave for the meeting from the rear entrance rather than the more public front entrance.

It was a gamble. Christopher did not know what kind of person he should be looking for and he did not know how far away from The Ritz the 'usual place' might be. He hoped it was nearby so that, if he picked out the right target, he could follow on foot.

Time passed.

He almost followed a tall cadaverous-looking man wearing the distinctive livery of a concierge. The job would afford the man good opportunities to spy on his clientele and he certainly looked furtive as he left the building. But would a paid informant advertise where he worked by attending a meeting with his handler wearing his uniform?

A young woman came out, looked up and down the street, and darted back in again before re-emerging and bustling off in the direction of the Rue St Honore. Christopher thought about following but decided she looked too young.

At twenty past four he saw a face he recognised. A small, balding, bespectacled man emerged and set off confidently northwards up the Rue Cambon. Although he wore a tie, he looked shabby. His shoes were dirty, his trousers were creased and his sports jacket had seen better days. Christopher would not have given him a second glance but for the fact that he had noticed the man on several occasions as someone to whom the lower staff of the hotel, waiters, barmen, porters and concierges, deferred. In one idle moment while waiting for a contact to meet him in the bar, Christopher had watched the man closely and surmised that he must be something to do with security at the hotel.

Security. The perfect position for an informant at a major international hotel such as The Ritz. Christopher was sure he had his man.

He began to follow at a safe distance but his prey was oblivious to him as he strode out purposefully, never once looking behind.

At the top of the road he crossed over and turned right up the Boulevard des Capucines and then took the first right down the Rue Daunou. He kept looking at his watch as though he were late for an appointment. Passing the Theatre de Daunou he turned in at the legendary Harry's Bar.

Bit of a fancy watering hole for you, thought Christopher, *and rather a public place to conduct clandestine business*. He satisfied himself with the thought that sometimes the most obvious and open meeting places provide the best opportunities to construct cover stories as, once again, he took up a position at a café opposite to watch and wait.

After half an hour he was rewarded with the sight of Pierre Charron leaving the bar and jumping into a taxi. He waited until the vehicle had turned the corner into Rue Louis Le Grand before crossing the road and entering Harry's Bar.

The small man with the spectacles was sitting alone at the bar looking glum. Christopher drew up a stool alongside him. 'Hello', he said cheerily, 'you don't know me but I do a great deal of business at The Ritz and I've seen you there on many occasions. I believe you are the big white chief of security, is that right?'

The small man blinked as though he had only just comprehended that he was being paid a compliment. He nodded. 'Hello', he said.

'Sorry, I didn't catch your name', said Christopher, extending his hand.

'Henri' said the other man shaking hands limply, 'Henri Paul'.

'Well, its very nice to meet you Henri', said Christopher, 'may I get you a drink.......?'

* * * * * *

London 6th December 1994

The photographers stood in a huddle gossiping and making lewd small talk to pass the time. They were gathered on the pavement in the shadow of Kensington's Royal Gardens Hotel.

To the average passer-by the reason for their presence was not immediately obvious. They were grouped around double wrought-iron gates which gave access to a service road running up the side of the hotel.

That road, in turn, led into the entrance courtyard of Kensington Palace, the home of the most famous woman in the world – Her Royal Highness the Princess Diana of Wales.

It was bitterly cold. The photographers stamped their feet, clapped their hands together, and blew on their fingers. A few yards away stood two elderly women, both expensively dressed. One carried an olive green plastic carrier bag bearing the word "Harrods" in gold lettering.

Next to the women stood a younger woman wearing a headscarf. She had a baby in a pushchair and was holding a small girl by the hand. The little girl held a Union Jack flag in her other hand and was waving it enthusiastically at a bird sitting in a leafless tree above her.

Kevin Donne was oblivious to the scene in front of him. His mind was playing pictures of Diana in his head. Diana smiling. Diana laughing. Diana dancing. Diana looking serious. Diana shaking his hand…and looking into his eyes.

He pulled the woollen beanie hat further down over his ears and thrust his hands deeper into the pockets of his bomber jacket.

'Here we go', said one of the photographers, as a police motorcyclist, blue lights flashing, roared through the gates and stopped the traffic in Kensington High Street. Kevin stepped to the edge of the pavement. Two more motorcycles swept by and then a large black limousine.

The photographers hit their shutter buttons in unison and the darkened windows of the car lit up with the flashes from a dozen or more flashguns. Diana looked as beautiful as ever. She smiled. Kevin knew it was for him alone. He smiled back. He did not wave back. That would not have been a manly thing to do. She was gone.

Kevin felt happy. He had shared her world and she had shared his for a fleeting moment. Just to be near her was enough. It had been the same last week and the week before and everywhere that he had managed to stake her out and catch her eye for the past five years.

He knew it was an obsession. He knew it was unhealthy. But he could not help himself. He loved Diana. It was pure love. Platonic. But passionate. It was slowly taking over his life. He wondered where it would all end.

Kevin felt a sharp jab in the small of his back. His reaction was instinctive and instantaneous. In one movement he whirled around, fists clenched. His right arm led with a scything left to right motion while a piston-pump action shot his left arm out in a powerful straight jab. At the same time his legs flailed upwards in a double karate kick – first the right, then the left.

He expected to see a gun or a knife flying through the air and a would-be attacker tumbling to the ground. But his assailant was also SAS trained and had dropped to one knee and swayed to his right out of reach of Kevin's flying fists and feet. Now he sat chuckling on the pavement.

'Hello you old tosser', he said, standing up. 'How the devil are you?'

Kevin threw his arms around him and grasped him in an affectionate bear hug.

'Spike Hughes', he bellowed. 'Good to see you, son. What are you doing here?'

'Just gonna ask you the same thing', said his old comrade. 'Nothing better to do than hang around trying to cop an eyeful of Her Royal sexy Highness, eh?', he grinned.

Kevin bridled at the suggestive tone in his friend's question. He was embarrassed but would not let his discomfort show.

'No, no', he said. 'I've been thinking about taking up this photography lark.

'I spent all those years learning skills like tracking and intelligence gathering. I reckon it's about time I used them to earn a living. These guys make pretty good money taking pictures of celebrities and flogging them. It can't be that difficult. So I just thought I'd suss out how they go about getting pix of the biggest celeb around'.

'Yeah, I thought it must be something like that', said Hughes. 'I spotted you here last week actually – Thursday I think. I was on a bus so I couldn't stop for a chat'. He smiled knowingly.

Kevin changed the subject. 'Blimey, it's a long time since I've seen you mate. Whatcha been up to?', he asked.

'Oh, this and that, you know', said Hughes. 'Listen, if you've got the time, let's have a drink and a natter'. He gestured towards The Goat Tavern on the opposite side of the road.

'Okay', said Kevin, 'I'll have a coffee with you but I've been dry for quite a while now'.

For the next half-an-hour the two men reminisced happily about old times. Spike was sympathetic when Kevin revealed that he was out of work and finding it hard to make ends meet.

'You should make your mark with the outfit I work for', he said. 'Now that really would be putting your army training to good use'.

'Yeah? What's that then?', asked Kevin.

'It's a security company called HSA based somewhere in West London', said Spike. 'I've never been there. Only employs guys like us. Mainly ex-Firm. Run by an ex-Colonel in one of the jock regiments. Good guy. It's not fulltime work but there's almost always something on either here or abroad'.

'What kind of work?', asked Kevin.

'All sorts', replied his companion. 'Bit of soldiering, bit of intel gathering, bit of detective stuff, bit of prot. Actually, quite a lot of prot'.

'Prot?', said Kevin.

'Protection. Body guarding', said Spike, scribbling a telephone number on the edge of a cardboard beer mat. 'Ring this number. It's a guy called Andy. Another jock. He's also ex-Firm. Tell him I sent you. He'll fix you up'.

'Thanks, I'll do that', said Kevin pocketing the mat and draining the dregs of his coffee.

'Actually', said Spike, 'one of the contracts they've got is supplying prot for that geezer who owns Harrods. You know that Mohomed El Fayeed bloke. They're looking for an extra body to join the team right now'.

'Oh no, I don't reckon I could work for an Arab', said Kevin.

'Hey, he's not an Arab', said Spike, 'he's an Egyptian. They come from an ancient civilization and do not regard themselves as Arabs. I was talking to Kenny the other day. You remember. Kenny Lumsden? He's working for him.

'He reckons he's very demanding but the money and perks are good and there's plenty of foreign travel'.

Spike downed the last of his pint of Guinness.

'Should be right up your street', he said. 'You'll never have a better opportunity to get close to your little Royal girlfriend.

She's always in Harrods shopping and El Fayeed hangs out with her quite a bit from what I gather'.

He winked and stood up.

Kevin refused to react to his companion's blatant tease.

The two men shook hands. Spike headed towards the underground station.

Kevin put his hand in his pocket and fingered the beer mat. He crossed the road and made for the public telephones in the Royal Gardens Hotel.

Chapter Eleven

Paris, 1st March 1995

Breakfast at La Chaise au Plafond was a daily routine for Christopher.

He could have breakfasted at home. He wasn't too lazy to look after himself. In fact he loved shopping for bits and pieces in the Patisserie and the Boulangerie down the street. The bachelor life suited him.

But living in the heart of the bustling, cosmopolitan, sophisticated Marais district, it seemed a shame not to take every opportunity to soak up the atmosphere. So each day began the same way. Shower, shave, dress, while listening to the radio. Pick up the papers, English and French, at the kiosk on the corner. Orange juice, black coffee and croissants at the café La Chaise au Plafond just a couple of hundred yards from his front door.

He accepted, indeed almost relished, the solitary, isolated nature of his profession. He was fond of quoting Ernest Hemmingway's exhortation to his students: *"A writer is always alone...always an outsider"*; as a description of his own role in life. But he was a gregarious soul at heart and loved to start his day among the chattering clientele of his local bistro.

The regulars knew he was English. They called him *"Christophe"* or *"L'Anglais"*. They did not know what he did for a living and they never asked.

For his part Christopher happily immersed himself in the minutiae of their lives. The ailments of their pets and their complaints about the price of food, he listened to them all with patience and the sympathetic air of a family doctor. It amused him to note that no matter how depressed the French became they never blamed it on the weather – unlike the British.

Today's topic of conversation was a 1960's pink American Cadillac convertible with white walled tyres and number plates bearing the name Elvis. It was parked across the street from the café and speculation as to its ownership and sudden appearance in the neighbourhood was running wild.

When the guessing and theorising died down Christopher suggested: 'Perhaps Elvis really is still alive and has come to live in Paris'. The customers and staff all roared with laughter. *Crazy Englishman. Does he take us for fools?* But the expressions on one or two faces suggested that they were prepared to give serious consideration to the idea.

Christopher had been living in Paris for almost ten years – on and off. The transfer from MI5 to MI6 seemed to have worked out well. He travelled a good deal, especially when London needed his linguistic skills on an operation, and he had been assigned to several short-term postings. But he was beginning to regard himself as a Parisian. He saw the French capital as home.

Christopher was a cultured man. He loved the Marais with its 17th century buildings and elegant stores and restaurants. He revelled in his close proximity to the Place des Voges, the Picasso Museum, the Carnavalet Museum, and most of all, the Louvre. Where he lived, in Rue du Bourg-Tibourg, he was just five minutes walk from the Seine.

Home was an air-conditioned and beautifully restored apartment in a registered historical building, which dated back to 1663. It had terracotta tiled flooring, exposed wooden beams and arched picture windows in the living room and bedroom. Christopher had furnished it tastefully in his own style with antique furniture from the Napoleon III and Louis Philippe periods.

He took another gulp of coffee and paused, transfixed, over an open copy of Paris Match on the table in front of him. A familiar face beamed back at him from the society pages. Between President Mitterrand and a junior finance minister stood a statuesque blonde in a black evening dress with a plunging neckline. She looked radiant. The caption told him that Mademoiselle Marielle Norstrund had joined the President at the Elysee Palace for a gala dinner in honour of King Hussein of Jordan.

Christopher finished his coffee, scooped up his newspapers and headed for the Metro station.

Today looked like being a fairly routine day. Apart from calling in at the office to pick up his mail Christopher was due to have lunch with a contact at The Ritz hotel. His job was all about contacts – paid informants, trained agents, people in high places or well-connected jobs who didn't know that Christopher was a spy and had no idea why they told him things that they shouldn't.

He held most of his business meetings in the large hotels. But he preferred The Ritz. He found the Georges V too ostentatious and the Crillon too pretentious. For all its glitz he thought The Ritz had an understated elegance and an indefinable style about it. He spent a lot of time there. And now that he had an agent in place there his job was made all the easier.

But there was something else which gave Christopher a spring in his step today. He was going to see Giselle.

Tonight they were going to the opera. Christopher had tickets for 'Le Chevalier a La Rose' at the Opera Bastille and afterwards they would dine *a deux* at Bofinger.

Then home to bed. The end of a perfect evening. Giselle would share his king-size bed.

Christopher smiled at the thought. It had been a while.

When he arrived at his office in the British Embassy the Commercial Attaché's secretary, Sonia, had a file for him to read. The encrypted contents had been transmitted via a secure telex line from London overnight. A cipher clerk had already deciphered it and a cassette tape, which had also arrived overnight in the diplomatic bag, accompanied it. Christopher's boss wanted him to absorb the contents and report his impressions as soon as possible.

He made himself a cup of instant coffee and settled down to read.

The file detailed an undercover operation run by PTCP - MI6's Production Targeting Counter-Proliferation department – the section which gathered intelligence on pariah nations, like Iran and Iraq, and disrupted their attempts to obtain biological, chemical and nuclear weapons of mass destruction. Most of their operations took many years to complete.

In this case the sequence had begun some five years earlier with the arrest at Heathrow Airport of a Monaco-based Israeli businessman whom MI6 suspected of having links to Israel's much vaunted spy organisation, Mossad. During a routine search of his briefcase Customs officers had found plans, which appeared to be for the production of mustard gas. The man claimed that he was an agricultural engineer and that the formulas were for a new insecticide. He was not believed but there was insufficient evidence to charge him with any crime so he was barred from entering Britain and put on a plane back to the south of France.

MI6 asked the DST to keep an eye on the Israeli and through telephone intercepts on his home they discovered that, a year earlier, he had obtained the plans for a mustard gas plant which he had sold at considerable profit to an American-based Iraqi. The CIA had been watching this individual because they had an idea that he was masterminding the build up of chemical weapons for Iraq's dictator Saddam Hussein and it soon became clear that he was pressurising the Israeli to come up with the specialist equipment and chemicals needed to actually build the plant.

The French noticed that the Israeli frequently telephoned a woman – a Mrs Margaret Daintree – at her home in a small village just outside the English cathedral city of Lincoln. As a result MI6 obtained the necessary warrants to intercept her telephone and her mail and set about closely looking into her background.

They discovered that Mrs Daintree, twice married with teenaged children, was a most unlikely businesswoman. She had spent most of her working life as a secretary at a local stationery and office supplies company, which she had bought from her boss when he retired. She had proved to have real business acumen and, having initially established stationery supply contacts in China, she quickly diversified into chemicals and pharmaceuticals.

Having met her through one of his business contacts, the Israeli was impressed with Mrs Daintree's versatility and work ethic and set about cultivating her as his 'cut-out' – someone who would unwittingly carry out the Iraqi's dirty and quite probably illegal work.

Margaret Daintree, in her innocence, had been delighted to be introduced to a new business partner and flew to Paris to meet the Iraqi in The Ritz hotel. He asked her to buy a couple of tonnes of thionyl chloride – a building block chemical used in the manufacture of many legitimate products but also an essential ingredient for making mustard gas and several nerve gas agents.

After six months of research, phone calls, and two trips to remote parts of China, Mrs Daintree was able to complete the thionyl chloride shipment to Iraq.

Her contact was delighted and tasked her to obtain some of the equipment for his new plant. He gave her blueprints and asked her to see what she could do. But she was out of her

145

depth. She had no technical training and could not understand the specifications and drawings. So she turned to an old friend of her husband, Thomas Carpenter, a former engineer who was working as a commodity trader with Haq Trading – an import-export trading company based in the City of London.

Carpenter needed the extra cash and readily agreed to take on the assignment. He and Mrs Daintree arranged a rendezvous at a motorway service station where two MI6 agents, posing as travelling salesmen, sat at an adjacent table and recorded their conversation through a directional microphone hidden in a briefcase. It was clear that Carpenter did not understand the drawings either but he was determined to be part of the deal so he took them away without letting on.

At this point the PTCP section head faced a dilemma. He needed to establish a contact with the Iraqis so that he could infiltrate and disrupt their operation. But he could not risk attempting to recruit Margaret Daintree because he reasoned that she would simply panic and pull out of the deal. And Thomas Carpenter was of the old school. So loyal to his friends that he would be bound to let on to Mrs Daintree that he had been taken on in a spying role.

So it was decided that an MI6 agent would approach the pair undercover, win their confidence and trust, and hope that they would recommend him to their Iraqi ringmaster.

But that was easier said than done. Mrs Daintree worked alone at home and was not accessible via intermediaries. Besides telephone intercepts showed that she was wary of strangers and only accepted them if they were recommended by friends.

But as luck would have it, the managing director of Haq Trading was already on MI6 books. He was being run as an informant by the head of the Middle East natural cover section. He agreed to take an MI6 man on as a temporary employee without anyone else in the company knowing about the operation.

The plan worked and, having convinced Carpenter that he was a qualified chemical engineer who could interpret the technical drawing and knew where to acquire the components, the MI6 agent had become friendly with Mrs Daintree who, in turn, introduced him to her Iraqi contact by telephone.

Christopher left the file open on his lap as he slotted the cassette into a tape machine on the desk in front of him. It was a recording of an intercepted telephone call between Mrs Daintree's Lincolnshire farmhouse and the Iraqi's office in Baghdad. Christopher pressed the 'Play' button.

After a series of clicks and a ringing tone the phone was picked up and a man's voice said: 'Hello'. Mrs Daintree could be heard introducing her newfound adviser on chemical engineering matters and then she handed the telephone over to the MI6 agent.

'Hello Mr Shafiq, I'm Mark Hensby', said the agent, 'nice to talk to you. Sounds like a terrific project you've got planned'.

The voice on the other end was cultured. Educated. The characteristic middle-eastern accent was tinged with distinctive American overtones.

'I'm delighted to be speaking to you too Mr Hensby. Margaret tells that you are just the guy to help us...'

Christopher listened intently to the brief conversation twice and then checked the name on the file. The Iraqi was named as Balaam Abu Shafiq.

Chapter Twelve

St James's, London, 22nd November 1995

The gentlemen's clubs of London epitomise the stereotype of
a capital city peopled by men clad in pin-stripe suits, smoking
cigars and drinking port. Their archaic rules and rituals have
survived the encroachment of the modern world and the strict
and elaborate membership restrictions, which preclude
women, are still proudly in place.

Principal among them all The Carlton Club stands out as an
establishment behind whose doors more epoch-making
decisions have been taken over the past two hundred years -
more plot and counter-plot - than ever took place in the
debating chambers of Westminster and Whitehall less than a
mile away.

If there were to be a headquarters of that mythical entity the
British like to call 'The Establishment' then it would surely be
the grand and exclusive Carlton.

Founded in 1832 it has been the private dining club, drinking
den and hub of skulduggery for the Conservative Party, in and
out of office, ever since. Now located at No 69 St James's
Street after the original building in Pall Mall was bombed
during the Second World War, the portraits of every Tory
Prime Minister adorn its walls, including Margaret Thatcher
who had to be made an honorary gentleman in order to be
allowed membership.

Today's meeting – it was a Wednesday - had a distinctly
clandestine feel about it. There was mystery and intrigue in
the air. The Library, discreetly located on the lower ground
floor, had been hurriedly booked the night before by Sir
Tristram Grainger who had spent much of the previous 24
hours urgently summoning a select group of like-minded men
to convene in the club at twelve noon, precisely.

At the appointed hour Sir Tristram rapped his glass on the green baize tablecloth and gazed balefully around him. The room itself conveyed a sense of foreboding. The walls were lined with dark oak bookshelves from floor to ceiling containing bound copies of Parliamentary debates and Hansard going back to 1826.

Tristram Grainger was a tall, rangy, figure with steel-grey hair swept back from his forehead, a neatly clipped moustache and formidably bushy eyebrows hooding ice blue eyes. He wore a pin-stripe suit over a blue shirt with a stiffly starched white collar and a Special Forces Club tie. A scarlet silk handkerchief tumbled foppishly from the breast pocket of his suit and, although Remembrance Day had passed eleven days earlier, a red poppy was still pinned to his lapel.

Like all but two of the twelve men seated around the table, Sir Tristram had a military background. Decorated for gallantry while a young officer with the King's African Rifles during the Mau Mau uprising in Kenya in the 1950's, he had seen distinguished service with the Special Air Service in Cyprus and Oman. Having attained the rank of Lieutenant Colonel he had spent five years seconded to Buckingham Palace as Equerry to Prince Philip, Duke of Edinburgh followed by a spell as Director of Military Intelligence at the Royal Military Academy, Sandhurst and had recently retired, as a Brigadier, from a post as strategic adviser to the Chief of Defence Staff at the Ministry of Defence in Whitehall. He now held a non-executive directorship with The Queen's bank, Coutts, in the City.

Although he had left Buckingham Palace some years previously Sir Tristram maintained very close links with the Royal Household. He had the ear of the Queen's most senior courtiers and it was generally accepted by his peers that when he spoke on constitutional matters he reflected the views of the innermost circles of the court and was probably voicing the personal opinions, if not of the Monarch herself, then undoubtedly those of the Royal Family.

'Gentlemen', he began, 'we all know why we are here and I need hardly remind you that the usual Chatham House rules apply. As I mentioned when inviting you to this meeting, the situation at KP is completely out of hand and has become very grave indeed. Something must be done about that woman before she does irrevocable damage to the institution of the monarchy, if indeed, she hasn't already done so'.

When uttering the words 'that woman' he spoke without venom, simply cold disdain.

'I propose that we begin by reviewing Monday night's programme and discuss its implications for the constitution before looking at ways in which the problem might be resolved'.

The others in the room nodded and muttered agreement. Although in their different spheres many of them held, or had held, positions of power and influence far beyond that of Sir Tristram they instinctively deferred to him as unelected chairman of their ad hoc grouping.

'You will all be well aware', he went on, 'of the furore this thing has caused in the papers and indeed the extraordinary shemozzle it has stirred up in the international media. I watched the damn thing myself out of academic interest and was utterly appalled. But I realise that we may not all have seen it so I have asked Tommy to provide us with a transcript of the interview'.

Thomas Crampton was the Director-General of MI5. He had come a long way since the early days of Operation Ephesus. His mentor, Sir Granville Sleight, had groomed him well over the years having seen, in the fastidiously studious young fellow, a perfect successor to himself.

Crampton was a dapper little man with suspiciously perfect black hair and steel-framed glasses. He wore a plain navy blue suit in keeping with the anonymity of his position. From

a black leather attaché case he drew a sheaf of papers –
photocopies of the same document neatly stapled together –
and began to pass them round the table.

'I have had the key words and phrases highlighted for the sake
of brevity', he said.

'Yes, no need to read the whole thing or we'll be here all day',
cut in Sir Tristram.

The men around the table, all of a similar age and bearing,
gazed at the document before them.

It was headed 'Transcript: BBC1 - Panorama. H.R.H the
Princess of Wales interviewed by Martin Bashir. Recorded at
Kensington Palace. Transmitted Monday 20 November 1995'.

For the next few minutes nothing could be heard except the
rustling of paper and the occasional snort of derision.

'Bloody BBC, absolutely typical. Just another example of
their determination to undermine and destroy everything that
is good about this country. Bunch of queer, over-educated,
Communists. My God, the influence we have allowed them to
gain. Should have been dealt with a long time ago'.

The speaker was William Tannadyce. Lord Tannadyce of
Pennycuik to give him his full title. A billionaire financier
with homes on all five continents, he had mostly made his
money from armaments. He was chairman of the multi-
national Tannadyce Ordnance Corporation and a major
shareholder in the American arms giant The Castle Group.

His colleagues were used to intemperate outburst of this kind.
His view of the world was unsophisticated and somewhat
outdated and his political opinions rooted in a time of simpler
choices and greater certainties. Bill Tannadyce was a doer not
a thinker but they needed him for the financial muscle he
brought to the table.

151

'Quite, quite. Point taken. Absolutely Bill', said Sir Tristram. 'But on this occasion I think we are less concerned with the motives of the messenger than we are with the consequences of the message'.

'I have had the circumstances surrounding the setting up of the programme analysed', said Crampton, 'and I am satisfied that the impetus came almost entirely from the lady herself. Indeed it was she who virtually solicited the BBC to conduct the interview and she who dictated the line of questioning thus allowing her to deliver the answers she wanted to give'.

He spoke with the conviction of a man who had been privy to conversations neither he, nor his organisation, ought to have overheard. He was not about to reveal that his intimate knowledge of the lady in question stretched back fourteen years to the earliest days of her marriage.

'It seems to me', broke in Sir Tristram, 'that the important passages are at the end, firstly when she talks about the Monarchy needing to change or die and then when she says Prince Charles will never be King. I refer you to page 18 at paragraph 8. She has already said that the public is indifferent to the Monarchy and the Royals are afraid to adapt then she calls for change '...*there are a few things that could change that would alleviate this doubt and sometimes complicated relationship between monarchy and public*' she says '*they could walk hand in hand as opposed to be so distant*'. There is an implied threat here that if they do not go along with her recipe for a monarchy of the proletariat they will be discarded by the public – almost a call for revolution.

'Then at the top of page 21 she says of Charles' accession to the throne, '*because I know the character I would think that the top job would bring enormous limitations to him and I don't know whether he could adapt to that*' and when she is asked if the crown should pass directly to William she says '*My wish is that my husband finds peace of mind and from that follows other things, yes*'.

'Bloody woman is deranged. A complete fruitcake', spluttered Lord Tannadyce.

He was the only man to have removed his jacket and as he spoke he rocked back in his chair and pulled his scarlet braces forward in a characteristic gesture.

His thoughts flew back to a secret discussion, which had taken place over dinner at a Royal Palace some twenty years earlier. Then the convenor of the meeting had been Colonel David Stirling, the legendary founder of the SAS, and the host had been Prince Charles' uncle, Lord Louis Mountbatten. Then, as now, the heads of both MI5 and MI6 had been present. Then as now the company was largely made up of former army officers fiercely loyal to the Queen. They had been plotting a coup to overthrow the Labour Government of Harold Wilson. History would never record how close they came.

Bill Tannadyce's musings were interrupted by a sharp knock.

'Would you like me to bring lunch now, sir, or shall I just serve drinks?', asked an elderly steward poking his head around the door.

'No, fetch lunch, thank you George', said Sir Tristram, 'but take a drinks order before you go. I'll have my usual, gin and water.

'I've taken the liberty of ordering roast beef and horseradish sandwiches and a couple of bottles of club claret. We'll have cheese and port with the coffee later'.

When the steward had withdrawn, James Sutherland spoke. He had been a colonel in the Royal Scots Guards and now ran a private security company, the Halcyon Security Agency, which employed former soldiers – mostly paratroopers, marines and other Special Forces commandos. His company was engaged by multinational corporations and governments to undertake mercenary operations in trouble spots around the world and now included on its payroll former SAS trooper, reformed alcoholic, and obsessive Diana-watcher, Kevin Donne.

'I'm sorry Bill but I don't agree'. Sutherland spoke in a cultured Scottish accent. 'The lady is very far from deranged. This is cold and calculating. She has an agenda and this is the first step towards achieving who knows what? The overthrow of the monarchy? Perhaps'.

'This is hysterical nonsense', said Tannadyce, 'just ignore the stupid girl and she'll go away. She couldn't lead a revolution even if she wanted to. She wouldn't know how. She has no powerbase'.

'Of course she has a powerbase. She is speaking direct to the people, and they love her', retorted Sutherland. 'Just take a look at the opinion polls today. The support she has is phenomenal. I think this is just the start of her campaign. It is almost as if she is storing up something with which to destroy Charles and with him the monarchy. She'll be manipulating the media to make much more trouble before this is over, I'm sure of it'.

Everyone shifted in their seats. There was a momentary silence. Then the gruff voice of Lord Tannadyce.

'All right, how about destroying her credibility with the public – tarnishing that angelic image? What about her infidelity? She's now admitted adultery on television and we all know that the woman is as libidinous as a warren full of rabbits. I'm sure Tommy's people can arrange to have her sexual adventures exposed?'

'Actually we have had some success in placing evidence of Her Royal Highness's infidelities in the public domain', said Crampton, 'but it has proved counter-productive. The public see her as a victim and seem to side with her even more. In fact she is admired for her sexual adventures, as you put it Bill'.

'What about the international dimension, David?', asked Sir Tristram, turning to the Chief of the Secret Intelligence Service, MI6.

To look at him, with his dishevelled hair and crumpled suit, the casual observer would not have been able to divine that Sir David Langdale was Britain's top spymaster. But when he spoke the depth of his intellect was clearly evident.

'Whether by luck or judgement Her Royal Highness has established a very high profile internationally and her influence on the world stage is growing at an immense rate', he said gravely. 'Her public pronouncements are accorded considerable weight by a number of governments, especially in third world countries, and there are elements within the United Nations inclined to take her seriously.

'The issue of landmines, which she has espoused so vigorously, is of major concern in some quarters. I know that HMG is privately very uneasy about the long-term effect of her campaign in this regard and it is causing our friends over the water a great deal of alarm'.

As he said this he glanced across the table at Lord Tannadyce but the munitions tycoon studiously avoided his gaze.

'Proposals gentlemen?', said Sir Tristram. 'How can this loose cannon be stopped? Will Uncle Sam help, David?'

'As I have said, there is concern on that side of the Atlantic, and a monitoring operation in relation to the target individual has been underway for some time. I am not at liberty to divulge the precise nature of that operation but a good deal of useful intelligence is being gathered and shared with us on the usual reciprocal basis.

'I sense a mood for action in this meeting', he went on, 'but I must caution against anything precipitate which might exacerbate things. I'm sure you would agree Tommy'.

Crampton nodded. 'Yes, the level of surveillance, together with monitoring both by the Americans, and us is already very high. I will ensure that the threat assessment, by that I mean the degree of threat which she poses to the Crown and the State, is kept up to date and, if necessary, report back to you Tristram'.

'Well gentlemen, I think we are all agreed that something must be done', said Sir Tristram.

There was a murmur of assent around the table.

'If this woman will not desist from her traitorous talk and actions she must be stopped by whatever means is within our power. *In extremis* I take it we could raise manpower, James?', he asked.

Sutherland nodded.

'And funding?'

Lord Tannadyce nodded.

There was a knock at the door and the steward entered again.

'I'm sorry my Lord but we've run out of the Laphroig', he said, 'will Lagavulin do?'

Lord Tannadyce exploded.

'No it will not do. Good God man, I mentioned to the bar manager last week that the Laphroig was getting low. It is utterly monstrous that a place like this should run out of malt whisky...of any kind!'

* * * * * *

Washington D.C., 15th January 1996

The atmosphere in the Pentagon's basement conference room was buzzing with anticipation. Fierce strip lighting and invasive air conditioning added to a feeling of foreboding not eased by the thick inward-sloping walls and ceiling fans, which reminded everyone, that this was actually a bunker built to withstand nuclear attack.

Allowing for the buttons, braid, and cap furniture there was enough brass in the room to equip the wind section of a small orchestra. All three armed services were represented and, apart from the men in suits, no one ranked lower than a general or an admiral.

This was a sub-committee meeting of a powerful grouping the Americans quaintly like to call The Intelligence Community – a loose alliance of sixteen government agencies whose remit in some way or another includes spying.

Today key personnel from just six of those organisations – the Central Intelligence Agency, the National Security Agency, the National Reconnaissance Office, the National Imagery and Mapping Agency, the Defense Intelligence Agency and the State Department Bureau of Intelligence and Research – had gathered to discuss a matter of global significance.

The chairman, a two-star general with a brush cut and a sour-faced expression, called the meeting to order.

'Gentlemen', he said, 'we are here to take a look at the latest tricks that Mr Sad Man Insane is getting up to and consider the way forward.' It was his own little joke. He thought he was very smart to have come up with a bastardised version of the Iraqi dictator's name and he trotted it out on every possible occasion.

There were weary smiles of recognition around the table.

'In the folder in front of you are prints of the reconnaissance material that NIMA has provided which should help us as we go through the satellite images on the screen. I have asked Hank to lead this first part of the discussion. Hank?'

Hank Scheidegger was in his late thirties with rimless spectacles and the intense look of a mad professor. He had been senior analyst with the National Reconnaissance Office for just over a year.

'Thank you, General', he said. 'Gentlemen, the prints in front of you are numbered one through thirty-five and I will deal with them in sequence. They each represent single frame images taken during three passes over the Persian Gulf on three separate dates within the past month. They are the best images we have though the quality in the third sequence is less than perfect because there was cloud cover on that day and we had to rely on the penetration of our short-wave radar satellite, Lacrosse.

He turned towards a flickering electronic screen, which had been lowered through a slot in the ceiling.

'You may find it easier to follow on the screen, gentlemen', he said pointing a hand-held remote control towards a black box in the corner of the room and pressing the button.

The screen filled with a black and white picture, which, at first, was difficult to decipher for the untrained eyes of the viewers in the room. It looked a like a relief map covering a barren and somewhat mountainous terrain.

'This is Kurdish northern Iraq', said Hank. 'You are looking at an area about fifty kilometres from Mosul almost directly due north of the city. I want you to pay particular attention to the area top right of your screen which will move to a more central position and become enlarged as we go through the sequence.'

Everyone leaned forward straining to make out anything which might be a recognisable feature on the remote landscape. One or two studied the photographs on the table in front of them.

What appeared to be two roads snaked their way through the mountains. One led to a cluster of small white oblongs. As the pictures became larger these appeared to be a group of low buildings.

For the next five minutes the room was silent save for the voice of Hank as he interpreted the satellite pictures.

'The reason we believe that this is a chemical weapons facility', he said eventually, using a pointer to indicate the side of a mountain a short distance from the buildings, 'is that we have seen exactly this configuration before.'

Again everyone in the room leaned forward.

Looking from directly above the perspective was skewed. Hank's pointer was indicating a steep cliff face at the bottom of which were two creases, which appeared to be entrances into the rock. Wide tracks led towards them.

'Are those tunnels going inside the mountain?', asked a heavily tanned man wearing the uniform and insignia of a U.S. Air Force general.

'Yes sir. We reckon they are something like that', said Hank. He flicked the sequence on a few frames. 'At this angle, if you look at the shadow cast by the upper edge of the openings on to the ground and calculate a comparative measurement, both these openings would be approximately twenty feet high and fifteen feet wide. Big enough to get a large truck, an oil tanker or even a military vehicle through.'

'Okay Hank, so tell us what evidence you have for saying that this is a chemical weapons facility', said the chairman.

Once more the analyst pointed his remote control towards the box in the corner and pressed the button. The screen cleared and a fresh picture appeared. It was also a satellite image but of a different mountainous region. In the middle of the picture was another cliff face and two more creases almost identical to those the group had been studying just moments earlier.

'This is Tarhunah in Libya, sir', he said. 'Forty miles southeast of Tripoli. Colonel Gaddafi's nerve-gas plant. Inside the mountain there is an underground chamber some three storey's high so that the plant is secure from air attack.'

'Virgil, remind me of the situation. Where are we on that one?', asked the chairman turning to one of the CIA field directors sitting to his left.

Virgil Grant was quick to oblige.

'You will recall, General, that we were successful in getting Gaddafi's chemical weapons plant at Rabta closed down in 1990', he said. 'But four years ago we detected this new facility at Tarhunah and together with our allies we were able to prevent any of the large machinery needed to complete the construction from reaching Libya so work on the site has now ceased.

'But, sir', he went on, 'in relation to today's discussion it is important to note that it was Iraqi engineers and scientists who were leading the Libyan chemical weapons programme at that time and many of them are still there. The Iraqi's are seen in the Arab world as experts in this field'.

The chairman looked around the room. 'Thoughts, gentlemen?', he asked.

There was a general murmuring.

'I gotta hundred bucks says it's a nook facility', said the Navy representative, a cantankerous old admiral who had hitherto said nothing but simply chomped on a fat cigar.

'You may be right, Henry', retorted the chairman, 'but right now all we got is a bunch a pictures taken from outer space that prove nothin''.

Virgil Grant raised his hand. 'Sir, if I may....?', he asked.

'Go ahead', said the general.

'Two things. First, prior to Desert Storm, this was the area around Mosul where Saddam Hussein, with support from the West, was developing his ballistic weapons industry, Project 395. The Condor Two missile. You will remember that the research, manufacturing and testing facility Saad 16 was located there. So there is already the infrastructure in the area and a skilled work force in place for this kind of activity.

'Second, we have just received a highly classified report from the U.N. Weapons Inspectorate team which has recently returned from Baghdad. They were not permitted to travel to Mosul or within 100 kilometres of the city and they suspect that is because there are programmes under construction in the area which may be for either germ or chemical warfare or possibly even a nuclear research programme.

'But much more significantly the leader of the delegation also claims to have clear evidence that the French are secretly supplying vital components to the Iraqi WMD programme against the letter and spirit of the latest UN resolutions and behind the backs of the rest of the world.'

The chairman frowned.

'You gotta give me more than that', he said. 'I can't go to the Secretary of State and the President with any kind of a recommendation based on all this guesswork. We need much more specific intelligence.'

'We do not have the people in place on the ground right now', said Grant, 'but the British do and the British have much

161

closer links with France so they are in a better position to monitor what is going on there. Maybe we should get them involved in the problem'.

There were nods of assent at this and affirmative grunts from around the table but the chairman was not convinced. He shook his head.

'The trouble with the goddam British', he said, 'is that they always demand a quid pro quo for everything they do, and right now we got no collateral to give them.'

'I think maybe we do, sir', said Virgil Grant. 'The material on Lady Di?'

The general exploded.

'Get outta here', he yelled. 'You gotta be kiddin' me. That is Mickey Mouse stuff. You cannot be serious if you think that the British would be interested in a trade for that junk. We'd just make ourselves look stupid.'

'I am serious, sir', ventured Grant after a pause. 'Talking to their people here I get the impression that this lady is becoming a serious domestic problem for them. Far more serious than she is for us on the international scene right now, though I know we still have issues there'.

The chairman glared at him and sighed.

'Okay', he said, 'give it a try but let me see what you propose to give them before you hand it over. I don't want them having all our best intelligence. It may be useful in the future.'

Chapter Thirteen

Mosul, Iraq. 18th April 1996

It was a hot, dry afternoon and traffic leaving the city had delayed Christopher longer than he intended. But he reckoned there should be just enough time to take a look at what he had come to see and still get back to the hotel before nightfall.

At first the road, running alongside the river, had been a four lane highway crammed with all manner of vehicles – cars, trucks, buses, motorbikes – all jostling for position amid a cacophony of tooting horns and angry curses. Then, on the outskirts of the city, it had narrowed to two lanes as they passed mile after mile of houses stacked against the hillsides like piles of casually discarded shoeboxes.

Heading north on the main road towards the Turkish border traffic was lighter. Lorries, laden with bulging sacks of grain piled higher than looked safe, teetered from the centre of the road to the dusty verge and back again, and the occasional car transporter thundered by. Military vehicles of various types passed in convoy every few miles.

But once they left the main road and set off towards the mountains they were all alone.

Christopher was driving the Landrover jeep just because he knew the way. Alongside him sat Faisal, his interpreter. They did not converse much on the journey but when they did speak to one another it was in French.

Christopher had never been on this journey before but he knew the way because he had memorised the route. A daylong briefing session at MI6 headquarters in London, studying maps and aerial photographs, had given him a clear mental picture of the terrain. He was having no trouble finding his way.

The operation had been put together in a hurry. The British were being pressed for assistance by the Americans and for some reason Washington's timetable was of the utmost urgency.

Christopher was the agent chosen to carry out the operation on the ground for two reasons. Firstly he had never been on an operation in the Middle Eastern sector and so his face was entirely unknown. And, secondly, he was normally based in France and spoke fluent French without any trace of an accent which might be detected by a Frenchman as belonging to a foreigner.

The French connection and Christopher's part in it was significant.

Ever since Saddam Hussein's ill-fated invasion of Kuwait, six years earlier, Iraq had been regarded as a pariah state and was subject to strict international sanctions, controls and monitoring. But there were suspicions that France did not share the rest of the world's revulsion.

Both Britain and America had an inkling that, while publicly joining in the allies' condemnation of the Iraqi dictator, President Mitterrand was privately cosying up to Saddam. And MI6's Paris Station, where Christopher was second in command, had been working for months to confirm the tip-off from his informant Marielle that France was quietly helping Iraq to develop its weapons of mass destruction programme.

Now the Americans had satellite imagery which appeared to show the construction of a chemical or nuclear weapons facility hidden inside a mountain to the north of Mosul. It was time that someone took a look.

The method that MI6 devised for infiltrating Christopher into Iraq had been a stroke of genius dreamed up by the Natural Cover section.

The United Nations oil-for-food programme designed to help the ordinary people of Iraq recover from the Gulf War had been established a year earlier and was awaiting ratification. But, in the interim, various UN agencies were sending delegations to Iraq to provide practical aid on the ground. One of these was a French agricultural mission, which planned to go into the more remote region north of Mosul to teach local farmers how to inoculate their livestock against debilitating disease.

The British intelligence services had long maintained a 'sleeper' presence within all the United Nations agencies and their agent working at a senior level in the U.N. Food and Agricultural Organisation tipped off his paymasters in London that the Mosul mission would present an excellent opportunity for spying provided that someone who could pass as a French veterinary surgeon could be found. He would make all the arrangements to get such a person into the delegation.

And so it was that Christopher found himself on a crash course in the treatment of rare ailments afflicting sheep and goats in hot climates. His new identity as a French vet, complete with fake qualifications, passport and supporting documentation had been scrupulously researched and seemed to fit him like a glove. The other members of the mission accepted their new colleague without question even if one or two of them might have wondered why they had not come across him before.

This afternoon had been scheduled as a rest period so Christopher was able to slip away telling the head of the delegation that he needed to check out one of the areas the team would be visiting later in the week.

Now they were on a dusty track, which wound its way through the folds in the mountains. The clean-cut surfaces of the rock face at the side of the road indicated that it had been recently constructed and its width suggested that it was designed to accommodate vehicles wider than might normally be found on a mountain track.

They were climbing higher and higher and could see a steep-sided cliff face ahead of them. Christopher engaged a lower gear. Suddenly they rounded a sharp bend and spotted a small squat concrete structure set into the rock face about a quarter of a mile ahead. There was a black slit-like opening running across the front of the building. It was obviously a blockhouse or sentry-post of some kind.

Christopher stopped and apologised to Faisal, explaining that they had taken a wrong turn and needed to go back.

Inwardly he was cursing himself. From the aerial reconnaissance photographs he had noted a rough track, which led to an area of scrub and boulders a few hundred yards from the road at about this point. He had planned to leave his vehicle hidden among rocks in this area and make his way on foot for the remaining mile or so to a vantage point from which he could take long-range photographs of the installation – for this was the site which was exercising the Americans – without being seen. He had not picked up the presence of a guardhouse. It was the same colour as the surrounding rock and being built into the cliff it had not shown up on the satellite pictures. Perhaps it was unmanned.

Hoping they had not been spotted, Christopher slipped the jeep into reverse.

Almost immediately there was a loud bang and the windscreen shattered, showering the cabin of the vehicle with glass. Momentarily there was silence and then a burst of noise – crackling sounds, whistling, rattling – all in quick succession.

Someone was firing an automatic weapon at them.

Faisal let out a yelp of pain and began to scream.

Christopher had never been under fire before. His mind was a jumble of confusion. He could not see his attackers and he could not judge how many there were. He twisted to look behind him. There was no room and no time to turn the vehicle around. He began to back away down the track.

There was another rattle of gunfire and he felt one of the tyres burst. The steering wheel jerked out of his hand and the jeep plunged sideways into a rocky culvert at the side of the track. It came to rest almost immediately, slewed over at a crazy angle with the tailgate resting against a small boulder.

They were sitting ducks.

The vehicle was tilting alarmingly towards the driver's side. So much so that Christopher feared it might topple over completely. He unlatched his door and it swung away from him towards the ground. He scrambled out and ducked into the culvert calling for Faisal to follow. But the interpreter was cowering in the front foot well of the passenger seat whimpering like a wounded animal.

A fusillade of bullets whistled around Christopher as he crouched beneath the jeep, whining as they ricocheted off the rocks and making a pinging sound when they hit the vehicle.

Once more he yelled at Faisal, beckoning as he did so. But his companion simply stared back with terror-filled eyes and shook his head.

Christopher leapt back into the cab diving full-length across the driver's seat. He grabbed Faisal's collar in one hand and his belt in the other. With one strenuous heave he pulled the petrified man back out of the driver's door, falling backwards himself as he did so. The pair of them landed in a heap on the floor of the culvert.

'For fuck's sake move', he yelled at Faisal. 'We've gotta get out of here now. So fucking move. Just go, go, go, you fucking useless raghead twat'.

Christopher was shocked. From somewhere in his subconscious came a sense of deep revulsion and self-

167

loathing. His carefully nurtured persona of cultured urbanity was just a veneer. It had been stripped away in an instant by the powerful combination of fear and adrenaline. He was no better than the next man. He was a primitive. And a racist primitive at that. Under stress he had instinctively used what his mother would have called 'the language of a guttersnipe'.

Momentarily he was back at Prep School, aged eight, standing in the Headmaster's study – head bowed, hands clenched behind his back, face reddening with embarrassment – being severely reprimanded for using foul and abusive language. 'I'm sorry, I'm sorry, I'm sorry', he mumbled to no one in particular.

Christopher felt ashamed. And horrified at the lack of professionalism, which had caused him to blow his cover by reverting so naturally to his native tongue when, he was supposed to be a Frenchman.

Another burst of gunfire brought him out of his reverie with a jolt.

The firing appeared to be coming from above them and to the right. They needed to get the jeep between themselves and their assailants but there seemed no obvious way that they could get out of the line of fire.

He looked around. To his left, about fifty yards away, was a dry stone wall. If they could get behind that they would be better protected than they were, crouching in an open culvert alongside a vehicle, which might topple over on top of them at any moment.

He grabbed Faisal by the arm and gestured towards the wall. He could have spoken to him in French but somehow he felt that all verbal communication between them had been broken by his outburst of uncontrolled swearing.

This time, however, the interpreter understood without language and nodded his agreement. Crouching as close to the ground as they could get, the two men began running for the wall. Their unseen attackers opened up an even more ferocious wave of gunfire.

Christopher got to the wall first and dived over it, landing awkwardly on the rocky ground and grazing his shoulder in the process. When he turned back Faisal was slumped over the wall, wailing pathetically. He pulled the stricken man over on top of him and noticed a large wound in his leg, which was beginning to pump blood. As they lay side by side, panting, Christopher tore the sleeve off his light summer shirt and tied a tourniquet just below Faisal's knee in a makeshift attempt to stem the blood flow. It appeared to work.

It seemed that almost every time either of them so much as twitched a few more rounds were discharged in their direction, fizzing past their ears and sending up clouds of dust just yards from where they lay.

For Christopher the fear was beginning to take on a physical manifestation. His mouth was dry but his face was cold and clammy with sweat. His chest was tight and painful. He could smell urine. He glanced at Faisal but looking down at a spreading stain on his khaki bush trousers he realised that it was he who had lost control of his bladder.

Every breath he took was accompanied by an involuntary grunt. He knew the sound. He heard it every year when he accompanied his mother on her annual pilgrimage to the All England Lawn Tennis Championships at Wimbledon. It was the sound made by professional tennis players when serving or returning service.

In their case, he knew, the grunting was an expression of aggression. In his case, he knew, it was an expression of total abject fear – rather like a small child whistling in the dark. He tried to moderate the grunting, fearing the snipers would hear it and be better able to pinpoint his whereabouts. It was irrational. His tormentors were far too far away to hear him.

Christopher propped himself up with his back to the wall, taking care to keep his head out of sight, and tried to think.

They were trapped. They could not drive away and they could not run away without being picked off by sniper fire. There was certainly more than one gunman. Two or three Kalashnikov rifles and at least one machine gun, he reasoned. Possibly a good deal more firepower if the installation was as important as the Allies suspected.

He could not understand why the soldiers, if indeed they were soldiers, had not simply moved in to capture them. He had not returned fire so it was obvious that he and his companion were unarmed. He wished that he had brought his regulation Smith & Wesson pistol with him but instantly dismissed the thought as ridiculous. What would he have done with such a gun against this formidable firepower? He could have shot himself, he supposed.

He looked up at the sky. The sun was rapidly lowering behind the mountains. Six or seven large black birds, which he took to be vultures, wheeled and floated high above. Not a comforting sight.

The snipers were toying with them. Keeping them pinned down until it got dark. Then they would move in for the kill. Christopher's fear gave way to a crushing sense of despair. He must do something to save himself. Gradually a plan came to him.

Taking a few deep breaths he jumped up, vaulted the low wall, and sprinted towards the Landrover. Once more the bullets flew around him as he zigzagged across the stony ground. When he reached the vehicle he threw himself across the front seat and began scrabbling in his canvas holdall. After what seemed like an age he found what he was looking for – a large black felt-tipped magic marker pen which the United Nations team used for drawing diagrams when giving instruction to the Kurdish tribesmen and Iraqi farmers they had come to help. He grabbed the largest piece of paper he could find – a road map of the region – and scrawled the two letters "U N" in bold capital letters on the back of it.

Gingerly he ducked beneath the open door and then, under a sudden hail of bullets, leapt on to the bonnet of the jeep. The windscreen was missing but he managed to trap the bottom edge of the map under the windscreen wipers and jabbed the radio aerial through the top so that the crude legend he had scrawled was facing towards the sniper fire and could be clearly seen by the gunmen.

There was a pause in the shooting. He ducked back into the cab and waited. They would be studying his banner through binoculars he imagined.

Suddenly there was a prolonged round of firing. It was sustained for more than a minute. Christopher's plan had not worked.

He gathered himself for a moment before making another run for the relative safety of the wall. He was just pondering on the fact that he had miraculously escaped injury thus far when he heard the sound of an engine approaching up the track from the direction in which he and Faisal had come an hour or so earlier.

Now they would be captured. Would they be summarily executed on the spot or would they face torture and a show trial before being hanged? Christopher remembered the fate of the British journalist Farzad Bazoft who had been accused of spying on Saddam's regime and had met such an end. He shivered.

Around the corner came a large black four-by-four vehicle. There was no dust on it at all. It was gleaming and new. From the radio aerial flew the familiar pale blue and white United Nations flag. On the doors and on the roof the letters "U N" were painted in large white lettering. But the windows were tinted black so that the occupants could not be seen from the outside.

As the vehicle drew level with Christopher's jeep it stopped and the driver flashed his lights towards the snipers position.

From the corner of his eye Christopher caught sight of Faisal clambering over the dry stone wall. He was weeping and hobbling towards the direction from which the firing had come. His arms were above his head in the universal gesture of surrender and he was intoning the name of Allah as if in a trance. Christopher called out to him but he was beyond noticing.

He reached the middle of the track about a hundred yards in front of the jeep before they cut him down. Two shots rang out. Faisal slumped to his knees then jerked upwards and fell over on his side where he lay motionless.

At the sound of the shots the doors of the black four-by-four flew open. Two young men wearing jeans and T-shirts leapt out and both dropped to one knee. They each carried automatic rifles and began to strafe the sniper positions with a steady stream of fire.

A third man jumped from the rear of the vehicle and ran towards the jeep.

'C'mon Chris, let's get outta here', he yelled. 'Goddam it you asshole, move yourself. You're gonna get us all fuckin killed'.

Christopher did an involuntary double take. After almost twenty years working in the unreal world of the secret service he thought that nothing could surprise him. But the sudden appearance, here, now, of CIA special agent Greg Krushelnycky was unexpected to say the least. He ducked his head and sprinted towards the open rear door of the vehicle. He dived onto the back seat and sat hugging himself to stop from shaking.

For the next hour they drove in silence – bumping and bouncing, twisting and turning over rough terrain and tiny mountain tracks scarcely wide enough for a goat let alone a large vehicle. Had he not been so pumped up Christopher would have found the journey pretty hair-raising. It was becoming progressively darker as they went but the pace was relentless. *Like one of those crazy cross-country motor rallies through the Scottish Highlands*, thought Christopher. The driver was obviously highly skilled but, when it became pitch black outside and he did not slow down, Christopher realised that he must be wearing night-vision goggles. He imagined what the rocky track might look like, picked out in photo-negative grey-green tones.

The man in the front passenger seat occasionally spoke. He spoke in short, sharp, bursts of alphanumeric code. Christopher realised they were grid-references giving their position to an unseen and unheard controller on a scrambled radio frequency, which he hoped was secure.

When they eventually slowed and came to a halt Christopher sensed, from the feel of the vehicle, that they were on flat ground in open space. Krushelnycky tapped him on the shoulder and they both got out. Christopher could see nothing. There must have been cloud cover. There were no stars to be seen. No moon.

In the distance he could hear the tuck-a-tuck-a-tuck-a clatter of a helicopter approaching. The noise grew louder until it was almost deafening. The aircraft was hovering right over him and the downdraught from the rotor was tugging at his shirt but still Christopher could see nothing.

Suddenly the pilot switched on the landing lights. A pool of fierce, brilliant, light spread out around the men on the ground, illuminating the area for a radius of some fifty yards.

Christopher blinked as his eyesight adjusted. The helicopter was about fifty feet up and descending. Krushelnycky tugged at Christopher's sleeve. They both retreated out of range of the rotor blades.

As soon as the aircraft touched down Kruschelnycky cupped his hands against Christopher's left ear and yelled above the noise: 'Keep real, real low and follow me. But stay real low if you wanna keep yer fuckin head'.

The pilot had slowed the revolutions but was obviously not going to kill the engines altogether. This was a quick in and out job.

The rear door of the aircraft was already open. Krushelnycky crouched until he was almost on all fours and began a rapid sideways, crab-like shuffle. Christopher aped him. The engine noise was loud enough to hurt his eardrums and the screaming rotor blades whistled above his head at a distance which felt like inches rather than feet. The wind almost knocked him over several times. He was mightily relieved to heave himself into the cabin alongside Krushelnycky as unseen hands slammed the door shut and the aircraft began to rise.

He buckled his seatbelt and looked out of the window. There was nothing but blackness again. The landing lights had been switched off the moment the two passengers were safely aboard.

This was going to be tricky. Christopher knew it. They were in hostile territory. Enemy territory. This was not a war zone. There was no war. But they had no permission to be there. They were intruders and the Iraqis would have every right to shoot them down...if they could find them.

He'd had no time to examine the helicopter from the outside but he assumed it was a Sikorsky Blackhawk, which he knew was the workhorse of the American Special Forces. These were infiltration aircraft equipped with the latest aids to enable them to carry out stealth missions at speed under cover of darkness. The pilot would be flying on instruments, keeping

174

as low as possible, zigzagging and hugging the contours of the mountains to fool Iraqi radar.

Christopher made a few calculations in his head. They would be flying due north – the shortest distance to the Turkish border – he felt sure. He guessed their starting point would have been roughly a hundred miles inside Iraq. The Blackhawk had a top speed of a little over two hundred miles an hour so he would have about thirty minutes to wait before he could relax.

A low infrared glow illuminated the interior of the aircraft. Christopher noticed that Krushelnycky was wearing a set of large earphones with a microphone mouthpiece projecting on a stalk from the front. A similar headset was hanging by the side of his own seat. He put them on. The effect was to reduce the intrusive sound of the helicopter engines but otherwise he could hear nothing. He did not look at his watch.

Suddenly there was a burst of static in his ears and an American voice, he assumed the pilot's, began recounting positions, altitude and speed readings to an air traffic controller who sounded curt but efficient...and friendly. They had broken radio silence. They must be out of Iraqi airspace.

Christopher's mind was full of questions. He tapped Krushelnycky on the shoulder and gestured towards his microphone. His companion held up a small button dangling from the wire below his mouthpiece and pressed it.

Christopher did the same and began to speak: 'How did you...?'

Krushelnycky held up a hand and said: 'Don't go there. You don't wanna go there'.

Christopher stiffened. 'This is a British operation', he said. 'You had no right to...'

'Hey, we saved your butt back there', said Greg. 'You were gonna get roasted. How about: Thanks a lot buddy. I'll buy you a beer when we get home?'

Christopher was in no mood for this. 'How dare you interfere with on of Her Majesty's...

Greg interrupted. His voice was calm but his words were angry.

'Listen, Mister pompous British asshole', he said. 'Your cover was shit. You got busted. You gotta buncha eye-rack-ee blue-eyes blinkin' all over ya. They knew you were comin. Didn't you ask yerself why there was no traffic on the road up to the facility? Huh? They were watching your sweet ass every step of the way'.

Christopher was in no position to argue with this statement but he remained defiant.

'Rubbish', he said. 'How could you possibly know that?'

'Bin sandbaggin the ragchew', said Greg. 'Copyin' the mail?'

Christopher looked at him blankly for a few moments and then shouted: 'Oh for God's sake will you at least try to speak English for five seconds. This is serious'.

'Well it looks to me like somebody in Paris was telling tales', said Greg, 'but I could be wrong about that. As a matter of fact we picked up some radio transmissions about you – the Arabic listening service. It seems your French colleagues did not believe that you were a veterinarian. Naturally the Iraqis were bugging your mission, as they do with every UN mission, and they overheard a couple of guys speculating that you might be a spy, planted on them. The Iraqis did their homework and Bob's your uncle, they gotcha'.

Christopher shook his head. 'I don't believe you', he said. 'That level of electronic surveillance is satellite-based and it is

176

processed through GCHQ. If my people knew my cover was blown why not just abort the mission?'

'Search me', said Greg. 'I dunno, but they were certainly gonna leave you to fry'.

There was an awkward silence.

'Listen I'm no expert on British foreign policy', said Krushelnycky, 'but you know what? I reckon it would suit the Brits to have you busted right here, right now. See, your people don't want a direct confrontation with Uncle Saddam. They don't want another war. But if you got captured and put on a show trial, they could make a huge fuss in the United Nations and the press would do the job for them by exposing all the bad stuff he is getting up to'.

Christopher looked puzzled. He said nothing for a long time. Then he spoke.

'But why the rescue mission?', he asked. 'Don't tell me the boys in Washington sent you all the way over here just to get me out of a pickle'.

'No, no', said Greg with a chuckle. 'We got a Delta Force unit embedded in Ninawa Province just a couple of weeks ago with a specific job to do. I was in Turkey acting as liaison, getting transport and equipment back-up to them and ready to process the material we hope they're gonna get. The SUV we used today, for instance, I got in through Jordan on a transporter taking in agricultural vehicles.

'Since your mission began we got new intelligence about a more important facility than the one you were looking at. Looks like yer good ole French buddies are secretly helping to equip it too. So we couldn't risk compromising the work we're doing in that area by having you captured and drawing attention to what you guys were up to 'cos the Iraqis might start to second guess how much we know.

'When you told your head of mission that you were taking the afternoon off to check out an area North of Mosul, alarm bells rang in Baghdad and Washington for different reasons. My people decided to mobilise our guys on the ground to get you outta there pronto'. He winked. 'And 'cos everyone knows that you and I get along real well, they asked me to ride shotgun on the trip'.

There was a long silence.

'I guess we're quits now, huh?', said Krushelnycky. 'I owed ya one, right?'

Christopher said nothing. He looked out of the window. There were lights below them. They were about to touch down. He didn't need to be told where they were. The NATO airbase at Incirlik had never looked so inviting.

PART TWO

"…Dark Forces…"

Chapter Fourteen

Paddington, London 24th May 1996

The stiletto heels were impossibly high. The mini-skirt was ridiculously short. The blouse was disgracefully low-cut. But it was the fishnet stockings which gave the game away. The young woman was a member of the oldest profession.

She slouched in a shop doorway, languidly smoking a cigarette and chatting idly to her girlfriend. They turned their heads and gazed with expressionless eyes as a car pulled up at the kerb opposite. The driver kept the engine running. Dull light from the street lamp cast deep shadows but they could just make out that it was a dark-coloured BMW saloon.

The women nudged each other excitedly and tottered across to the passenger side of the vehicle. The electric window slid silently down. A small, nervous-looking, man sat in the passenger seat. The driver was a young blonde woman wearing a baseball cap which partially hid her face. She leant across her passenger.

'Hi Kathy, how are you tonight?', she asked.

The tubbier of the two women put both hands on the roof of the car and bent her head towards the window.

'Mustn't grumble, Princess Di, how's it going with you darlin'?'

'Oh, I'm fine thanks', replied the young blonde driver, as the streetlight briefly illuminated her features beneath the peak of her cap. There was no mistaking her identity. It was the Princess of Wales.

'And how are you, Jan?', she asked the other, slimmer woman. 'Is your little Gary any better?'

'Nah, can't sort out his cough. He's still got it...keeping him off school. But thanks for asking, Di love', replied the second woman.

'Can't the doctor do something?', asked the Princess with a concerned expression on her face. 'You have taken him to the doctor, haven't you?'

'Oh yeah', said the prostitute. 'He just give him some pink muck to drink but I don't reckon it done much good. Anyway how are your two little buggers getting' on?'

'Oh, you know, going through the naughty boy phase', replied the Princess with a glow of motherly pride. 'They're home for the half-term holidays at present so I see more of them, which is nice'.

The man in the passenger seat shifted uncomfortably.

'My God, you actually know these people', he said *sotto voce* out of the corner of his mouth.

'Oh, I'm so sorry. Kathy, Jan, this is Paul, my butler', said the Princess introducing him. The prostitutes thrust their hands through the car window and shook hands.

'Have you been busy?', asked Diana.

'Nah', replied the second woman. 'It's been quiet but we'll stick around. Gotta work ya know Princess'.

'Now I've brought something for you Kathy', said Diana reaching on to the back seat of the car. 'I know this is the wrong time of the year for a heavy coat but you were so cold last winter and I found this in my wardrobe today so I thought I'd give it to you while I remembered. I never wear fur and I have no use for it'.

182

She thrust a light-coloured bundle through the window and watched as the first woman unfolded it to reveal an ankle-length sable coat. She put it on and pulled up the large collar until it almost swamped her face.

'Thanks Di, you are a bloody angel, you are', she cried.

'No problem', said the Princess. 'Now look girls, why don't you take the night off'.

She leant across her butler and passed two crisp fifty pound notes out of the window.

'Off home to your kids now, okay?, she said.

Both women nodded and waved as the window slid back into place and the car pulled slowly away from the kerb.

Fifty yards further up the road Police Constable Ricky Arbuthnot had just rounded a corner and was strolling purposefully towards the two prostitutes with his hands clasped behind his back. He noticed the BMW as it passed him but did not break stride. He recognised the number. Every policeman in London knew that number. It was more than their jobs were worth not to know that number. That number was attached to the private car owned by Diana, Princess of Wales.

'Come on girls, move along now', said PC Arbuthnot. 'You know the rules. No soliciting in the street. Just shift it or I'll have to nick ya'.

'All right, darlin', keep yer hair on we're just going', said the larger woman as she turned to leave.

'Oi, hang on a minute, Kathy', said the policeman. 'Where'd you get that fur coat? It's far too good for you and wearing it in the summer too. Don't tell me you nicked it. I bet you've been rippin' the punters off again, haven't ya?'

'No, she give it me', scoffed Kathy.

'Who?', asked the constable.

'You know who', said the prostitute. 'I saw you clockin' her car and I know The Old Bill know every car she drives. So don't come it with me, mate'.

'Princess Diana gave you that coat…to keep?', said PC Arbuthnot with a note of incredulity in his voice. 'You're having a laugh'.

'No, straight up. And she give us dosh 'an all', replied Kathy.

'How much?', asked the constable.

'Ain't tellin' ya', said Kathy.

'Fifty quid each', interjected her companion.

'Blimey', said the policeman. 'Well you two don't need to work again tonight so why don't you do us both a favour and piss off home before I take you down the nick'.

As the women tottered off, muttering obscenities, PC Arbuthnot undid the button on the breast pocket of his tunic and took out his notebook. His night shift would now be prolonged. He would have to write a full report of the incident he had witnessed when he got back to Paddington Green Police Station. And he would have to make sure the grammar and spelling was correct, too. This report was bound to find its way to the Commissioner's office at Scotland Yard. He knew it.

* * * * * *

Chicago, 5th June 1996

'Hi, I'm Marcie, I'm gonna look after you all this afternoon.
How're you gennilmen doin today?'

It was a rhetorical question. Part of the patter. Without
pausing even to consider whether a reply to her inquiry might
be forthcoming, the waitress gushed on breathlessly.

'May I tell you the specials today? We have...'

Christopher held up his right hand as though swearing an oath
in court.

'No. Thank you. I don't need the specials. I'll have a stuffed
pizza. Cheese and shrimp. Small. And a Greek salad but
without vinaigrette. Just some olive oil'.

Marcie beamed her most winning smile, revealing an ugly row
of wire and zinc bracing on her top teeth. She fished in the
pocket of her black apron with the 'Giordano's' logo on the
bib and produced an order pad.

'All right. That's fine. Would you care for an appetizer, sir?'

'No thanks'.

'May I get you a drink?'

'Decaf coffee, large'.

'Cream and sugar?'

'No. Black. No sugar'.

'Sure. And what may I get for you, sir?'

Christopher's companion was not ready to order. He had not
looked at a menu. His hands were clasped together in front of

185

him and resting on the table in an attitude of prayer. His eyes were fixed on Marcie's chest.

'Uh, oh, I need a couple more minutes', he stammered as she turned her mouthful of ironmongery towards him.

'Sure. You go right ahead and take as long as you want. I'll be right back', she said, flicking her blonde ponytail as she turned away.

Greg Krushelnycky gazed intently at her pert buttocks encased in skin-tight black trousers as she wiggled her way back towards the bar.

'Pretty cute buns, huh?', he exclaimed.

Christopher sighed with irritation. It had been almost fourteen years since Belfast but his American counterpart had not changed. As far as women were concerned he had never grown up. He still treated every encounter with a member of the opposite sex, however fleeting, with the same sleazy, schoolboy approach, which Christopher found so distasteful.

Of course Greg was older and greyer now and the ponytail, which had served him so well in his undercover role as a minor drugs baron, had given way to a more sober businessman's cut. He wore spectacles too.

It had been Krushelnycky's idea to rendezvous at Giordano's pizza restaurant. His favourite branch of the world famous chain was on West Randolph Street close to the theatre district and he had given Christopher precise directions.

As was his wont, Christopher had arrived early, and picked out one of the wood panelled booths against the wall as the most discreet location for their meeting. A row of coat hooks separated one booth from the next so that conversations could not be overheard. Large fans rotated silently just below the ceiling and large posters with a distinctly Chicago theme covered the walls. It was not his style of restaurant but when in Rome do as the Romans do was his philosophy.

Now the two men sat side by side on the green and red striped faux leather bench seat looking out at the other diners.

'Great to see ya again, buddy', said Greg. 'How'ya bin?'

Christopher was brusque, almost rude.

'Listen, I'm very well, thank you, and it is lovely to see you again too, but can we just deal with the business in hand before we get to the socialising, please?', he said.

Greg recalled how the Englishman's matter-of-fact manner had irritated him the first time they met. He smiled.

'Okay. Let's do it. You first. Shoot'.

'Well, I'm not sure my people would want me to be talking to you', said Christopher, 'but...

A fresh-faced teenager wearing a green polo shirt and carrying a jug of water and two glasses containing ice cubes appeared at the table. Christopher broke off while the bus boy poured the water and withdrew.

'I'm guessing why you are here in Chicago at this particular time and I expect you can make an educated guess as to why I've come, too'.

'Well I reckon we're coming at this from different angles because what the US wants in this regard is slightly different from what you guys need to have happen', said Greg. 'But we are both here looking at the same areas of activity for sure'.

He looked down at the heavy plastic tablecloth and traced a large figure of eight with his finger around its garish cream and maroon squares.

187

Marcie arrived with the pizzas and placed them on a large wooden cube in the centre of the table.

'Well we know the target is here in the city and I've got a watching brief', said Greg.

'I've got a watching brief, too', said Christopher, 'but mine is close contact. See who the target meets and follow if appropriate. I may need a little help. I know you have the toys in place so if you can give me a read-out on movements and key conversations later that would be extremely helpful.

'Dunno 'bout that', said Greg. 'I'd need authorisation'.

'Look, I don't know what data you have but I have detailed specifications of the technology involved and I can get details of the finances and the governments which are in play and which have dropped out of the game', said Christopher.

'Okay. That could be interesting', said Greg shaking more oregano on to his pizza. 'We're getting good intelligence out of Paris. The French are playing a very dangerous game on this one, you know'.

Christopher pointedly put down his knife and fork and stared at Krushelnycky.

'I'm based in Paris, or had you forgotten?, he asked with studied contempt. 'We may be just a little ahead of you'.

His companion stared back.

'Hey, are we talking about the same job here?', he asked. 'My target is staying at The Drake Hotel'.

'So's mine', said Christopher taking a mouthful of pizza.

They completed their meal in virtual silence, although Krushelnycky tried valiantly to engage his companion in a futile conversation about the difference between baseball and cricket. Then Marcie was back.

'Would you gennilmen care for any dessert? We have Tiramisu, cheesecake, cannoli, ice cream and chocolate cake', she said.

Christopher looked up at the clock over the bar. "Pizza Time" was emblazoned on the face in red lettering. *How very tacky. How very American*, he thought.

'No, that will be all. Thank you', he said. 'Would you please bring me the bill?'

'Check? Sure. You got it'. Marcie hovered momentarily, and then she asked; 'Say, are you from England?'

Christopher nodded.

'I think your Lady Di is fantastic. What a doll. And the stuff she does for the poor an' all. All that work she does for charity. She's an angel.

'You gonna see her while she's here? She's at the Drake Hotel and she's gonna talk to a buncha people at a breast cancer fundraiser later on. I'm gonna go down there when I'm through here. See if I can catch her'.

Christopher glanced at Greg but he was transfixed by Marcie.

'No. I'm on business and I'm only in the city for a couple of days. I've seen the Princess Diana before, in London, actually', he said.

'Say, did anyone ever tell you what a pretty smile you have?', asked Greg.

Marcie blushed, flashed him a broad metallic grin, and tottered away, giggling.

Christopher raised his eyes heavenward in exasperation. As he did so he caught sight of a familiar female figure on the flat television screen mounted on the wall opposite. Wearing a candy pink business suit she appeared as radiant as ever though with a sad, haunted look in her eyes. Christopher remembered that her divorce was imminent.

The caption scrolling silently across the bottom of the picture read: "Fox News: Princess Diana in Chicago. British Royal boosts breast cancer fight".

'And that's not all you've been boosting, is it your Royal Highness', muttered Christopher under his breath. 'One of these days you'll be punished. You naughty girl'.

There was a loud pop to his left. Greg Krushelnycky had squeezed the wrapping on one of the vacuum-sealed cinnamon candies supplied at the Maitre-d station and was loudly sucking the pink and maroon striped ball on a stick.

'Whatcha say?', he inquired.

'Nothing', said Christopher. 'We've got work to do. Let's go'.

Ten minutes later he stepped out of a taxi on Walton Street some fifty yards short of the main entrance to The Drake hotel. The driver had heard that there were traffic problems in the vicinity and had suggested approaching the building from Oak Street but Christopher was in no hurry. They could not drive right up to the entrance, however, because a small crowd had gathered in the approach at Walton Place and the police had put striped wooden barriers in the roadway.

Christopher paid off the cab driver and marched towards the police line. A gum-chewing officer stepped forward and enquired – more politely than Christopher was accustomed to from the Chicago police – where in the hell he thought he was going. Christopher's sarcasm was so subtle and genteel that it sailed right over the officer's head. He thought he was going

190

to the hotel in which he was staying and to the room in which he had left his belongings, he replied. The officer grudgingly stepped aside and motioned him towards the entrance where he was obliged to go through the same routine with another burly cop who kept fingering the gun on his belt and never looked Christopher in the eye.

Waiting for his room key at the reception desk he found himself standing next to a man whose aftershave gave off a subtle hint of aromatic spices, a touch of the East. Christopher glanced at him. He was swarthy with a full head of rich, wavy, black hair. His suit looked as if it had been spun from extruded steel. The cufflinks were of a simple design but obviously gold. His silk tie was neatly tied and looked very expensive.

The stranger's head was bowed as he concentrated on filling in his registration card.

Christopher took a peep.

Balaam Abu Shafiq, was the name.

Christopher noted the room number and turned away towards the elevator.

Chapter Fifteen

Paris, 21st October 1996

Balaam Abu Shafiq took an olive stone out of his mouth, placed it delicately in the ashtray, and replaced it with a cashew nut from the porcelain dish in front of him.

He was a handsome man in his late forties with an understudied hint of style about him which spoke of wealth. He did not look out of place in The Hemmingway Bar of the Ritz. It might have been his natural habitat.

Born in the city of Mosul in Northern Iraq, the son of a Chaldo-Assyrian Christian teacher, he was a rarity among his peers as the only Catholic in the inner circle of Saddam Hussein. His membership of the Ba'ath Party had brought him into contact with the President and his international network of connections quickly made him indispensable to the dictator of Baghdad.

Like many young men from the Middle East before him, Balaam had the Americans to thank for an extremely good education. Graduating Summa Cum Laude in Law from Boston College he had gone on to complete a doctorate in aeronautics and astronautics at the Massachusetts Institute of Technology.

His name did not appear on any diplomatic list but he had a roving commission as a fixer for his country and since security was of paramount importance to Iraq, Balaam Abu Shafiq was effectively Saddam Hussein's chief security adviser.

A waiter brought the Dubonnet he had ordered and politely inquired if there would be anything else. Abu Shafiq explained that he was expecting company and would doubtless increase his order when his guest arrived. He checked the diamond-encrusted gold Rolex oyster watch on his left wrist. His contact was late.

When he did arrive it was in a flurry of apologies about the state of Paris traffic. His chauffeur had attempted numerous shortcuts and back routes from the Ministry but all to no avail. He was terribly sorry to have kept his host waiting. He accepted a Campari and soda.

Abu Shafiq would normally have indulged his visitor by making small talk for a while to put him at his ease and allow him to regain his composure. But he had a dinner date. And, besides, they had met before and the Iraqi knew that the man sitting in front of him was effectively speaking for the President of France personally when it came to the business at hand. So he cut to the chase.

'I believe you have a business proposal for me', he said raising his glass in salute before taking a sip.

His guest, a young man with slicked-back hair and wearing tinted glasses and a neatly pressed grey pin-striped suit, leaned forward wringing his hands together in a nervous gesture which belied the confidence with which he spoke.

'*Au contraire*', he said. 'I think you have a need to conduct a little business with us'.

Abu Shafiq smiled. 'My apologies', he said. 'I put that rather clumsily. I believe we have a mutual interest in doing business and I am hoping that we can find a formula which will satisfy everyone's needs in this matter'.

His French contact sat back and took a sip from his drink.

'Perhaps you would care to give me a rough outline of what your requirements might be', he said. 'I am not a technical man, as you know, but I have sufficient knowledge of our industrial capabilities in the field where you require assistance to be able to say how far we might go to meet your needs'.

'We are looking at an inertial guidance system', said Abu Shafiq. 'In essence an up-dated version of the package designed and supplied by your Sagem corporation for Project 395 in 1988. Missile technology has advanced a great deal over the past eight years so naturally we will need to develop a guidance system which can keep pace. I can provide a detailed specification if we reach agreement'.

The Frenchman gave him a knowing look.

'The diplomatic landscape has also changed over the past eight years as you well know, my friend', he said. 'The climate of world opinion has grown a little chilly and these things are much more difficult to achieve.

'Before Kuwait your missile programme was paid for by the Americans and Sagem was just one company giving assistance to the project. You will recall better than I do that the Germans, the British, the Italians, the Austrians, the Swedes, the Egyptians, the Argentineans, everybody was involved. It was an international aid programme'.

He paused.

'Nobody can do this kind of business anymore. There are sanctions. There are United Nations resolutions. There are weapons inspectors crawling all over your country'.

Abu Shafiq crossed his legs and leaned back in his chair. When he spoke it was in the language of a diplomat. He spoke slowly. Ponderously.

'The people of Iraq are indebted to France for the invaluable support this great nation has given during a time when we have suffered great deprivation because we dared to stand alone against the avarice and greed of the most powerful nations on earth who have sought to plunder the wealth of our oilfields for their own corrupt purposes', he said. 'The

194

President will always be grateful for the courage of President Mitterrand in standing with us in these difficult times'.

His companion ignored this last remark.

'I have made some inquiries' he said, 'and there is certainly the technical expertise available to provide the kind of system you describe. But, were they to become aware of such a contract, our European partners would be bound to disapprove of any dealings with Baghdad on this scale. And we would certainly face considerable difficulty at the United Nations'.

'I fully understand', said Abu Shafiq. 'This matter is extremely delicate and the utmost discretion must be exercised. We too would not wish the details of this project to emerge. It must be treated as top secret.

'All documentation, from contract stage downwards, would designate the purpose of the system to be support for an advanced automatic high-speed railway signalling project. The hardware would be delivered to a neutral country with which we have reciprocal diplomatic arrangements and shipped on in packaging containing agricultural equipment, which is permitted under current United Nations sanctions'.

The Frenchman sucked his teeth.

'Sagem could not undertake this project', he said. 'That would attract too much attention in the inquisitive electronics world. But there is another French company, CDI, less well known on the world stage, which has the capability and would benefit from such a contract.

'However', he added, 'in view of the advanced technology involved and the need for absolute secrecy this is likely to be a very costly project'.

Abu Shafiq said nothing. He simply nodded.

'We would need to have the specifications', said his companion, 'but estimates vary between a quarter of a billion and a billion dollars'.

Again Abu Shafiq nodded.

'And my principal wishes you to know that there would be a commission payable too', said his guest.

Abu Shafiq gave him the full benefit of his very expensive dental work. He beamed. His perfect white teeth positively glowed against his sallow complexion.

'In the Middle East we have long understood the value of a bargain', he said. 'It is only right and proper that the intermediary who concludes a business deal should be rewarded for his part in the transaction'.

He paused and leant forward confidentially.

'I must point out to you, however, that not only has the diplomatic landscape, as you put it, changed but so has the political landscape in your country. I am sure that your new President would not require any personal inducement to conclude a deal which will bring very good business to his industrial sector'.

The Frenchman shook his head.

'You do not understand', he said. 'I have explained the delicacy of this matter and the need for secrecy. Chirac does not need to know of this. It is better if he doesn't. Chirac cannot deliver this deal. Mitterrand's people still can. You know we can'.

Abu Shafiq stared at him for fully twenty seconds then he spoke almost in a whisper.

'You may tell your principal that, as a token of our gratitude, we will be happy to pay him the usual ten per cent of the final contract price'.

He leaned across and shook hands with his guest.

'Do you have time for another drink?', he asked.

* * * * * *

Paris, 19th November 1996

Christopher had long since relegated Marielle Norstrund to the bottom of his list of priorities. Indeed he had virtually forgotten her. She was officially listed as one of his informants and he had religiously filed a report following both their previous meetings but he had become resigned to the fact that it might be many years before he heard from her again.

He could not make her out. She was who she said she was. He had checked her out. She was a director and principal lobbyist for one of the largest arms manufacturers in France. And he had pictorial evidence that she rubbed shoulders with the most powerful figures in the land.

But on the two previous occasions when they had met she had talked in riddles and vague generalities. She seemed to have good information but declined to deliver the detail. She simply teased him with promises of more the next time. *She was flaky and not to be trusted,* decided Christopher.

Yet here she was back in his life after seven years and he was on his way to meet her. This time he would take a tough line and demand answers or he would cut her off forever.

He spotted the blonde pigtail as he approached the café. She was seated with her back to him so he adopted her own approach and bent down to give her a peck on the cheek as he drew up a chair and sat down.

'Lovely to see you again, Marielle', he said. 'How are you?'

'Fine but I need to talk', she said in a rush.

Christopher stopped her with a hand gesture. 'No. I need to talk first', he said. 'Today you will give me names and details. You will tell me why you are doing this and there will be none of this "I'll tell you more next time" nonsense. Do you understand? If you don't give me straight answers I don't want to meet you again because you are wasting my time'.

'Okay', she said in a firm tone. 'They knew you were there'.

'There you go again', said Christopher impatiently. 'Who knew I was where?'

The Cabal. They knew you were in Iraq. They tipped off Saddam's people about you. They wanted you killed'.

Oh great, thought Christopher. *The entire world and his bloody wife knew I was in Iraq. No wonder I didn't get very far. My own people wanted me captured and put on trial. The French wanted me killed. Thank God for Greg and the Yanks.*

'And what have your people got to do with all this?', he asked.

'Well, as you know, Saddam Hussein is building this underground facility inside a mountain somewhere', said Marielle, pushing her sunglasses on to the top of her head. 'I don't know if it is for chemical or nuclear weapons but we have been contracted to produce an inertial guidance system for the long-range rockets which will deliver the payload, whichever it is. Our engineers are working on the specifications as we speak. The hardware will be shipped to Jordan. The documentation will describe it as components for automatic railway signals'.

'And the cost?', asked Christopher.

'Something in the region of half a billion dollars', replied Marielle, taking a sip of coffee. 'The Cabal will take a ten per cent commission, as usual'.

'Look, why are you telling me all this?', said Christopher. 'You have not asked for money so that is not your motivation. You are French. If you are troubled about corruption why not go to your own authorities?'

Marielle looked at him with sad eyes. 'I know that the cabal was run by several people close to Mitterrand but I have never known precisely who they are and I have no real way of finding out now that he is dead', she said. 'I would not know who to go to with this information. I would not know whom to trust. The cabal people have their own contacts within the DST. Speak to the wrong person and you will die a mysterious death. Remember Francois de Grossouvre?'

Christopher wracked his brains for a moment. Then he remembered the details. Francois de Grossouvre had been Mitterrand's friend, confidant and political adviser for over 40 years. Two years ago his body had been found in his office at the Elysee Palace. There was a bullet in his head.

'Yes, de Grossouvre. A case of suicide', said Christopher.

Marielle shook her head. 'He found out about the cabal and tried to do something about it', she said. 'You asked about my motivation. My father was Norwegian but my mother is a Jewess. I am Jewish. I hate what the Arabs are doing to the Jews and I hate the thought that we are arming Saddam with weapons to attack Israel. I cannot expose it myself but perhaps the British can'.

'And the main man?', asked Christopher gently.

Marielle's eyes misted over.

'He is my *"cinq a sept"*, she said with a tremble in her voice. 'You do not have this tradition in England. Between five and seven in the evening you have a cup of tea. In France that is the time when we meet our lovers before returning to our husbands or wives. We call it *"cinq a sept"*. The main man, as you call him, has been mine for many years.

'He pays for my apartment in St Germain and my company pays for me to buy him expensive gifts, like handmade leather shoes, for instance. The big defence contracts come to my company and everybody is happy. I am more than a mistress. I am a whore. I am not proud of it. But I have come to love him…' Her voice trailed away.

'But who is he? I need to know if I am going to help you Marielle', said Christopher.

Marielle stood up. 'Maybe next time…'

'No, now', yelled Christopher, standing too.

Marielle looked into his eyes for several seconds. 'Le Begue', she said as she turned and walked away.

'Le Begue?', said Christopher to himself. 'The Stammerer? Who the hell is that?'

* * * * * *

Paris, 2nd December 1996

Greg Krushelnycky was a sucker for gadgets.

Ever since he was a small boy he'd been fascinated by the idea of remote control. He'd flown his first radio-controlled aeroplane straight into the ground at the age of eight and immediately turned his attentions to jet-propelled model powerboats. By the time he was a teenager he was experimenting with drag racing cars – operated through a radio signal at a distance of up to a quarter of a mile – racing them round a track on his uncle's farm in Louisiana.

So the demonstration taking place in front of him had him completely captivated.

Mounted on a pedestal in the centre of the workshop was a scale model of a motorcar. Greg guessed it was about one quarter size. The little car had wheels, an engine and a chassis but no body. It was a skeleton. The engine was running and the wheels were rotating. The electrics were also working as the lights at front and rear of the model indicated.

'Before we conduct the experiment, Monsieur, I will just show you that the brakes and steering are working', said a swarthy man wearing greasy blue overalls.

He leant across and rotated the steering wheel first right then left. The wheels responded to his touch by moving in the correct direction each time. He slipped his arm through the chassis and pressed down manually on the brake pedal. All four wheels stopped spinning and the tiny brake lights at the rear of the model glowed red.

'Monsieur, if you please to take this control panel and stand over there', said the mechanic. 'You will press the button when I give you the signal'.

He handed Greg a small black metal box about the size and shape of a house brick. It had a red button mounted in the centre.

Greg retreated to the corner of the workshop and waited. The mechanic made an adjustment to one of the wheels and then raised his thumb in Greg's direction.

Greg pressed the red button. Nothing discernable happened.

201

Once again the mechanic pushed his arm through the car's framework and pressed down hard on the brake, keeping the pedal depressed. Once again the brake lights glowed but the wheels continued to spin. He turned the steering wheel as he had done before but this time the wheels did not move out of alignment. They remained locked in a straight line ahead.

Greg was impressed. One press of a button and the car's brakes and steering had been disabled...remotely. Simple.

'This is incredible Olivier', he said. 'You're a goddam genius. The Company has been using the Boston Brakes system for this kind of thing for years but it is so clumsy – the scuba diving compressed air cylinder and that kids' joystick control arrangement. It is difficult to install and even harder to retrieve afterwards. Gotta hand it to you. I asked you to come up with something better and you did. Way da go, Buddy'.

He scratched his head and blew out his cheeks.

'What's the range of this thing?', he asked.

'It depends', said the Frenchman. 'I have tested it up to two hundred metres but it must be, how do you say, so you can see it?'

'You mean line of sight. It only operates on line of sight. Right?', said Greg.

'Oui Monsieur', said Olivier, 'line of sight. But it is not one hundred per cent. I told you I have a simple device you can attach to the exhaust and it fill the car with carbon monoxide. The driver will go unconscious very soon. Perhaps it is better, non?'

'No, no', said Greg. 'I don't want to get into that right now. It's detectable. It will leave a trace of carbon monoxide in the bloodstream. I like the look of this thing. So show me the size of the gizmo you put in the engine'.

Olivier leant into the engine compartment and withdrew a plastic-covered package about the size of a packet of cigarettes.

'Fantastic', said Greg. 'So small. So simple'.

'I need to make the control unit smaller. It is of course, only a prototype at the moment', said the mechanic, adding: 'I will not confuse you with how it works but essentially it blows the fuses and knocks out the hydraulics on the brakes and puts the power steering into overdrive so that it freewheels.

'But remember I told you it will only work on cars with onboard computers or very sophisticated electronic control systems'.

'Yeah, I know but I need to use it…', Krushelnycky corrected himself… 'May need to use it, on a Mercedes S80 saloon. Can you do that?', he asked.

'I think so Monsieur', said Olivier. 'I will get hold of the electrical specifications tomorrow'.

'Okay, your turn now Laurent', said Krushelnycky, turning to a tall young man who had been standing quietly behind him watching the demonstration in silence. 'We've got to get the thing into one of those Etoile Mercedes in The Ritz car park and run a test. Today's Monday. Can we get up and running by Thursday?'

'Yep, if Olivier is going to be ready by then I'll get the chauffeurs' rotas for Thursday from my man and arrange to have him fit the equipment into one of the cars', replied the young man.

They all shook hands and left the workshop.

Three days later the trio found themselves together again sitting in an anonymous-looking Citroen car parked at the rear of The Ritz in Rue Cambon. Laurent was in the driver's seat,

Olivier in the front passenger seat and Greg Krushelnycky sat on the back seat with the control box on his lap.

It was four o'clock in the afternoon and raining. Olivier held a piece of paper on which a car registration number had been scrawled in pencil.

Several cars came and went through the entrance to the Ritz underground car park. No one spoke.

Eventually a large black Mercedes limousine emerged with a liveried driver sitting behind the wheel.

Olivier checked his piece of paper. 'That's him', he said. Laurent pulled the Citroen quietly in behind the departing vehicle.

'Okay, so this is just a test, right?', said Greg. 'I don't wanna hurt anybody or get anybody killed. So I need to do this when he is in traffic so he can bounce off other vehicles. And when he's not going too fast because we need to get him stopped somewhere where we can get the kit back pretty easily.

'I'll tell you when I reckon we're in the right place and you lemme know when we're doing about fifty clicks. Okay?'

'Okay', said Laurent.

The Mercedes in front of them headed off in the direction of Charles de Gaulle airport. It was rush hour and traffic was heavy.

By the time they had filtered on to the Paris ring road, the *Peripherique*, they had come to a standstill in three lanes of traffic.

'This would be perfect if we were just rolling', said Greg. As he spoke all three lanes of cars began to move forward.

'Give me a speed check', he said to Laurent.

'Thirty kilometres per hour', said the driver. 'Forty. Fifty'.

Greg hit the red button.

Nothing happened. Then brake lights further ahead began to come on. The Mercedes' brake lights came on but the car did not slow down. It began to snake wildly from side to side.

Greg let out a whoop of joy.

'Alright baby', he yelled, 'Houston, we gotta problem'.

The Mercedes cannoned into a car on its left, bounced across to sideswipe a car to its right and came to rest with its front nearside wing embedded in the boot of a large Peugeot sedan.

'Damn. Don't you just hate it when that happens', chortled Greg. But he was talking to himself. Olivier and Laurent were already out of the car and sprinting towards the Mercedes.

The chauffeur was also out of his car. He looked shaken but appeared unhurt.

'Monsieur I am a mechanic', said Olivier. 'I just need to disable your engine to make sure there is no risk of fire'. He leant inside the car and released the bonnet catch.

Laurent put his arm around the chauffeur and suggested that he might like to sit down in the back of his own car until help arrived. Moments later Olivier tapped him on the shoulder, raised his eyebrows, and patted the hip pocket of his overalls. Both men withdrew to the Citroen.

'Nice job, guys', said Greg. 'Now let's get outta here. I got an appointment. I gotta go see my sweet lady ambassadress. The Honourable Pamela Harriman herself, no less'.

He gazed glassy-eyed into the middle distance.

'I don't think she likes me real good', he said. 'Leastways I don't think she likes the kinda stuff I gotta do for Uncle Sam now and again'.

Olivier and Laurent were not listening. They were discussing ways of disentangling themselves from the traffic jam, which now engulfed the Citroen.

Greg stroked the black box on his lap.

'I may never need to use this but at least we know it works', he said. 'And next time...it could be fatal'.

Chapter Sixteen

Angola, 15ᵗʰ January 1997

Diana, Princess of Wales was walking through a minefield –
literally and metaphorically.

She looked beautiful and vulnerable as she stepped lightly
along a path in the African bush wearing a white shirt and
cream chinos – the picture of casual glamour, which had
become her trademark. Yet there was something incongruous
and disturbing about her appearance because she also wore a
green flak jacket and a protective helmet with a clear visor.

She was doing what she did best. Doing what came naturally.
Providing a photo opportunity for the world's media and at the
same time creating an iconic image, which would convey a
serious message. Contrasting her own beauty with the
ugliness of war.

She was in Angola on a three-day visit as a guest of the
International Red Cross to see for herself the devastation
caused to the lives of innocent civilians by the scourge of
landmines and to highlight the ineptitude and unwillingness of
the international community to deal with the problem. It was a
humanitarian cause. It was her cause.

The eyes of the world were on her but not everyone looked
upon her mission with admiration and support.

After a visit to a remote hospital in which she saw appalling
injuries to women and children who had inadvertently
wandered into minefields while going about their daily lives, a
deeply distressed Princess made an impassioned plea for a
worldwide ban on the use of anti-personnel devices.

Back home in Britain the Conservative government were not
best pleased. Their Labour opposition had been calling for

such a ban but Prime Minister John Major would not support a ban until all the countries of the world agreed. He was deeply embarrassed by Diana's outspokenness because she had been briefed in advance by the Foreign Office on Britain's position and the Queen had personally endorsed her visit.

Within hours a junior Defence minister, Lord Howe, was publicly denouncing her remarks describing her as 'ill-informed' and a 'loose cannon' who had angered the government by failing to understand the delicacy of the negotiations they were engaged in on the subject.

By contrast the Americans were loving every minute of it. In secret cables sent on the diplomatic wires to the Secretary of State, Madeline Albright, in Washington, two United States ambassadors could not prevent themselves from gloating over the discomfort the episode was causing to the British.

Admiral William Crowe, United States Ambassador to Britain wrote: "*She bested a political furore in London when a junior minister criticised her understanding of the landmine issue and her call for a general global ban on them which deviates from UK/NATO policy. But PM Major and Foreign Secretary Rifkind stepped in to cool things off.*

"*Government officials immediately scrambled to repair the public relations damage and issued statements affirming the government's commitment to 'working towards a worldwide ban on landmines'. A Downing Street spokesman was quoted as claiming there had been a 'misunderstanding' and that the Princess's remarks were not inconsistent with government policy*".

Crowe went on: "*Controversy and/or room for misunderstanding was inherent in the Princess's trip given the Red Cross calls for an immediate ban on APL's worldwide*".

His colleague, Donald Steinberg, US Ambassador to Angola, gave his boss an even more detailed report of the visit after talking to the British Ambassador, Roger Hart.

"The Princess refused to do anything not connected with the Red Cross or the landmine cause", wrote Steinberg, admiringly. "She wanted a serious visit, not to be seen wining and dining with the social elite. The daughter of the King of the Lundas wanted to meet with her British counterpart, but failed. The Princess accepted a dinner invitation hosted by First Lady Ana Paula dos Santos on the condition that it be small (26 guests ate from a catered Chinese food buffet), short (it ended at 8.10 pm) and there be no press or speeches. Hart also managed to get the local directors of Shell, BP and De Beers invited. Hart himself held only a dinner for her and some Red Cross officials".

There was more than a little hypocrisy in the Americans' glee at the political hornets nest which Diana had stirred up, however. As major manufacturers of landmines, like Britain, they too were dragging their heels and hoping that calls for a worldwide ban would go away.

Both ambassadors reported on the extensive press coverage of the visit but they failed to recognise the impact that pictures of the Princess in a flak jacket were having on public opinion worldwide.

The Diana bandwagon was rolling. It would not be long before both London and Washington began to worry about the political power and influence of the leggy blonde with the shy smile and perfect teeth.

* * * * * *

Washington D.C., 21st January 1997

The hiss from the air-conditioning was barely audible. Imperceptible sound. An attentive dog might just have picked it up. More ambience than noise.

The wall-to-wall carpeting was of a pile so deep that even the heaviest of footfalls could not be detected. The leather on the chairs so soft and pliable that it didn't even rustle let alone squeak when sat upon.

The floor-to-ceiling smoked glass, which constituted the outside wall, was double-glazed, four inches thick, and bulletproof. The sounds of traffic on Pennsylvania Avenue beneath could not penetrate.

The room was hermetically sealed.

The walls were panelled with finest Cedars of Lebanon timber. The thick coffin-shaped table, with platinum plated legs, was made from South African stinkwood so highly polished that even the lightest of touches would leave a fingerprint mark clearly visible without the aid of zinc powder dusting. And on the walls...two original Canalettos.

It was opulent. The whole place spoke of wealth...of mega-wealth...of riches beyond imagination. And power.

This was the boardroom of The Castle Group.

Joel Butcher stood at the window gazing absent-mindedly at the Stars and Stripes fluttering atop The White House two blocks away. A light dusting of snow on the trees beyond gave the scene a distinctly Christmas card look.

It had been but a handful of years since Butcher was a daily visitor to The Oval Office. Back then he held the office of United States' Secretary of State with power and influence across the globe. Now he was Chairman and CEO of The Castle Group. His visits to The Oval Office were a little less frequent and his power and influence a little less discernable to the general public. But his reach was still global.

Every man in the room came from a similar background. Now that The Castle Group had been discovered by the world's media, that fact was the subject of much moralising, contention and debate.

In just a few short years The Castle Group had stealthily amassed a private equity investment portfolio which now had an estimated 40 billion dollars under management worldwide. But virtually every director, counsellor, or adviser had been handpicked because he or she once held a position of pivotal political importance either in The White House, on Capitol Hill, or in one of the great offices of state. The company even boasted three former heads of state on its international board and a former British prime minister headed its European operation.

The controversial thing about The Castle Group was its core business in the aerospace and defence sector where companies enjoying its patronage were competing for major governmental arms and ordnance contracts, which required political intervention. This was where the high-powered political networking of its senior management team came into its own. Critics called it political arbitrage of the worst kind.

'Last item on the agenda for today, gentlemen…anti-personnel devices', said Butcher. 'As you know the President has committed the United States to back any international agreement which seeks to ban the stockpiling, production and use of landmines. But I get the impression that the President's heart is not in this and I am sure that his advisors have not thought through the strategic and financial implications of such a course of action. I believe we need a strategy of our own on this.'

He turned towards a thin man with black-rimmed spectacles and a grey crew cut.

'Ed, remind us of the facts would you please?'

Edward Kaempfner III had been Defense Secretary in the previous administration and his ties to The Pentagon remained close. He spoke like a schoolboy reciting a piece of memorised homework.

'Some 110 million anti-personnel landmines are currently laid in approximately 70 countries', he intoned, 'and are manufactured in some 54 countries, principal among which are China, Russia, Belgium, Italy, South Africa and, of course, the United States.

'The average cost of manufacture ranges between three and fifteen dollars per unit but the cost of removal from site is approximately one thousand dollars per unit.

'Annual production is estimated to be one hundred million units worldwide and the annual turnover for the industry is approximately two billion dollars of which our companies have about a one third share.'

'Thank you, Ed', said the chairman. 'The United Nations is becoming quite exercised on this issue and public opinion is building up quite a head of steam after all the tear-jerking publicity the protestors have generated. As you know, several manufacturers in the U.S. have declared that they will cease production directly and a number of countries have already pledged to support the banning treaty scheduled for later this year.

'However it is an important part of our sector and we have major contracts in the pipeline from Sri Lanka, Nicaragua, Mozambique and, just this week, the government of Iran, I believe. I wanted to put this matter before you now so that we can consider a campaign to win hearts and minds in the places which matter before this sector of the industry is wrecked completely.'

Kaempfner was next to speak.

'Mr Chairman, The Pentagon is essentially of our mind on this', he said. 'They have some 10 million devices stockpiled and would be loathe to destroy them. They are preparing to offer the United Nations a compromise in the form of alternate devices which might be less indiscriminate and cut down on civilian casualties'.

'That would require a research programme, wouldn't it?' asked Robert O'Hara.

'It certainly would, Bobby, and I think I know where you're coming from', replied Kaempfner.

O'Hara had been Director of the US Office of Management and Budget; he could smell an opportunity to make money a mile away.

'A proper research and development programme would be a costly operation and worth a deal of investment. We should have a couple of our companies bid for the tender'.

'In the meantime the State Department ought to be reminded of the effect on the economies of some of the smaller manufacturing countries if we withdraw our investment in their armaments industries', cut in Jack Marshall, retired former White House Chief of Staff, 'not to mention the political leverage supplying these weapons gives us with some of our beleaguered friends in hostile parts of the world'.

'Just a moment, gentlemen, this may not be so simple', came a gruff voice from the end of the table. The speaker was Max Carlotti, whose term as Director of the Central Intelligence Agency had been marked by controversy and conflict. He sucked a knarled briar pipe as he spoke and his dark eyes were hooded with foreboding.

'You spoke of winning hearts and minds, Mr Chairman', he said, 'but I think it is too late for that. I think the hearts and minds have already been won…'

He paused. '…by the British princess. Di'.

Everyone in the room looked at him.

'She may be only a girl on her own but look at the impact her personal appearances and visits to landmine clearance areas has had', he said. 'Only last week – those pictures from Angola? Powerful, emotive images. She certainly knows how to push the buttons on the PR machine. The world loves this kid and will do anything she says. Countries are flocking to sign up to the treaty because of pressure from their citizens who simply can't get enough of Princess Di. Crazy but true'.

Butcher was nodding.

'I have been thinking along the same lines, Max.' he said. 'I'm not sure what we can do to stop her bandwagon rolling, except to exert what influence we can with the decision-makers who matter'.

'Look, she may win the landmines argument but then what?', asked Carlotti. 'She's a very determined young woman and obviously believes that she has a destiny to do good in the world and be remembered for it. Her idol is Mother Teresa of Calcutta. She wants to leave an even bigger legacy to mankind. My God, she's even been nominated for a Nobel Peace Prize for Pete sakes. That should give the kid a helluva lot of chutzpah!

'Suppose she decides to go totally peace loving and hippy and sets out to shut down the armaments industries worldwide, one by one. How about mortars or smart bombs next? Okay, I exaggerate, but this kid could do one heck of a lot of damage before she's done'.

'What do you suggest?', asked Butcher.

'What about Big Billy Tannadyce? He practically runs Great Britain', said O'Hara. 'The guy's a Lord for God's sakes. He even knows the Queen. Lemme talk with him; get him to kick some ass'.

'I don't think this situation is susceptible to you're usual kick ass approach, Bob', said the chairman. 'It needs something a little more subtle, a little more decisive, in a persuasive sort of way. Max?'

'I'm sorry Joel, I did not mean to hijack this discussion', said Carlotti. 'You are absolutely right. A systematic programme of lobbying to keep the pressure on in the right quarters is the right approach for now.

'But as my old high school football coach used to say, "hit 'em hard, hit 'em low, and hit 'em early". I believe in keeping one step ahead of my opponent. With your permission I will ask The Company to use their good offices to monitor the lady. That way we may get a clearer idea of her intentions and future plans so that we can move to curtail them before they gain momentum'.

There was nodding and a murmur of assent around the table.

'You don't need my permission, Max', said Joel Butcher, 'but thank you. You will doubtless keep us informed. If there is no other business the meeting is closed. Thank you, gentlemen'.

* * * * * *

The Ritz Hotel, Paris 5th February 1997

The breasts, once her glory and the object of lustful desire from the most wealthy and powerful men of her generation, lay limp and flaccid, putty-coloured against her rib cage.

There is no dignity in death, thought Henri Paul, *only ugliness and sordid degradation.*

She was dead, of course. Not quite. But everyone present knew it was only a matter of time. She lay motionless on the mosaic tiles by the side of the pool. Her floral bathing costume had been pulled down to her waist so that the Paramedics could work on her chest. A small white plug protruded from between her grey lips where they had attempted mouth-to-mouth resuscitation.

It had worked. She was breathing imperceptibly but all her other vital signs were almost undetectable. The ambulance men would arrive in a few minutes to remove her virtually lifeless body to hospital.

Henri Paul thought there must be worse places to die than the Ritz Hotel. Sudden death was a matter of routine to him. Elderly guests collapsed and died relatively frequently – usually in the privacy of their own suites. There were procedures to be gone through. He did his job. It didn't affect him.

But this lady was different. She was special. He knew she was not young but there was a vibrancy about her that convinced him she was too young to die.

He looked around him. It was a stylish place to expire. The Greco-Roman style décor. The warm-toned frescoes on the wall. The wealth of columns and potted palms.

She came here every morning to start her day with an invigorating swim. Perhaps it was fitting that she should end her days in these peaceful surroundings, which she loved so much.

No. Something was nagging at the back of Henri's mind. *She was fit ands healthy. There had to be something wrong. She should not be dying. Not in his hotel. Not now.*

'Excusez-moi Monsieur'. The ambulancemen had the body on a stretcher. 'I need a name for our records. Who is this lady?'

'That', said Henri gravely, 'is the Honourable Pamela Harriman, United States Ambassador to France'.

The ambulanceman raised his eyebrows, picked up one end of the stretcher, and turned away. 'Merci', he said.

Henri Paul returned to his daily duties and was saddened, though not surprised, to hear on the lunchtime news that Pamela Harriman was dead. She had suffered a massive stroke while taking her customary morning swim at the Ritz Hotel health club, the newsreader said.

Later that afternoon a woman telephoned from the Ambassador's residence to ask if she could collect the few belongings, which Mrs Harriman had left behind in her changing cubicle. The concierge, who took the call, offered to have them delivered but the woman insisted that she wanted to come personally to the hotel.

When she arrived Henri Paul was summoned to meet her. He found an elegant woman in her seventies wearing a fur stole and a pearl choker. In a soft Mid-Atlantic drawl, she announced herself as Pamela Harriman's secretary and companion and said that her name was Valerie. Her immaculate make-up was disturbed around the eyes, which were red and watery. In her hand she clutched a lace handkerchief which appeared to be more than a little damp.

Pitying her distress and instantly sympathetic, Henri invited her to take tea with him in the Bar Vendome. While they were being served he sent for the dead woman's belongings which arrived in three Ritz carrier bags – one containing her winter overcoat, one containing her shoes and clothing, and one containing her handbag.

Valerie had been at the hospital for most of the day and it was clear to Henri Paul that she was traumatised and needed this excursion to rid herself of the pent up emotions. He gently encouraged her to talk about her friend.

217

It all came pouring out. Some of it he knew, much of it he didn't.

Born into the English nobility Pamela had been a great social beauty who married Winston Churchill's son Randolph but found it impossible to remain faithful. She had three marriages in all and countless affairs with men of wealth and prominence. She had become an American citizen and such was her skill as a courtesan and hostess that President Clinton had asked her to take one of America's most important diplomatic postings as their Ambassador in Paris.

Between occasional outbursts of sobbing, Valerie insisted on going through the list of Pamela's lovers. They included Greek shipping tycoon Stavros Niarchos, the celebrated American broadcaster Ed Murrow, Jock Whitney owner of the New York Herald Tribune, the Aga Khan's son Prince Aly Khan, Baron Elie de Rothschild and Gianni Agnelli the billionaire owner of the Fiat motor company.

When there was an appropriate lull in the conversation Henri politely asked if Valerie would mind checking that all the belongings were accounted for. In particular he wanted her to check the contents of the handbag.

She fished absent-mindedly in the handbag and began to spread the contents out on the table in front of her.

'Oh, What's this?', she asked suddenly holding up a business card. 'Jean-Jacques Iversen. Parfaite Image Press', she read. 'I don't know what Pamela would be doing with him. Anyway it's no good to her anymore, or me for that matter. You might as well have it. Do you know this person?'

'Oh yes, I know him', said Henri wearily. But Valerie wasn't listening.

'Oh my, look at this. Isn't it lovely?'

218

She held up a delicate gold fountain pen encrusted with diamonds.

'A present from Princess Diana', she said, dabbing her nose with a tiny lace handkerchief. 'Oh dear, the poor child will be devastated. They are very close you know. Diana regards Pamela as a very dear aunt. She thinks their personalities and lives are very similar. She needs Pamela for advice and comfort. She knows that Pamela understands the unreal world she lives in and she looks up to her. When they meet they spend hours just chatting'.

She paused to dab her eyes.

'Diana once said that the only other woman she thought she might have had the same relationship with was Grace Kelly. But of course she died before they could develop a proper friendship. I think that was a stroke too...'

Her voice trailed away.

Henri Paul looked at the business card in his hand. The ubiquitous Monsieur Jean-Jacques Iversen, eh? *Had he already seized his photo opportunity with the Honourable Pamela*, he wondered, *or would he have to be satisfied with photographing her funeral?*

That would be right up Iversen's street, thought Henri. He was still boasting about the brilliant pictures he had taken at the funeral of Princess Grace of Monaco...the friend of Princess Diana...who, like Pamela Harriman had also died of a stroke.

* * * * * *

219

Paris, 3rd April 1997

Marielle sounded breathless. 'I need to meet you, but not anywhere in public', she said.

'Okay', said Christopher, 'where do you suggest?'

'The underground car park in the Boulevard St Germain near Place Maubert. I think it is number thirty-seven. On the second floor down. That is always empty. I'll be driving a silver grey Porsche Boxster. We can sit in the car and talk or drive around. Meet me there in an hour'.

'I think I know who Le Begue is but I can't be certain', said Christopher.

'Not now', replied Marielle. 'It is getting too close to me. You should be looking at Saddam's contact man. His name is something like Sharif. They meet in The Ritz. He's coming to Paris again soon. I'll tell you more when I see you. I've got to go now'.

Christopher heard the sound of a doorbell chime as she put the phone down.

Three hours later he sat behind the wheel of the British Embassy's general purpose Renault Espace people carrier with his eyes fixed on the down ramp leading from the first basement floor of the Boulevard St Germain car park. He had been parked there for over two hours. Cars had come and cars had gone but there had been no sign of a silver grey Porsche Boxster.

Christopher got out of his car, pressed the button on the key fob zapper to lock it, and made for the exit stairs. As soon as he emerged at street level he took out his mobile phone and dialled Marielle's home telephone number.

220

It rang for a long time before someone picked it up. 'Allo', said a man's voice.

'Is Marielle there?', asked Christopher.

'Who is this?', said the man.

'A friend', replied Christopher.

'One moment'. There was a muffled conversation in the background and then the man said: 'She is busy right now. She will call you tomorrow'. The phone went dead.

She will call who tomorrow?, thought Christopher. *He didn't ask my name.*

He knew where Marielle lived. He had taken the trouble to have her telephone number traced and had double checked her address on the voters' register while he was checking out her credentials. He had never been to her apartment but he guessed that it was no more than ten blocks away from where he stood. He decided to leave his car where it was and walk.

St Germain was a swanky part of The Left Bank and Christopher imagined that Marielle must live in a fairly luxurious apartment if a wealthy lover had bought it for her. He strolled down the Rue Lecourbe and counted the streets until he came to Rue Rousselet.

As he turned the corner he saw police cars drawn up outside the 19th Century apartment block. A silver Porsche Boxster was parked among them. A gaggle of curious onlookers stood huddled together gossiping on the opposite pavement and a piece of blue and white tape was strung across the entrance to the building. Behind the tape stood a solitary policeman wearing the uniform of a gendarme and glowering menacingly at anyone who came too close. Christopher walked up to him.

'Excuse me officer', he said. 'Where is the Inspector? I need to see him urgently'.

'He is busy, Monsieur', said the policeman. 'He is conducting an investigation. You cannot see him at the moment'.

'No, no. You don't understand', said Christopher. 'It is about this matter that I need to see him. I need to go in there and see him'. He pointed to the entrance of the apartment block.

'Monsieur, this is a crime scene. You cannot go in. Who are you anyway?'

Christopher pulled out his wallet and withdrew his official diplomatic credentials. It was a pass he carried for identification in emergencies but he rarely used it.

'*Corps Diplomatique de Grande Bretagne*', he said with as much pomposity as he could muster. 'This is a government matter. I must enter at once'.

The policeman took the pass and squinted, first at the photograph, and then at Christopher.

'Very well, Monsieur', he said at length. You may enter. Do you know where you are going?'

'Yes', said Christopher, 'fourth floor'.

'You cannot use the lift, Monsieur', said the policeman. 'You will have to use the stairs'.

When he reached the fourth floor, Christopher paused on the landing to catch his breath. The door of Marielle's apartment was open and he could hear voices coming from inside. He walked into the hallway.

It was, as he had expected, a beautiful home. The walls were all painted cream and the floors were polished wood, which, along with the high ceilings, gave an airy feeling of spaciousness. He could see right through the living room to the balcony and a pretty view over the garden behind the Clinique St Jean de Dieu.

One man was bent over the dining room table writing labels for various items he had placed in plastic evidence bags. A smaller man, whom Christopher took to be the Inspector, was standing smoking a cigarette, silhouetted against the floor-to-ceiling net curtains at the far end of the room.

Christopher stepped forward. And then he saw her.

A slight movement caught his eye as he passed the open door of the kitchen to his left.

Marielle was barefoot and wearing a pale blue denim smock with flowers embroidered across the yoke. Her blonde hair was dishevelled. He could not see her face because her head was slumped onto her chest… and she was hanging from an oak beam…suspended above the kitchen table with a rough piece of hemp around her neck.

'Hey, you. What are you doing in here? Get out of here at once'.

It was the voice of the smaller man. Christopher turned and saw that he had a Mexican-style Zapata moustache drooping down beside the corners of his mouth. He was red-faced and looked angry.

Christopher produced his pass once more and held it out for inspection.

'I am from the British Embassy, Commercial Section', he said. 'I have…had… an appointment with Mademoiselle Norstrund to discuss a business transaction with her company'.

'Well you cannot come in here. I am conducting a criminal investigation', said the man with the red face. 'You will have to make another appointment with the company. Now get him out of here', he yelled at the second man.

'But...', said Christopher, gesturing towards the kitchen.

'Suicide', said the moustachioed detective matter-of-factly. 'It happens'.

Yeah, right, thought Christopher. *And I'm a monkey's uncle. Didn't I just hear you say you were investigating a crime?*

Chapter Seventeen

Marylebone, London, 21st May 1997

At Daniel Galvin's hair salon in London's fashionable Marylebone High Street they are used to dealing with celebrity.

The man, who gave his name to the business, has built up a reputation as the world's foremost exponent of natural hair colouring. As a result, anybody who considers themselves to be anybody automatically beats a path to his door whenever they feel in need of a hair makeover.

He numbers among his clients some of the biggest names in Hollywood and some of the largest egos jostling for position in the gossip columns of the tabloid press. They all cheerfully pay top-of-the-range prices just to see and be seen in his colouration studio.

Daniel makes sure that every one of his high-profile customers is treated as a special individual by his staff. They are pampered and cosseted from the moment they cross the threshold until they leave, looking a little more glamorous and feeling a lot better about themselves.

There was one customer, however, for whom nothing was too much trouble. The treatment she received was consistently a cut above the others. That customer was Diana, Princess of Wales.

When she let it be known that she wanted Daniel Galvin to work on her hair, his business was given a major boost. Hairdresser to the stars is one thing but the man who does the hair if the most photographed woman in the world? You cannot buy that kind of cachet.

Over the years Daniel lavished hours of personal care and attention on the princess's hair and she returned the favour by being one of his most loyal and long-standing customers.

But she had moved on from the man himself, whom she adored, and now felt comfortable with one of his senior colourists, Vanessa, a young woman of her own age with whom she enjoyed an easy familiarity. There was a relationship of trust between the two. Diana insisted on being attended by Vanessa.

Today she was having fresh highlights put in her blonde bob.

The atmosphere in the salon was both professional and cosy. Discreet concealed lighting cast a pale glow over the cream-coloured walls and stripped pine flooring. The chrome and stainless steel surrounds of the mirrors picked out the black edging of the basins and contrasted tastefully with the black and sable of the styling chairs. There was a low murmur of conversation set against a soothing track of canned muzak playing quietly in the background.

Vanessa was wearing a tight-fitting trouser suit in chocolate brown over a candy-striped open-necked shirt. Her jet-black hair was neatly swept back into a tight ponytail held in place by a gold ring. As always her make-up was faultless. She prided herself on taking an hour to apply it each morning. From the eye shadow, which matched her clothing, to the scarlet, highly glossed, lipstick there was not a brushstroke out of place. It was truly a work of art – a lurid work of art.

'Is this a tape, Ness?', asked Diana pointing a perfectly manicured fingernail towards the ceiling.

'The music? No my love', replied Vanessa. 'I think it's a CD darlin'. D'you wannit changed? I can get sunnink better for you if you like'.

Essex girl Vanessa had tried to improve her native Estuary English when she first got a job with Daniel Galvin. Aware that she would be mixing with the rich and famous, and not wishing to appear ignorant and uneducated, she took a short course of elocution lessons in her hometown of Southend-on-Sea. But her teacher was no Professor Henry Higgins. Vanessa found herself standing in front of the bathroom mirror mouthing phrases like 'How now brown cow' and dissolving into fits of giggles over the ridiculous faces she was pulling to avoid strangulating the vowels. She gave up and decided just to be herself.

'No, I meant is it a record, or is it the radio?', said Diana. 'Can you get the radio on your system?'

''Course we can darlin'', said the colourist. 'Is there sunnink you wanna hear?'

'As a matter of fact there is', replied her client, glancing at her wristwatch. 'I'm told there is a very important announcement from the government which will be made on Radio Five Live in about five minutes. I'd really like to hear it if that is possible'.

'Marlon, 'ere a minute, love. Can you do us a little favour darlin'?', cried Vanessa.

A smartly dressed black youth with a diamond ear-stud got up from one of the styling chairs where he had been reading a copy of *Hello* magazine and ambled over with the exaggerated gait he had copied from his peers – up on the left toe, dragging the right foot like a cripple, while rocking the hips and rolling the shoulders ostentatiously. In the South London area of Brixton where Marlon lived such a walk was *de rigueur* among teenaged boys. It was a code, a badge of honour. It marked you out as one of the "bruvvers".

'Yeah. Whatcha want?', asked Marlon. He sounded surly but he was giving both women an affectionate smile, which showed off a gleaming set of white teeth – and one gold one.

'Can you get rid of the music and get Radio Five on the radio?', said Vanessa.

'Live', corrected Diana.

'Yeah, BBC Radio Five Live', said Vanessa. 'Can you do that for us darlin'? The Princess needs to hear sunnink on the radio, alright?'

'No problem', said Marlon as he hobbled and bobbed away towards a cupboard in the corner of the salon.

Diana sipped her herbal tea.

The tinkling music stopped abruptly. There was a brief silence and then a series of jerky, disjointed, stuttery sounds as the dial zipped through several radio stations before coming to rest on the perfectly enunciated vowels of a BBC announcer. He was introducing a statement from Her Majesty's Secretary of State for Foreign Affairs.

The sudden loss of a musical backdrop to their conversations made other customers uneasy. The babble of gossip and small talk between the staff and their clients dropped to a respectful whisper. Only Diana was listening to the radio.

The sound of the new Foreign Secretary was very distinctive and reassuringly full of authority. Robin Cook had a deep, rich, resonance to his voice and his educated Scottish tones rolled out of the speakers in the salon ceiling, oozing gravitas and sincerity.

'Every hour another three people lose their life or lose a limb from stepping on a landmine', he said. 'Thousands of children who ran into a landmine are left unable to run ever again. Landmines have limited military use, but create unlimited civilian casualties'.

Diana leant forward in her chair clasping her hands together. She was looking at herself in the mirror but seeing the image of maimed children in her mind's eye.

'Today we are announcing a complete ban on any British trade in landmines and a moratorium on their operational use with British forces', went on Mr Cook. 'The moratorium will remain in force until existing stocks are destroyed by the year 2005 or by the entry into force of an effective international agreement banning the use of landmines'.

'Yes! Yes! Yes!', cried Diana, punching the air in triumph. Everyone in the salon turned to look at her. They had not been paying attention. Her uncontrolled delight was a mystery to them.

The Foreign Secretary began to drone on again and the customers and staff once more turned their attention to more mundane matters.

'Britain will play a full part in the Ottawa Process to achieve an international ban on landmines. We will also redouble our efforts at the Geneva Conference on Disarmament to get the main export countries to stop selling landmines', said Robin Cook.

Diana closed her eyes. *This new Labour government were starting to deliver their promises. Perhaps they would be good for the country after all*, she thought.

'Our twin commitments to a ban on trade and a moratorium on the operational use of landmines will enable us to speak with authority at the negotiating table and to lead by force of example', concluded the Foreign Secretary.

'Too right', squealed Diana. Her eyes were sparkling and she was grinning broadly. She bounced up and down in her chair so that the foil wraps protecting her highlights waved and rustled against each other.

'This is fantastic. We're on our way. We're going to get there', she shouted at the mirror.

Vanessa bustled across to stand behind Diana's chair. She loved the military click of her own stilettos on the pinewood floor. It was her favourite sound. She couldn't get enough of it. She had not been listening to the radio, and wouldn't have understood the significance of the announcement if she had, but she was wreathed in smiles.

'That's absolutely brilliant darlin'', she gushed. 'Well done you. I'm so happy for ya. You must be over the moon. Now, we'll just give it another five minutes and then we'll wash. Okay?'

* * * * * *

Paris, 18th June 1997

Christopher sat on the balcony of his apartment with a bottle of chilled Sauvignon Blanc and a dish of pistachios while the sun slowly faded and dipped behind the Paris skyline. His summer was turning out to be busier than he had anticipated.

The Chief himself, no less, Sir David Langdale, had personally briefed him for a special assignment.

MI5 surveillance operatives had picked up intelligence that the wealthy Egyptian owner of Harrods department store, Mohamed Al Fayed, had invited Diana Princess of Wales and her two sons to join his own family for a holiday at his villa in the South of France. Buckingham Palace had apparently approved the plan and the Princess had accepted the invitation. Departure was scheduled for 14th July.

The Director-General of MI5 had requested assistance in monitoring this escapade from his opposite number at the Secret Intelligence Service.

Christopher was ordered to carry out a detailed reconnaissance of the Al Fayed residence, the family yacht, and any other venues in the St Tropez area, which the Princess might frequent during her stay. A full surveillance was to be mounted on her every movement while she was in France and Christopher was authorised to recruit extra manpower for the task. It was anticipated that she might spend some time in The Ritz Hotel in Paris, which was also owned by Mr Al Fayed.

Christopher could see no point in the exercise but from his early days in MI5 he had known the rumours about Tommy Crampton's obsession with Diana. There seemed no reason why Crampton should drop the subject now that he had reached the dizzy heights of Director-General. Obviously he hadn't.

The loss of a romantic weekend with Giselle four years earlier just to satisfy Crampton's whim by spying on Diana's shopping expedition still rankled with Christopher. He thought the whole thing a stupid waste of time and manpower but he was obliged to follow orders.

Actually it was an unwelcome distraction from his main pre-occupation – tracking the illegal French arms trade with Iraq.

London was becoming increasingly interested in his reports on the subject and he was being pressed to identify the ringleaders behind the corrupt government cabal as soon as possible.

He took another sip of wine. Who was 'Le Begue'? The question had puzzled him ever since Marielle threw out the name as a clue to the identity of the cabal's leader. It was a French nickname. He knew that. It meant 'the stammerer' and it was used mostly by schoolchildren as a cruel jibe against any child with a speech impediment. But he knew of no French public figure with such a soubriquet. He thought he had cracked it when he noticed a prominent politician, with close links to Mitterrand, stuttering explosively during an interview on television. It was this man's name he was going to put to Marielle on the day she was murdered.

Since her death, however, he had learned that the man was a rampantly promiscuous homosexual and thus highly unlikely to have been Marielle's mysterious lover.

He shelled another pistachio and popped it into his mouth. What were the last words Marielle had spoken to him? Something about watching Saddam's man. She had got the name slightly wrong. Christopher knew all about Balaam Abu Shafiq. No, she had said something about it all getting too close to her. Well 'Le Begue' was her lover. That would be close.

Close to her? Close to her? Christopher tapped his index finger against his lips. Suddenly he sat bolt upright. A thought had come to him.

For a reason he could not quite remember he had kept the issue of Paris Match magazine which contained the picture of Marielle posing with President Mitterrand at an Elysee dinner.

He darted into his living room and began to rummage through a jumbled pile of publications haphazardly jammed into a bamboo magazine rack. Eventually he came across what he was looking for. He had had the foresight to turn down the corner of the page with the picture he needed. Yes, there it was, the President, Mademoiselle Marielle Norstrund and... he looked at the caption. The other man was named as a minister in the Ministry of Finance. Christopher looked back at the picture. The minister was young and handsome. He was smiling broadly and his arm was clasped around Marielle's waist in an intimately familiar way. *I wonder*, thought Christopher.

232

'They meet in The Ritz'. That was what Marielle had said. Christopher made a mental note to brief his Ritz informant about Shafiq and the minister. He needed to know if they ever met at the hotel.

But for now he had packing to do. He had an early flight to Nice in the morning.

Oh Diana, what have you done to upset the spooky boys at Thames House, he thought.

* * * * * *

Covent Garden, London, 9th July 1997

Lord Tannadyce swilled the wine around his palate allowing it to engage his taste buds as he inhaled slowly through his nostrils to maximise the effect of its rich aroma. A Chateauneuf du Pape it was, but a rather superior one. Domaine du Vieux Donjon. He rolled the ruby red liquid around in his glass and held it up to the light before swallowing and nodding his approval to the sommelier.

He was not a great wine buff but he knew what he liked and he reckoned this would go nicely with his favourite steak, kidney and oyster pudding. He knew his companions had ordered game of some sort so his choice ought to be satisfactory to them as well. If not they could choose their own wine.

Once the waiter had finished pouring the drinks and withdrawn Sir Tristram Grainger got to his feet and said: 'Gentlemen we have serious business to attend to today so I intend to break with protocol and propose the loyal toast now, at the beginning of the meal. I think it is appropriate in view of the occasion and the subject matter before us'.

233

There was a scraping of chairs as they all rose, raised their glasses and turned towards the portrait of Queen Elizabeth II which occupied a prominent place on the wall behind Sir Tristram's seat.

'The Queen', said Sir Tristram and they all solemnly intoned 'The Queen', in reply.

Lord Tannadyce added: 'God bless her'.

The John Betjeman Room on the first floor of London's oldest restaurant, Rules, had been his choice for today's meeting of the men who now believed, more firmly than ever, that the preservation of the British monarchy and all it stood for lay in their hands and theirs alone.

It was an intimate oak-panelled room with just one leaded-light window, heavily shrouded by crimson brocade curtains, an oval mirror above the fireplace, a trophy cabinet, and the walls were festooned with period cartoons and portraits both large and small. It was discreetly tucked away at the top of a narrow staircase and perfect for a secret tryst.

The table in the middle could accommodate ten diners but just eight men were present.

'Things appear to be coming to a head, gentlemen', said Sir Tristram. 'Our friend seems determined to up the ante'.

He held up a copy of *The Daily Telegraph* newspaper bearing the headline: 'Princess confronts press to demand holiday privacy'. Then, reading from a crumpled copy of *The Sun* newspaper, he said: 'Princess Diana revealed yesterday she is about to make a bombshell announcement on her future. Di told The Sun's Royal team, quote, you are going to get a big surprise with the next thing I do'.

He paused then continued with a note of gravity in his voice. 'Now we could all speculate about what surprise she intends, gentlemen, but there is clearly a threatening subtext here.

'The disturbing aspect is the contiguity of this statement with the new and, I am told, rapidly developing friendship with the young man Fayed. If her surprise relates to him, and I will ask David to expand on that in a moment, then there could be unhappy constitutional consequences.

'Marriage to a Muslim or, heaven forefend, impregnation by one is utterly unthinkable for the mother of the future King of England. There are deep and complicated issues relating to the Act of Succession and the Act of Supremacy here'.

'I cannot understand why Buckingham Palace has allowed the young princes to be taken abroad, unsupervised and unprotected, on such an ill-judged and highly unsuitable escapade', interposed Martin Chamberlain. 'After all William is second in line to the throne, what about security?'

Chamberlain was a retired Royal Marine officer with a colourful history in the Special Boat Service – the naval equivalent of the SAS. Now a wealthy industrialist he was a major benefactor of several charities sponsored by members of the Royal Family.

'Her majesty was graciously pleased to grant permission for her grandsons to escort their mother to France on this occasion', said Sir Tristram, adopting the stiff terminology of the Court. 'She took the view that not to do so would seem churlish and deny the boys the opportunity of a holiday. Al Fayed has his own security detail who are all former British soldiers with the appropriate training. He has pledged to provide a level of protection higher than the average'.

Chamberlain was not placated. 'Al Fayed's motives for extending the invitation must be dubious', he said. 'He is trying to inveigle his family into Royal circles through this silly girl. Can you imagine the situation if he, the wealthy foreign owner of Harrods, were to become step-grandfather-in-law to the King? This whole thing is compromising the independence of the Royal family'.

Lord Tannadyce was feeling impatient. 'Look, we all know the woman's a raging nymphomaniac', he said. 'She just wants a bit of holiday rumpy-pumpy with a good-looking gippo fellow. What's wrong with that? Good luck to her'.

'I am afraid it is much more serious than that, Bill', replied Sir Tristram. 'David?'

Sir David Langdale leant forward and clasped his hands together. The MI6 chief had not touched his food.

'We have assets in place who report that the relationship between Diana, Princess of Wales and Emad Fayed, colloquially known as Dodi, has every likelihood of leading to marriage', he said, 'and although there is no evidence, and it would be very difficult to prove at this stage, your reference to impregnation may not be so wide of the mark, Tristram'.

'My God you spooks are completely shameless', said Tannadyce. 'Poking and prying into other people's private business. The bloody girl is barking mad and should never have been allowed to marry the heir to the throne but what she gets up to on holiday is surely harmless fun'.

Sir Tristram Grainger treated this interruption as though he had not heard it.

Tommy?', he inquired, turning to the Director-General of MI5.

'As you know our friends overseas have had an ongoing monitoring operation in place on the lady for almost two years for their own purposes which have to do with geo-political issues of importance to them', said Thomas Crampton.

'Their satellite equipment is much more powerful and more sophisticated than ours but our facility at GCHQ which serves NATO is better at tracking signals than anything they have so much of the inbound material is routed through Cheltenham.

'This gives us the opportunity to take a feed and we have obtained intelligence from intercepted conversations which have taken place in St Tropez, both on land and at sea, over the past few days which indicates that there is a determination, in fact almost a collective commitment, within the Fayed family for a marriage to take place and an urgency to cement the union with a child. The Princess of Wales does not appear to oppose this proposition indeed she seems eager to comply'.

'The Princess's keynote speech to the Mines Advisory Group conference in London last month did not go down at all well in Washington', added Langdale. 'As a result the surveillance was stepped up and put on a round-the-clock footing which is, of course, of no concern to us. But one by-product is that we have, for the first time, been able to gain a better insight into her plans and what her intentions may be in terms of attacking the Crown.

'I have set up a specialist unit and one of my most experienced analysts is giving me daily reports'.

James Sutherland had been silent. Now he spoke.

'It is quite simple, he said calmly, 'the relationship must be broken up. Both of the parties are spending most of their time together abroad so whatever is done to achieve this will have to be done outwith these shores. I imagine that your operatives may be of some assistance, David, but it might be prudent to distance yourselves and HMG from any involvement or complicity.

'It may be best if any operation we agree on is strictly of a freelance nature. I have sufficient specialist manpower on standby and I am willing to undertake whatever action this meeting sees fit to authorise'.

Sir Tristram looked around the table. 'These are difficult times, gentlemen', he said. 'We must not be precipitate but I

237

think we are all agreed that things cannot be allowed to go any further'.

There was nodding and general agreement at this.

'I propose that James and I begin putting together a strategic plan to be actioned if needs be. We will monitor the situation on a day-by-day basis and consult with the rest of you as and when appropriate. I will not push the tit until we have taken a collective decision to go ahead. All agreed?'

All eight hands were raised in unison.

'Have a drop more of this plonk, Triss old boy, it's damned good', said Lord Tannadyce, filling the chairman's empty glass.

Later, when it came time for the lunch companions to take their leave of one another, James Sutherland and Sir Tristram Grainger found themselves momentarily alone together on the pavement outside the restaurant. 'Time is short, James', said Sir Tristram. 'We cannot afford to wait. We need to move, and we need to move soon'.

Sutherland looked him firmly in the eye. 'I hear what you say', he said, as he hailed a taxi. I need to speak to someone. There is an M.C.C. reception for the Australian touring party at the In and Out Club his evening. Call me there. After seven'.

Sir Tristram opened his mouth to speak but Sutherland was gone.

* * * * * *

Paris, 23rd July 1997

Christopher was intrigued.

He loved the Jardin du Luxembourg. It was one of his favourite parks. Strolling on a Sunday. Watching the children play with their radio-controlled boats on the Grand Bassin pond. Lingering behind the open-air chess players trying to anticipate their moves. Cheering another fine throw on the Jeux de Boules pitch. It was the essence of Paris at ease.

But as the venue for a meeting with a man he had known for years? A man he always met in a restaurant or a bar? He couldn't work out what Pierre Charron was playing it.

It all seemed so cloak and dagger. Far too melodramatic.

Stand facing the Fontaine de Medicis at precisely eleven o'clock reading a newspaper. Watch Pierre walk by and ensure he was not being followed. Then walk back along the path towards the Grand Bassin and sit on the third bench on the left. If that was occupied sit on the next unoccupied bench. If Pierre was being followed continue reading the paper. If not fold the paper and hold it in the left hand.

This was basic tradecraft. One of the first lessons. Juvenile stuff. They were professionals. Grown ups. They didn't need this nonsense. Pierre was his opposite number in the DST. His liaison man. They had been seen together in public on many occasions over the past twelve years. This was all very puzzling.

But Pierre had sounded troubled. He had called on Christopher's mobile almost pleading for an urgent meeting. He had not used the usual number at the British Embassy. He had asked that they meet in the open air and insisted on these extraordinary precautions.

Christopher liked Pierre Charron. They had crossed swords a few times. Pierre had not been too amused at the way Christopher tricked him by recruiting his best informant at The Ritz hotel from under his nose. But over all they trusted one another.

This was out of character. It must be serious.

The Jardin du Luxembourg was a short taxi ride across the river from the British Embassy and about the same distance from DST headquarters.

So here he stood on a brilliant sunlit day trying to keep his copy of Le Monde out of the fine spray, which a brisk breeze occasionally sent fizzing towards him from the top of the fountain. His watch read eleven o'clock precisely.

He saw Pierre approach from his right and pause to look up at the fountain. He was carrying a carton of coffee and a paper bag, which contained some kind of pastry no doubt. He strolled away casually as if looking for somewhere to sit and drink his coffee.

Christopher turned to face the direction from which Pierre had approached. A jogger came by. No. Hopeless cover as a surveillance tail. You had to keep running.

A girl in a green anorak came briskly into view. She was wearing dark glasses and talking on a mobile phone. Christopher opened his paper and pretended to read. The girl appeared to be following Pierre. Suddenly she threw out her arms and ran forward to embrace a dark–haired young man. They kissed briefly and then made off in another direction arm-in-arm.

Christopher waited for the cross-feed. If the couple had been following Charron a third member of the surveillance team would have to pick up the tail from the point where they left it. No one appeared. Pierre's fears had obviously been unfounded.

Christopher turned and walked back. He found the designated bench unoccupied and sat down holding the folded newspaper in his left hand. This was ridiculous. He felt embarrassed.

After five minutes Pierre Charron arrived and sat down. 'Thank you so much for coming, Christopher', he said. 'I have to talk to you but I cannot take any chances'.

He looked haunted and there was an indefinable raggedness about his usually pristine appearance.

'They are killing people', he said.

'Who are?', asked Christopher.

'The government', replied Charron.

Christopher remained silent. His companion was sounding like some left-wing student in the first flush of discovering radical politics. He half expected him to launch into a ranting polemic about the injustice of French foreign policy.

'They are assassinating people who have become an embarrassment or people who might blow the whistle on their corruption. It is wrong. Totally wrong and they have to be stopped. Exposed if necessary'.

'Yes but, they? The government?, asked Christopher. 'Who exactly? What evidence do you have?'

'This goes right to the very top', said Charron gravely. 'The President's own people were ordering these killings and de Champvieux was doing their bidding'.

So you are catching up at last, thought Christopher, *what took you so long?* He leaned back casually and stretched his arm along the back of the bench.

'Hang on', he said with an expression of indifference on his face. 'You know as well as I do that these things happen occasionally in our business. It is regrettable, but sometimes there are political imperatives which dictate that these things have to be done quietly and discreetly in the national interest or in the interests of political stability in a particular part of the world. You really shouldn't be talking to me about this. This is something I should not know and don't want to know'.

'No no', said Charron leaning forward imploringly. 'You don't understand. These are not wet jobs. This is not occasional. It is regular. These killings cannot be justified in the name of national interest or even political expediency. This was calculated murder at the whim of the President of France's closest associates to serve their own private, personal, purposes. To save their skins. To avoid embarrassing the office of the President. And it is still going on'.

Christopher was hearing nothing which surprised him, of course, but he was beginning to spot a potential advantage to himself in this fraught conversation. He still had not worked out who the main players were in the Franco-Iraqi arms profiteering cabal and with the loss of Marielle his chances of discovering the true identity of 'Le Begue' were very slim indeed. Perhaps Charron could lead him to his targets. He decided to take a more tactful line.

'All right, I hear what you say. What about evidence? Give me an example', he said.

'Beregovoy', replied Charron. 'Pierre Beregovoy. The prime minister. Mitterrand's chums wanted him out of the way so they had him killed'.

'Wait a minute', said Christopher, 'Beregovoy killed himself. Everyone knows it was suicide. The pathologist's report.....'

'De Champvieux ordered the pathologist to say it was suicide', cut in Charron. 'I know the pathologist. He told me. He is an

242

honourable man. He was devastated. He had clear proof that Beregovoy was murdered but because he works for the security services he was prevented from saying so in court'.

Christopher shook his head. 'But why would the President want to have his former prime minister killed?, he asked. A man he had worked so closely with for so many years?'

'That is precisely the reason', said Charron. 'It wasn't Mitterrand himself who had him killed. But he'd worked with Mitterrand's office too closely. He knew too many nasty secrets about the President's associates so they got rid of him.

'Remember Saddam Hussein's Project 395? Iraq's Condor Two ballistic missile and Saad 16 at Mosul? The mustard gas? Remember all of that? Well, Sagem were supplying the guidance system for the missiles, as everyone knows, but France was quietly doing a lot more to help Saddam's weapons of mass destruction programme. The contracts were huge and some of the President's advisers were secretly raking their own cut.

'Beregovoy was Finance Minister at the time and knew exactly what was going on. When the whole thing came under closer international scrutiny after the Gulf War, these Mitterrand acolytes were afraid that Bere would talk. He was also associated with the financial loans scandal involving two of Mitterrand's closest friends, if you remember, so his mouth had to be shut. He had to go'.

Christopher sat back and blew out his cheeks.

'People', he said. 'You said they were killing people. Who? How many?'

'Quite a few' said Charron. 'I am making my own discreet inquiries but obviously it is difficult. I have to be very careful. It is taking time. I was just so disgusted by the murder of Bere that I started to go freelance on this.

'I can tell you that Carina was one'.

'What? The singer?', asked Christopher, incredulous. 'Oh, that's just ridiculous. Why would the President want to kill one of France's most popular singers? Anyway, if my memory serves me, she also committed suicide'.

Charron simply raised his eyebrows and shrugged.

'It wasn't suicide. She'd had a long-running affair with Mitterrand and was blackmailing him. She was threatening to go public with all the lurid details. I think they probably killed de Grossouvre, too – remember his strange death – and there was a woman who apparently committed suicide in her apartment in St Germain in April. There wasn't much in the papers so you probably didn't hear of it, but she was a big public relations lady for CDI. You know who they are?'

Christopher nodded.

'Well they have been getting all the best contracts for supplying Saddam lately and most of it is either secret or illegal or both. This woman was up to her neck in all the deals. She knew Mitterrand and a lot of his cronies. I am convinced that her death was no coincidence. It was not suicide. I am sure'.

Charron paused and looked at the sky as if for inspiration.

'They have been using L'Appeau', he said. 'There's a link between him and all the killings I'm looking at. Certainly Beregovoy. He seems to have been in the company of each of the victims no more than a matter of hours before their deaths. In some cases a matter of minutes'.

'L'Appeau?', asked Christopher.

'L'Appeau', said Charron. 'It translates as The Decoy in English. It is a hunting term....'

'I know what a decoy is', said Christopher. 'Someone or something used to lure the game into a trap or at least within gunshot range'.

'Exactly', said Charron. 'We have employed The Decoy for years. He has the perfect profession for cover. He gets to meet all kinds of people in all kinds of unthreatening circumstances on a regular basis and they all trust him. Consequently he is obviously a wonderful source of raw intelligence but he can also entice people in the sense of getting them to go to places and do things where we are able to manipulate the situation in our favour.

'But I reckon de Champvieux has gone one step further and got The Decoy to flush out the prey he wants eliminated. He may have even used the guy to do the killing. I'm not sure'.

'Hmm', said Christopher. 'Why are you telling me this?'

'Just in case anything should happen to me', said Charron. 'I think I'm getting close to something here but I cannot trust any one of my colleagues. No one seemed as shocked at the death of Pierre Beregovoy as I was and I don't know who is close to de Champvieux and who isn't'.

'Well, you're certainly taking a big risk', said Christopher. 'You'd better be very careful indeed. If what you say is true and de Champvieux gets a sniff that you are on to it then you are not going to last long yourself'.

'I know that', said Charron. 'That is why I needed to tell you and hopefully keep you informed if my other inquiries lead me anywhere'.

'You said you were getting close to something just now', said Christopher. 'What?'

'Right up until his death Mitterrand was in bed with Saddam', said Charron. 'When the rest of the world boycotted him, France was secretly helping him to re-arm and continue his

WMD programme. And all the time a few of Mitterrand's rich and powerful associates were benefiting personally.

'Throughout that period Saddam's main weapons procurer and security adviser was coming regularly to Paris to negotiate bigger and bigger deals. And it is still going on. France is still secretly helping Iraq behind the backs of the international community. The United Nations must know because their weapons inspectors must have spotted what is going on. And I'll bet the Americans, with all their sophisticated eavesdropping technology, probably know too. But they're all just turning a blind eye'.

Christopher gazed into the middle distance and said nothing. He was wondering if Charron was so disillusioned, and frightened, that he might be recruited as a 'black agent' for the British – a totally deniable asset within the French secret service.

'The thing is, it is still going on even though Mitterrand is gone', said Charron. The present government is much more in line with international thinking on Iraq but there are still people who were in Mitterrand's cabal who are making money out of the situation. There are moves afoot to investigate all of this publicly but there are powerful people out there who have a vested interest in keeping things quiet. And de Champvieux is one of those.

'Saddam's man still comes to Paris regularly and I just need to find out who he is meeting…'

'Listen, you've said enough', cut in Christopher. 'I get the picture. Thank you for telling me. If you need to pass on anything at any time, feel free. I must go now. You take extra care. You're in a very dangerous situation. Okay?'

He shook Charron's hand and stood up to leave.

'Just as a matter of interest', he said. 'What is The Decoy's real name?'

'Some other time', said Charron. 'Maybe I'll tell you next time'.

He slipped a pain aux chocolat out of the paper bag and took a bite.

Chapter Eighteen

Sarajevo, Bosnia, 8th August 1997

'Diana, Diana...over here, look this way'...'Diana, give us a smile, love'... 'Are you missing Dodi?'... 'Are you in love, Diana?'... 'C'mon Di, let's see your smile'...

The whirr of the camera motor drives and the staccato crash of the shutters was almost deafening. A barrage of flashguns lit the scene like a cascade of mini lightning strikes.

The international press pack was in full cry.

Their prey, Diana, Princess of Wales, her blonde hair ruffled by the breeze, looked radiant as she stepped from a private aircraft on to the tarmac at Sarajevo Airport. Dressed in pale slacks, a light blue open-necked shirt, and navy blazer, the most photographed woman in the world appeared the picture of happiness and contentment.

As she strode towards the waiting cavalcade of cars she ignored the dozens of photographers, reporters and TV cameramen massed behind temporary barriers and jostling each other as they fought for the best angle and ran to keep up.

Instead she chatted amicably to her hosts while her faithful butler, Paul Burrell, walked dutifully a few paces behind.

Wherever she went in the world the self-style 'Queen of Hearts' drew large crowds and plenty of media attention. But this summer Diana's much publicised romance with the Egyptian playboy film producer, Dodi Fayed, ensured that the press presence surrounding her was even more intrusive than usual.

Today she was on a mission. The breathless, heady, whirlwind atmosphere of her new love affair had been left behind in London for three days while she attended to business. Her business. Her worldwide anti-landmine campaign.

At the back of the crowd of journalists stood Ken Darwin, his hands buried in the pockets of a gabardine raincoat. He did not want to be there. And he certainly did not want to be posing as a reporter on an assignment he saw as, at best, tedious and, at worst, totally frivolous.

But the order had come direct from CIA headquarters in Langley, Virginia. For some crazy reason Washington saw this beautiful girl with a willowy figure and a fashion plate smile, as a threat to United States interests.

So Ken was taking a break from monitoring the simmering tensions between Serbs, Croats, and Muslims, that continued to threaten peace in the region in the aftermath of the war, which had split the country.

His job over the next three days was to go everywhere the Princess went and report on everyone she met with an assessment of the impact her visit was making on the local political situation but more especially the world's media. He was also to take a close look at her hosts, the Washington-based Landmine Survivors Network.

The previous day Ken had read the SITREP reports, sent through from Langley to the American Consul, and also studied the 'CX' – as MI6 called raw intelligence – which had been thoughtfully shared by the British head of Sarajevo station. So he was fully up to speed on the political and security background to the visit.

He knew that the British Red Cross, which had sponsored the Princess's highly controversial trip to see minefields in Angola six months earlier, had withdrawn support for this visit. The President of the Bosnian Red Cross was the wife of the former Serb leader, and indicted war criminal, Radovan Karadic. It would have been virtually impossible for the Princess to avoid a politically embarrassing meeting with Mrs Karadic. The British Foreign Office had given the determined young princess the green light to go ahead with her mission, however, despite the fact that London had cut off diplomatic relations with Bosnia over its failure to meet peace deadlines.

Just three weeks earlier an undercover hit squad of British SAS commandos had been involved in the killing of one war criminal and the arrest of another in the town of Prijedor. Anti-British feeling was running high. Ken looked around him. To the untrained eye everything appeared normal but he could see that security cover for the pretty blonde lady was being provided at an unusually high level.

He fingered the fake media accreditation in his pocket. It was one of five phoney press passes he used as the occasion demanded. Today he was ostensibly reporting for The Christian Science Monitor. A girl with a blonde bob, a Louisiana accent, and more teeth than any one human being could feasibly have owned, handed him a printed sheet detailing Diana's planned schedule for the day. He thanked her and moved to his car to join the media cavalcade just setting off in pursuit of the celebrity visitor.

Over the next 60 hours Ken Darwin trailed everywhere in the wake of the Princess.

He watched her sombre, reflective, visit to a cemetery where landmine victims were buried. He travelled to the Northern Muslim town of Tuzla and stood outside a shabby council house for almost an hour while Diana had a private interview with a former soldier who had lost both legs and one eye in a landmine blast. He heard how she cried while listening to the story of a teenaged girl horribly maimed by a mine. He watched her mobbed by crowds in a Sarajevo shantytown. And heard a choir of children sing anti-mine songs to her.

When it was all over and Diana departed with her entourage for London, Ken returned to his office in the United States Consulate and began to compose his report.

It was a comprehensive document in which he expressed the opinion that Diana was well on the way to fulfilling her ambition to have a global role as a roving humanitarian ambassador. He also pointed out that the Princess was beginning to have a major impact on the future of the landmine industry. Referring to a statement by the United Nations spokesman in Sarajevo who declared that Diana's visit was drawing attention to the need for $16m to finance de-mining, Darwin noted that the very next day The World Bank had announced a $16.2m package of aid for de-mining efforts in the region.

He concluded his report by outlining what he assessed as a weakness in Diana's ability to carry out her campaigning strategy.

Under the heading "Weakness" he wrote:

"The subject's principal area of vulnerability remains her private life.

"Her romantic interests, though intense, are not sufficient distraction to prevent her from fulfilling what she sees as public duties and obligations viz. her current visit to Bosnia-Herzegovina. In terms of momentum for her campaigning stance the heightened media interest in her arising from such romantic interludes serves only to raise the international profile of her activities.

"However, it has yet to be seen what long-term effect the breakdown of such a relationship might have, both on her personally and in terms of her media popularity. The current affair may be temporary but if it is not, consideration should be given to a program of disruption aimed at ending it permanently so that the effects can be assessed".

He could have no idea what an impact those words were to have in Washington, in London, and in Paris...

251

* * * * * *

London, 20ᵗʰ August 1997

The sound system in the gym was pumping. Loud. It was mid-morning. Mid-week.

In the corner a skinny girl wearing a fluorescent pink leotard lay on an exercise mat rolling her hips from side to side. An elderly man, who ought to have known better, was straining every sinew to lift a set of weights which were clearly too heavy for him. The veins at his temple and on his neck stood out like ropes. He was sweating profusely and groaning with every repetition.

Spike Hughes paid no attention. He was focussed on his daily routine - pounding along on the running machine at a steady six miles per hour for a continuous thirty minutes. He was twenty minutes into the run breathing normally and scarcely having broken sweat. He looked straight ahead into the floor-to-ceiling mirror but he was not admiring himself. His steel-grey eyes were glazed in concentration.

Spike was supremely fit. You could tell that he was a soldier, or had been. His head was shaven and his body was taught and muscular. But the giveaway signs were the tattoos. One on each bicep. On the left the winged parachute insignia of the Parachute Regiment. And on the right the winged dagger of the Special Air Service.

The duty manager of the gym, a bronzed young man in shorts and a running singlet, poked his head around the door. He waved to attract Spike's attention and then held his closed fist against his ear.

Spike pressed a button on the electronic display panel in front of him and the treadmill slowed to walking pace. He jumped off, wiped his face with a towel and walked into the gym reception area. The telephone receiver was lying on the counter. He picked it up. 'Hello', he said.

A voice at the other end simply said: 'Job. Usual rendezvous. Sixteen hundred. Tomorrow'.

'Roger. Rodge', said Spike, replacing the receiver as he returned to the gym.

On the Brecon Beacons in a bleak corner of Wales, one hundred and eighty miles to the west, it was raining. Four new recruits to the SAS were in the second phase of their training. They were on a thirty mile route march over rough terrain carrying a 40lb back pack and a self-loading rifle each. Not only was this an endurance test but also they were being taught the 'arcs of fire'. They jogged along in a diamond shape. The point man at the front faced forward. The man to the left faced left. The man to the right faced right and the man at the rear rotated constantly keeping a close eye on what was happening behind him. Every so often an instructor would pop out from behind a rock or out of a gully to see if he could catch the soldiers unawares.

One of those instructors was Sergeant Danny McCormick, a barrel-shaped little Scot who was now a part-time soldier having left the regular army for a short-term posting with the SAS Territorials.

Danny had just successfully ambushed the tail end Charlie of the unit for the second time when he felt a vibration against his thigh. He fished inside his anorak and pulled out his mobile phone. 'Yep', he said.

'Job', said an anonymous voice. 'Usual rendezvous. Sixteen hundred hours, tomorrow'.

'Received', said Danny. He clicked the phone shut.

'Okay you little shits, lets move it', he yelled. 'You're all dead by now you useless bastards.'

Almost thirty hours later a group of men met at the Special Forces Club in London's Knightsbridge.

There were fifteen of them. They arrived separately within minutes of the appointed hour. They all came on foot, converging, one by one, from different directions, on the anonymous-looking Georgian terraced house in a quiet back street a stone's throw from Harrods department store. Each man checked up and down the street before pressing the entry buzzer at the door. Once inside they climbed the stairs past row upon row of black and white photographs depicting unsung and unknown heroes of special operations in wars and foreign conflicts long forgotten.

As a group they looked particularly incongruous. These were men accustomed to dressing casually. For most of them their daily working garb consisted of jeans, T-shirt, and trainers. Yet here they were dressed, to a man, in jacket and tie so as to comply with the club rules. Between them they wore a motley assortment of shirts, ties and jackets that mostly looked as though they had been picked up cheap at a church jumble sale somewhere. Even those who wore regimental ties had managed to team them up with lurid checked jackets or brightly coloured shirts that clashed horribly. They would have given any self-respecting fashion stylist apoplexy.

There were handshakes all round when they met up and a good deal of friendly banter but generally the atmosphere was serious. Professional.

The first-floor bar of the Special Forces Club had seen better days. The maroon carpet was threadbare in places and the cream-coloured walls could have done with a lick of paint. They were covered with picture frames containing a fascinating catalogue of British Special Forces' exploits over several generations – citations for bravery, sepia photographs of commandos in action, yellowing press cuttings detailing acts of heroism. One wall was dominated by a full-length oil painting of Queen Elizabeth, the Queen Mother, and on the opposite wall hung a dramatic painting of a night time parachute drop over France. The top of the bar itself was upholstered with quaint little olive-green faux leather cushions.

In the corner sat two elderly women chatting over a couple of glasses of wine. Their white hair was neatly permed. Their jewellery tasteful and their clothing expensive. Their handbags were placed on the floor alongside their chairs. They might have been a couple of dowager duchesses relaxing after a shopping trip to Harrods. But these were special ladies. A lifetime earlier, in the bleak days of the Second World War when they were just girls, they had both spent many hazardous months working under cover behind enemy lines displaying courage and self-sacrifice beyond imagination. Their nation owed them a debt of gratitude. They had more than earned their membership of the club.

As the men began to gather around a small table on the other side of the room the ladies ignored them. They had seen such gatherings before. The barman, too, stood back discreetly. He knew there would be no alcohol consumed. He provided bottles of water and went quietly about his business washing glasses.

Outwardly there was nothing remarkable about this meeting. But, had they known it was taking place, any journalist worth his salt would have given a month's wages to be a fly on the wall.

From time to time over the years newspapers had speculated on the existence of private armies in Britain – clandestine groupings of military men prepared to take armed action to right perceived wrongs which the government and the forces of law and order were unwilling or unable to tackle. Such stories usually emerged at times of national crisis and were quickly dismissed as the fanciful imaginings of unbalanced radicals.

Former British soldiers were known to work as mercenaries, paid to fight the battles of small-time dictators in third world countries, and several companies run by ex-army officers had been set up to supply specialist services of a military kind to foreign governments and multi-national corporations around the world.

But in recent years a persistent rumour had been circulating about a group called The Feathermen – a shadowy fraternity of retired special forces operatives acting as vigilantes against a gang of Middle Eastern assassins. Scepticism about the existence of such a group was widespread among the experts. A piece of far-fetched fiction, they surmised. Yet had they been able to eavesdrop on this gathering at the Special Forces Club they would have been astonished. For this was an operational briefing of The Feathermen in full session.

They were a band of brothers. Battle hardened. Unable to settle to careers in civilian life. They had all seen service in the world's hotspots from the Far East to Northern Ireland. When an Omani potentate put contracts on the heads of SAS soldiers he believed were responsible for the death of his son The Feathermen formed up to protect their comrades and deal with any death threats against them.

Actually "The Feathermen" was just a romantic title dreamed up by a former SAS officer who wanted to write a book about their activities without revealing too much. Within the ranks of the Special Forces they were known as "Group 13". They had initially gained a fearsome reputation as a specialist assassination unit but now the group had evolved into a do-anything-go-anywhere freelance outfit ready to undertake special missions which required speed, secrecy, and above all deniability.

A tall grey-haired man walked into the room carrying a briefcase. The men stood as one.

Kevin Donne was the first to speak. 'Good afternoon Colonel', he said.

'Good afternoon gentlemen' said James Sutherland.

'Good afternoon, sir', they all chorused.

'Please sit down chaps', said Sutherland as he opened his briefcase and handed a small folder containing photographs, maps, and an eight-page briefing sheet to each man.

'I can't tell you precisely when this job will take place', he said, 'because we do not yet have specific information on the movement of the principals. But I can tell you that the location is Paris and the target premises are the Ritz Hotel and associated buildings.

'We may see some action in the next few days but you will all need to be on the plot by next weekend at the latest.

'You will see from the photographs that there is more than one target individual', he went on, 'and it is not clear which one we will be focussing our attentions on when it comes to it. There is also more than one possible scenario so I need you to be familiar with all the likely eventualities before we move.

'Gordon will now take you through the details and allocate the logistics – vehicles, accommodation, equipment, weapons, egress and exit and so on'.

'Thank you, sir', said Gordon Frame. He was older than the others. In his late forties. A grizzled veteran. A former Major in the SAS. Decorated for bravery in Aden. He didn't smile.

He removed all the water glasses from the coffee table, spread out a floor plan of The Paris Ritz alongside an aerial photograph of the French capital's third airport, Le Bourget, and began to speak in a low monotone. He had the undivided attention of every man in the circle around him.

For the next three hours Gordon spoke. He referred frequently to the photographs. He drew pencil lines on the maps. He handed out addresses, railway tickets and car hire vouchers. He was interrupted occasionally when one or other of his colleagues raised their hand politely and asked a question.

While all this was going on various soberly dressed men and women entered the room, glanced towards the group and made straight for the bar where they studiously ignored the discussion behind them. They were familiar with this kind of gathering in their club and guessed it was a matter of the utmost confidentiality that was being planned.

Eventually, when Gordon had completed his briefing, James Sutherland asked if there were any questions. When none were forthcoming he stood to his feet and shook hands with all fifteen men in the group.

'Good luck, gents. I'll see you in Paris', he said as he gathered up his briefcase and left.

* * * * * *

Sardinia, August 27th 1997

From a distance the yacht looked like a piece of discarded flotsam carelessly tossed aside to spoil the surface of an otherwise perfect sea. But as they drew nearer it became a dazzling white object of beauty, its elegant lines and aristocratic bearing standing out majestically against the deep azure blue of the water.

It would have made a pretty picture on its own, but that was not the object of the exercise.

Inside the cramped cabin of the helicopter the engine noise was deafening. The pilot and his passenger both wore large headphones from which microphone mouthpieces extended on slender stalks around the front of their faces. Even with this facility the two men struggled to make themselves heard to one another.

The passenger tapped the pilot on the shoulder and pointed to the yacht far below. He yelled an instruction into his mouthpiece. The pilot nodded, gave a thumbs up sign, and banked the aircraft into a swooping dive.

The passenger picked up one of four cameras lying at his feet and trained the chunky-looking lens on the vessel. His profession was obvious. But this was no ordinary photographer.

Jean-Jacques Iversen was the best-known snapper in France and one of the leading paparazzi in the world.

A former paratrooper with a tough-guy image and a gung-ho attitude to go with it, the 53-year-old Vietnam veteran had a taste for the high-life and a love of fast cars, and smart women.

His international reputation had been built on two ultimately iconic photographs. One a picture of a Pepsi-Cola bottle on the Great Wall of China – the contrast between capitalism and communism captured in one image. And the other, Stavros Niarchos lying on his deathbed – for which he had paid a cleaner to smuggle a camera into the dying tycoon's bedroom.

He specialised in taking photographs of the rich and famous – film stars, politicians, and royalty – and often established a personal friendship with his subjects. In France his political influence was rumoured to be considerable. He had been the official photographer and confidante of Prime Minister Pierre Beregovoy until his sudden death four years earlier and was a motorcycling companion of socialist Premier Lionel Jospin.

For years Jean-Jacques Iversen had spent every August in St Tropez making a fortune out of photographing the beautiful people who flock to the French Riviera to while away their summers in an orgy of excess and opulence.

But this year was proving to be the most lucrative of all because the best known and, arguably, the best-loved woman in the world was in town. And, better yet, she had begun a brand-new love affair.

Iversen could not believe his luck when he discovered that Diana, Princess of Wales was bringing her two young sons, Princes William and Harry, to holiday at the St Tropez retreat of Mohamed Al Fayed, the multi-millionaire owner of Harrods. He was not the most favoured photographer of the British Royals, having once snatched a picture of the princes' nanny Tiggy Legge-Burke kissing Prince Charles on a skiing break in Klosters. But the now-divorced Diana was no longer protected by Royal bodyguards and even though he had several run-ins with Al Fayed's burly security men, Iversen's images of the princes and their mother disporting themselves on jet-skis and picnicking with the Fayed family were soon appearing in newspapers and magazines around the world.

Subsequent news that Diana had begun a serious romance with Al Fayed's handsome playboy son, Dodi, launched a media feeding frenzy with dozens of reporters and photographers converging on the South of France to capture the couple's every move for the inquisitive eyes of the world.

Once again Jean-Jacques Iversen was in the vanguard. This was his territory. He knew everyone from policemen to politicians, from maitre d'tables to millionaire gamblers. He had eyes and ears everywhere and was always one step ahead of the marauding press pack.

As the summer wore on and the love affair deepened the world's media became transfixed. The first pictures of a kiss were sold for millions of pounds. The relationship made headlines around the globe. And now, in a bid to win a few days of privacy, Diana and Dodi had set sail on board his father's luxury yacht The Jonikal.

For a while they were safe from prying eyes but even cruising off the Sardinian coast they were not safe from Jean-Jacques Iversen. It was typical of him that he should have used his contacts to track the progress of the yacht as it criss-crossed the Mediterranean and wholly characteristic that he should have been the only photographer to charter a helicopter to take pictures of what the press were calling 'Di's floating love-nest' from the air.

'Make one slow pass so that I can have a good look', he yelled into his mouthpiece. 'If there is anyone on the sundeck I need you to drop and hover. Okay?' The pilot nodded.

For the next half hour the little aircraft buzzed the yacht repeatedly. The pilot was later to describe the manoeuvres as being like an army exercise. 'It was as though we were plotting a military target', he told his friends. 'I don't know where this guy learned his trade but he was thorough. If it had been anything other than a private yacht I'm sure the air force would have been called out to see what we were up to'.

But for Iversen this was a potentially money-spinning assignment. He captured Dodi reading on a sun lounger. He caught Diana looking anxiously out from beneath an awning. He made a low pass and snapped the pair retreating below decks to avoid his unwelcome presence. He took pictures of the crew and bodyguards. He hovered over the sundeck and took close-ups of the food and drink the couple had been enjoying before he arrived out of a clear blue sky. And he even photographed the book Dodi had been reading in case it appealed to a diary editor on a newspaper somewhere. He would have liked more but his pictures would more than cover the cost of hiring the helicopter with a healthy profit to boot.

A cold smile crossed his face as the image of Diana peering up into his lens with a fearful expression in her eyes flashed through his mind. He recalled her oft-expressed fears for her own safety and her maudlin assertion that "one day I will go up in a helicopter and not come back".

'You are coming away in this helicopter with me', he said as he gestured for the pilot to return to base.

'*Au revoir, ma petit belle*', said Jean-Jacques Iversen with a hint of menace, 'I'll be seeing you again soon…very soon'.

Chapter Nineteen

Paris, 30th August 1997 (13.00 hours)

Henri Paul was elated. Today was a special day.

It had begun for him with a game of tennis at his local club and a couple of Coca Cola's in The Pelican bar near his home.

Now it was lunchtime and he was on duty behind the wheel of a large black Range Rover following a Mercedes 600 limousine as it weaved its way through the busy Saturday traffic. His colleague, Philippe Dorneau, the Ritz hotel's top chauffeur, was driving the car in front. They were in convoy heading to Le Bourget airport ten miles to the north of the city.

For Henri the day was special because he was going to meet the world's most famous woman and the man with whom she was in love - his boss. And if rumours whizzing around the corridors of the hotel were true they all might be celebrating an engagement before the weekend was out.

As acting head of security for one of the world's most prestigious hotels, Henri felt a sense of pride. He had met Diana, Princess of Wales, on several occasions because she was a frequent guest at the Ritz. Just five weeks earlier he had helped maintain a cloak of secrecy when she spent a clandestine weekend with her new lover in the hotel.

Now the secret was out. The boss with whom he had always had a special rapport, Dodi Fayed, son of the hotel's owner Mohamed Al Fayed, was in love with Princess Diana and the couple were on their way to Paris for an overnight stay at the end of their romantic Sardinian holiday.

Henri puffed out his chest and smiled to himself. Just then he noticed something in his wing mirror. A leather-clad motorcyclist with a black visor was zigzagging through the traffic behind him evidently trying to keep up. He checked the rear-view mirror. There were two more motorcycles both with male pillion passengers tucked close in behind the Range Rover. His heart sank. The paparazzi were on the case. His boss would be furious.

The private jet touched down just after three o'clock and taxied to a stand near the Transair terminal building which, by now, was over-run by photographers. Henri and Philippe drove their vehicles over to where the plane was parked and arrived just as the portable steps were being placed against the side of the aircraft.

One of the Fayed family bodyguards, Trevor Rees-Jones, was first down the steps followed by Diana who greeted Henri quite effusively. She was girlishly happy. It made the little Frenchman blush. Dodi, too, was in high spirits and shook hands warmly.

The party was just about to depart when a senior French policeman arrived and suggested that the *Service de Protection des Haute Personnalites* – a trained unit whose job is to move foreign dignitaries around Paris – should provide a car and escort to ensure the couple's safety and security. To Henri's delight Dodi refused the offer point blank, insisting that the security resources of The Ritz Hotel were more than adequate for such a task.

Dodi and Diana got into the Mercedes along with Rees-Jones. The other bodyguard, along with Dodi's masseuse, housekeeper and butler joined Henri in the Range Rover.

And so the cortege set off with an army of paparazzi photographers in hot pursuit. Before very long clusters of motorcycles and cars were buzzing around the Mercedes like bees around a honey pot. They found it difficult to take pictures through the darkened windows but it didn't stop them trying.

Alongside Henri Paul, the second bodyguard, Kes Wingfield, was talking constantly on a mobile phone to his colleague, Rees-Jones, in the lead car. Both men were concerned for the safety of the Mercedes in case one of the paparazzi vehicles got too close and caused an accident.

Henri eased the Range Rover forward and closed up to within inches of the Mercedes rear bumper. He was not a regular chauffeur but had been on an anti-terrorism defensive driving course run by the Mercedes car company. He was also a trained pilot and had confidence in his own ability to handle a big car at speed in tight situations. His girlfriend often complained that his confidence as a macho driver was misplaced but he ignored her. This was a situation made for him. He cursed the marauding paparazzi motorcycles loudly for the benefit of his passengers but inwardly he was purring with satisfaction.

By the time they reached the centre of Paris the bodyguards had agreed between themselves that the two vehicles would separate. Henri peeled away and headed for Dodi's luxury apartment in the Rue Arsene-Houssaye off the Champs Elysee to deposit the luggage and the domestic staff. The Mercedes made for the Villa Windsor in the Bois de Boulogne – the former home of the exiled Duke and Duchess of Windsor which had been restored by Dodi's father and was now leased by him from the French government. Dodi was going to show his girlfriend around the house in the hope that he could persuade her to marry him and set up home together in the villa.

By the time their tour was over Henri Paul had joined them and once again drove the Range Rover behind the Mercedes as the happy couple made their way to The Ritz. It was four thirty in the afternoon.

For the next two-and-a-half hours, while Diana and Dodi relaxed in the splendour of the Imperial Suite, Henri Paul went about his routine business. The antecedents of new guests had to be checked. The credit-worthiness of others had to be established. There was footage from the hotel's myriad CCTV cameras to be viewed and tapes of dubious telephone calls passing through the switchboard to be listened to. He also had to do his rounds, making sure that everything was in order from a security and fire safety point of view and listening to the various concerns of staff.

Just before seven he learned that Philippe Dorneau was about to take his boss and the Princess to Dodi's apartment. The party were going to leave by the rear entrance in the Rue Cambon in order to avoid the press pack massed in front of the hotel in the Place Vendome. He went to the door and saw them off.

Henri's tour of duty was over for the day and he had nothing planned for the evening. He was about to head for the bar to relax over a drink when his mobile phone warbled. It was an incoming text message.

He looked at the screen. It bore the single word "Queze". Henri flinched. It was a code word. He double-checked that he had not misread the word. He knew it meant an end to the quiet evening he had hoped to enjoy.

He flipped open his mobile phone once more and ran through the phonebook looking for a stored number. He knew he should not have stored the number in the first place. He should have committed it to memory. He just hoped that he had not deleted it, as he should have. He sighed with relief. The number was still there. He dialled the number. When it was answered he said nothing. Just listened.

After a moment he simply said, 'Oui. D'accord', and flipped the phone closed.

* * * * * *

Paris, 30th August 1997, (19.00 hours)

Henri Paul was troubled. He had recognised the codeword in his text message instantly but it was one which had not been used for some considerable time.

It meant "Contact. Urgent" but it was not the code used by his regular handler.

It was a trigger word given to him by his previous contact – a man he had not seen or heard from for more than three years.

At the time he had been told nothing about the change of handler. He just assumed the first man had moved up the DST chain of command.

The contact telephone number was the same, though. And the voice. He knew the voice the moment he heard it. But the meeting point was new.

In the past the man he had known only as David always wanted to meet in Harry's Bar. Now he wanted to meet some distance away. More discreetly. In Montmartre.

Henri considered his options. His car was at home. He had left it there when he came to work this morning knowing that he might spend most of the day driving his boss's Range Rover. He checked his watch. Twenty minutes to the agreed meeting time. He could afford to be a little late but he would never make it by public transport. Better take a taxi.

He turned to make towards his usual exit at the rear of the hotel. Then a moment of vanity overtook him. There was still a large crowd of onlookers and photographers gathered at the front of The Ritz hoping for a glimpse of Princess Diana. He must have been seen leading Diana's security detail earlier. Perhaps, if he left by the front entrance, he would be recognised. His very public departure might confuse the waiting paparazzi. They had just missed Dodi and Diana leaving from the rear of the hotel. Perhaps he could act as a decoy.

He pulled himself up to his full height and strode through the revolving doors out into the Place Vendome. He paused and looked around as he had often seen celebrities do when they expected to be photographed. It was his moment to bask in the reflected glory of his association with Diana. There was nothing. No cameras clicked. No one called out to him. No one even looked in his direction.

He glanced towards the gaggle of photographers gathered at the front of the crowd. He remembered several of their faces from earlier in the day. From the airport and the crazy drive back into the city. He recognised most of them. They often harassed his guests as they left The Ritz. He realised that he could not put a name to any of the faces. Except, of course, Jean-Jacques Iversen. He was famous. The celebrity photographer. Friend of princes and prime ministers. There he was. Bald and belligerent. Camera at the ready. He, too, ignored the little security man as he pushed his way through the throng.

On the edge of the crowd two casually dressed young men looked at one another. One, wearing a baseball cap, nodded curtly at the other. His companion acknowledged the gesture and turned to watch Henri Paul make off up the Rue de la Paix in search of a taxi.

Henri told the taxi driver where he was going but deliberately gave an address two blocks away from the place where he had agreed to meet his contact. He took a schoolboy pleasure in his work for the security services. He knew it was low-grade stuff. It was not real espionage. But he liked to pretend, at least to himself, that he was a spy. And so he behaved in the way spies behaved in the movies.

When they arrived in Montmartre he paid off the taxi and crossed the street so that he would be approaching the Bistro L'Epicurien from the other side of the road and could walk straight past if he spotted anything suspicious or anyone looking at him in a strange way. He made two passes up and down the street before crossing over and entering the café.

Bistro L'Epicurien was on a corner. Pierre Charron was sitting at a table with his back to the wall where he could not only see the door but also both streets through the large picture windows on each side of the entrance. He had a large milky coffee on the table in front of him and an unopened copy of Paris Match.

Henri knew this was not going to be a brush contact in the usual sense because it was clear that he was there to be briefed but he realised the magazine was there for a purpose – a purpose he had come across before. He ordered a pastis and walked over to the table. 'Bon soir, David', he said.

Charron replied: 'Bon soir', and immediately got down to business. He looked anxious. Stressed. Henri did not remember seeing that expression before.

'This man is staying in your hotel', he said, placing his hand palm downwards on the magazine in front of him. 'He arrived yesterday. You may know him. He is a regular.

'He will have a meeting with someone this evening. Within the next three to four hours. I need to know exactly whom he meets. It is very important. It is likely that you will know the person he meets. It may be a public figure.

'Tomorrow I will need a still from the security footage to confirm the identity. I will contact you. I will also need a copy tape of their conversation. I will arrange my own transcript. Hopefully the sound quality will be better than the last time'.

He paused and looked at Henri's face to make sure he was being understood.

'This matter is vitally important', he went on. 'You must inform me as soon as contact is established. Immediately. Do you understand?'

Henri nodded.

'The word remains the same but the number is different. Page 125. Yes?'

Again Henri nodded.

Charron tapped the magazine.

'You will find that your requirements are fully met. Bon chance', he said. Standing he drained his coffee and left.

Henri leaned forward so that his elbows were resting on the copy of Paris Match. He took his time to complete his drink then picked up the magazine and walked out into the street.

It took him a while to find a taxi. When he did, he ordered it to take him home.

It had been an exciting day and he was off duty. He was not going back to the hotel now. Not for David. Not for anyone. He could catch up with the mystery resident and his mystery guest tomorrow. He would get what was wanted without too much trouble. What could be so important about the meeting anyway?

He opened the magazine. A large buff envelope was tucked inside. The envelope contained a large black and white photograph and a smaller, bulkier, envelope.

Henri took the picture out of the envelope. A handsome Arab-looking man stared out at him. He knew the face. He'd seen the man around the hotel. He turned the picture over. The words "Balaam Abu Shafiq" were printed in pencil.

He tore open the smaller envelope and took out a wad of bank notes. They were dollar bills. He did not bother to count them but at a quick estimate he reckoned there could be more than a couple of thousand dollars there. This was going to be a good night after all. Perhaps he should pay more attention to Mr Abu Shafiq than he had at first intended.

He opened the Paris Match and turned to page 125. In the margin on the top of the page what looked like a mobile telephone number had been written in a very precise hand. Henri tore the corner off the page and put it in the breast pocket of his jacket.

He sat back in the taxi and allowed himself a smile of satisfaction.

At that moment his mobile telephone trilled. Another short conversation. Another rendezvous arranged for later.

Perhaps this was going to be an interesting evening after all. And lucrative.

* * * * * *

Paris, 30th August 1997, (21.00 hours)

Kevin Donne was restless.

It was not that he could not stand still in one place for hours on end. Sentry duty in the army had taught him that.

It was not that he could not concentrate on one surveillance subject for hours on end, either. There had been times when he had kept the sights of his rifle trained on one house or one person for a whole night.

He had undertaken missions of this kind in all weathers and in all kinds of terrain and in all parts of the world.

Kevin was irritated that he had heard nothing – no messages, no information, and no instructions – for more than three hours.

A tiny radio receiver no bigger than a button was squeezed into his left ear. It was not immediately obvious to the casual observer. But up close it looked like a sophisticated hearing aid. Under his shirt an equally tiny microphone was attached to his chest with a sucker directly beneath his mouth and close to his voice box. It was voice activated. A thin wire led from the microphone to a battery pack in his pocket.

He could hear other members of the team talking to one another, in the truncated verbal shorthand used by military men the world over, as they carried out various tasks in different parts of the city. Some were beyond the range of his receiver but mostly his colleagues were operating within a mile of his location. He was at a key observation point in the whole plan yet he seemed to have been forgotten.

Kevin's impatience was growing by the minute.

Group 13 had been in Paris for more than forty-eight hours. They came in ones and twos. Some on the Eurostar train from Waterloo Station in London. Some by car on the shuttle, which ran through the tunnel under the English Channel between Folkestone and Calais.

Kevin and his partner Danny McCormick had used this route but travelled on a powerful motorbike, taking turns to ride pillion.

Every man in the team was using a British passport – false of course – but, travelling from one European Community country to another, none of them had been asked to show their identity documents. All their vehicles had been hired from different companies in England and paid for in cash. The only paperwork showed the phoney driving licence details and untraceable addresses of the drivers. They had all been billeted, in pairs, in small, cheap pensions located in several of the more run-down parts of the city.

The team's leader and quartermaster, Gordon Frame, had arrived a few days before his colleagues and busied himself acquiring vehicles and weapons.

Once the whole team was assembled there were routes to be reconnoitred and several alternative scenarios of the 'hit' to be rehearsed.

Now it was watch and wait time.

Danny and Kevin were on lookout duty in the splendid Place Vendome facing the front entrance of The Ritz hotel. They had been there since early afternoon.

They had witnessed, and reported, the comings and goings of several important players in the main plot, which the team had rehearsed – including the principal target. Two hours earlier they had seen the hotel's head of security leave on foot and, so far, not return.

Elsewhere they could hear a shifting pattern of events as the team constantly moved from one location to another at short notice, prompted by an anonymous informant referred to in radio transmission simply as 'Zulu Kilo'. They both knew that 'Zulu Kilo' was Group 13's agreed codename for a former SAS soldier who now worked on the personal security detail of the Ritz Hotel's owner, Mohamed Al Fayed.

During the afternoon and evening a large crowd had built up outside the hotel. They mostly seemed to be tourists and passersby hoping to catch a glimpse of the celebrities coming and going from the hotel. There was also a hard-core of press photographers who had been there almost as long as Kevin and Danny.

The two men stood on the outer edge of the milling crowd where they could observe everything without getting caught up in the throng. They knew why the press photographers were there but ignored them. Neither man spoke to the other because to do so would open the voice channel on their microphones and broadcast their words into the earpieces of their colleagues elsewhere. They were trained soldiers not given to idle chatter when on duty.

But the inactivity and the silence was getting to Kevin. Even on the longest and loneliest stakeouts he'd experienced in the past the boredom was alleviated by fairly constant radio chatter.

Eventually he could stand it no longer.

'Eagle, Eagle receiving? Over', he said. Danny shot him a quizzical glance.

Gordon Frame's voice came back. 'Go ahead', he said.

'Target Alpha remains in the premises', said Kevin. 'No movement'.

'Received', came the curt reply. This was not going to be easy for Kevin.

'Anything on the security guy?', he asked.

'Stand by', said Gordon. After a few seconds he added: 'We've got him on obbo'.

Silence.

Well I didn't achieve much there, thought Kevin. *The hotel security man is under observation, one of our principal targets is not moving from the hotel and still there is no action. What about the other players?*

Suddenly a mood of excitement and anticipation began to run through the crowd. The photographers picked up their cameras and started to jostle one another.

'Eagle, Eagle receiving? Over', repeated Kevin.

Gordon's voice was deadpan. 'Go ahead'.

'Vehicles approaching', said Kevin. 'Stand by.......'

It was her. He knew it was going to be her. There she was. Getting out of the car. White slacks, black jacket, black top with a flatteringly scooped neckline. He froze the image in his mind. She looked fantastic. As always. He wanted to speak to her. Receive her special smile. The one he knew she reserved for him alone. He took a step towards the throng of photographers. He had the muscle to force his way through to her.

He felt a tug on his sleeve. He turned. Danny was looking at him with a concerned expression. Kevin rolled his shoulders and stretched his neck as though the move he had just made was an attempt to relieve cramp. *What was happening to him? He was an experienced, disciplined soldier on an operation. These feelings he had for this woman were irrational. Childish. It had to stop. He loved her but he knew his duty. He had a job to do.*

'Eagle, Eagle. Papa Delta housed. Action status remains amber', he said. 'I repeat, Papa Delta is in the hotel. Code amber'.

'Roger', came the curt reply.

Danny turned away, looked at the sky, and whistled.

* * * * * *

275

Ritz Hotel, Paris, 30th August 1997, (22.00 hours)

Henri Paul arrived back at The Ritz just after ten o'clock.

The night security manager Francois Tendil who was struggling to cope with the growing crowds outside the hotel and the mounting anger of his boss, Dodi, whose plans for a romantic evening with his girlfriend had been thrown into chaos, had summoned him urgently.

The call suited Henri perfectly. He needed an excuse to return to work so that he could carry out Pierre Charron's assignment without arousing suspicion.

This time he brought his own car, a nippy little Mini, because he would need transport later. He parked it at the rear of the hotel. The only space he could find in the crowded street was tight so he took care to give himself the extra few inches for a fast getaway. He might need to move quickly.

He went straight to the reception desk. Leaning over the duty receptionist's shoulder he tapped in a name on the computerised guest register - Shafiq. Up it came on the screen. Suite 128.

'Any new arrivals this evening?', asked Henri casually.

'Just one, sir', replied the girl, 'English. A Mister, er, Sutherland'.

'Uh huh', said Henri. 'Where from?' He wasn't really interested.

'Business address in London', said the girl. She checked the registration card. 'Halcyon Security Agency'.

'Good', said Henri absently. 'Suite 128. Is he in?'

'His key is not here, sir', replied the receptionist.

'Alright, give him a call', said Henri. 'If he answers ask him if he will be dining in the hotel this evening'.

'It is a little late for him to be dining now, sir', said the girl.

'I know that', snapped Henri. 'I just want to know if he is in his room or not. Make up some excuse about the restaurant being full and wanting to give priority to hotel guests for any late dining reservations.

'I just need to know if he is in his room or not. Page me with the result'.

He strode off and made straight for the security control room in the basement. It was his base. His environment. He felt comfortable there. Cocooned.

The uniformed security officer on duty looked up at the hiss of the electronic door opening.

'Anything'?, asked Henri. 'No', replied the man, and went back to watching the CCTV screens in front of him.

Henri ran his eye over the bank of screens. He could see a man pacing the corridor outside the Imperial Suite. It was Trevor Rees-Jones on guard.

The scene in the Place Vendome hadn't changed much in the past three hours. The photographers and the tourists were still there in large numbers – if anything larger numbers. Two men at the back of the crowd caught his attention momentarily. One was wearing a baseball cap. They seemed familiar for some reason. Henri could not put his finger on it.

He moved to the other end of the room and sat down at a large console, adjusting his position in front of the keyboard. The computer screen before him was filled with a screensaver, which bore the familiar starburst motif adorning the wrought iron balustrades over the entrance to the hotel.

He clicked the mouse once and the screen cleared, leaving a simple frame containing a number of empty boxes. In a box marked 'Suite' he entered the number 128 and hit the return key. The legend asked 'Extension link. Y/N'. Henri typed the letter 'Y' and again hit return.

An intercept link between the hotel switchboard and the telephone in Suite 128 was now set up. It was a facility which was available for the security department to use in rare cases of extreme emergency. Henri Paul knew that he was exceeding his brief and should not be taking such action without higher authority but, nonetheless, he switched on the voice activator, which would automatically start a recording as soon as a call was made to or from Abu Shafiq's room.

'Let me know immediately if there are any calls on that line', he said to the security officer, pointing to the illuminated light on the console, and left the room.

Since beginning to work for "David", Henri Paul had made one other personal decision to break with the hotel management's strict privacy guidelines. In each one of the bars he had secretly hidden a small voice-activated Dictaphone beneath one of the tables. The bar staff were unaware that the devices were there but whenever Henri wanted to record a specific conversation he would instruct the bar staff to seat his targets at the tables he knew were bugged. Every few days he would check and rewind the tiny tapes. Once a cleaner had found one of the recorders but the person she reported the matter to was…Henri Paul.

Back at reception Henri once again checked the guest register. Balaam Abu Shafiq had been in residence for thirty-six hours.

He scratched his head. How did his handler know that Shafiq was due to meet someone this evening without having access to the usual services, which he himself provided? And there

278

was another question nagging at the back of his head. How did his other contact, the one who had called him in the taxi, also appear to know about this particular guest's plans?

He shrugged and began a quick tour of the reception, concierge, and front door staff. To each he addressed the same question. 'Do you know Mr Shafiq?' The Ritz staff prided themselves on knowing every regular guest by sight and by name. Shafiq was a frequent guest so Henri received an affirmative answer in every case.

'If he comes down from his room I need to know immediately where he goes', was his instruction to everyone. 'If anyone comes in and asks for him, direct them to the Hemmingway Bar, and advise Mr Shafiq that his visitor is there. If he leaves the hotel ask him where he wants to go and get him a taxi. Then let me know'.

In the bars he gave similar instructions, telling the barmen and waiters which specific tables he wanted Shafiq and his visitor to be seated at.

That done he made his way to the Vendome Bar and ordered himself another pastis. He might be in for a long wait. Dodi's bodyguard Kes Wingfield joined him. He was taking it in turns with Trevor Rees-Jones to stand guard outside the Imperial Suite.

The boss was in a foul mood, reported Wingfield. He'd had plans to entertain Diana at Chez Benoit, one of her favourite restaurants, but had cancelled when he heard the place was under siege by press photographers and had diverted to The Ritz. The clamour outside the hotel as they entered had alarmed Diana and done nothing to lighten Dodi's spirits. And the last straw had come when the couple were driven from the hotel's Espadon Restaurant by gawping diners and had taken refuge in the Imperial Suite where they were now dining alone. Best they be left alone for the time being.

Henri checked his watch. Eleven fifteen. Balaam Abu Shafiq's meeting was going to be very late or perhaps David's information had been wrong. He needed to find out soon because he had an important assignation of his own after midnight and this contact would be expecting the same intelligence as David – for which he, too, would pay handsomely.

Once more Henri did the rounds of the staff. Had Mr Shafiq met anyone in the hotel in the three hours he himself had been missing, he wanted to know. They all answered in the negative.

His pager buzzed. He went to the nearest house phone and connected to the security control room. The phone in Suite 128 was active.

By the time he reached the basement the call had been completed and disconnected. But, re-winding the tape and listening to it, Henri discovered that Shafiq had been talking to a private aviation company based at Le Bourget airport. From the tone of the conversation it was clear that the businessman was a regular customer. A sudden change of plan meant that he must attend an urgent meeting in Corsica the following morning. He would need an executive jet to take him there first thing. He needed to leave at six. The charter company assured him that his requirements would be met. They would file a flight plan immediately.

While Henri Paul was listening to this conversation the telephone in Suite 128 was picked up again. Mr Shafiq was asking for an alarm call at five o'clock and a taxi to collect him at five thirty.

Henri was relieved. There would be no meeting at The Ritz that evening. But David would have to be informed at once about Shafiq's new plans. Clearly whoever he had been due to meet that evening was now in Corsica.

He felt in his breast pocket for the piece of paper bearing David's new mobile telephone number. It wasn't there. Damn. He'd changed jackets while he was at home earlier and left the number behind. He flicked open his mobile phone and scrolled through the address book. Nothing for it. He'd have to use the old number.

He dialled. The phone rang for a long time before he heard the voice of his former handler. 'Oui', he said. He was breathless as though he had been running.

Henri identified himself. The voice at the other end was furious. 'I gave you another number', he screamed. 'Why did you call me on this number? You shouldn't have used this phone'.

Henri apologised and explained the situation. He just managed to blurt out the new information about Shafiq's travel plans before Pierre Charron cut him dead.

'Listen', he said with a note of panic in his voice, 'this is a serious matter, a matter of life and death. My life is in danger and yours may be too if this call is being monitored. Destroy the other number and never use this number again. Now get off the line'. The phone went dead.

Henri was confused. He did not know what to make of the situation. He knew the man he had just been speaking to – the man he knew as David – was a senior agent in the DST. He was no fool. He sounded serious. He sounded genuinely scared. What on earth had Henri got himself mixed up in?

His thoughts turned to his other handler – the one who would be waiting for him in a club in the Pigalle in just over an hour. He, too, had made it clear that the identity of Balaam Abu Shafiq's mystery contact was of vital importance to the security interests of his country. He would have to be told of the new arrangements.

But how? He was not contactable by phone and while Dodi and Diana remained under siege at The Ritz their safety and security was Henri Paul's responsibility. He could not leave.

Gradually an idea took shape.

Henri knew that his boss had intended that he and Diana should spend the night at his own apartment. It was his home. It had a more relaxed feel to it than the opulent grandeur of the Imperial Suite. Henri had spoken to the housekeeper earlier and he knew that Dodi planned to end the evening with a champagne nightcap for his lover.

If he could persuade the couple to fulfil that plan he would still be able to make his appointment after he had dropped them off. The only problem was the pack of paparazzi, which had terrified Diana and forced Dodi to take refuge at the hotel.

Henri checked his watch again. Eleven forty-five. If he was going to act he must act now.

He picked up the house phone and asked to be connected to the Imperial Suite. When Dodi answered he apologised profusely for the intrusion and expressed the hope that dinner had been satisfactory. He knew his boss liked him and he traded on that relationship. He said that he had a suggestion which he hoped might help make amends for the disappointment of Dodi's ruined dinner plans and asked if his employer might spare him a few moments to explain in person. Dodi agreed and invited him up to the suite.

A few moments later Henri Paul knocked politely at the door of the Imperial Suite and was admitted to the lobby.

'Forgive me, sir', he said. 'I know that you are comfortable here right now but I understand that you had intended to spend the night at Rue Arsene-Houssaye?'

Dodi nodded.

'Well, since all your luggage is there and the room has been prepared and the drinks are ready to be served I'm sure the Princess would feel more relaxed if we arranged for you to go there'.

His boss seemed about to interject when he went on: 'You left by the Rue Cambon entrance earlier, sir, and were able to avoid the photographers at the front. I thought, if we sent Phillipe and Trevor and Kez to the front with the two cars the press would think you were about to leave from there. Then I could take you quietly from the back in another car. We have a spare vehicle downstairs in the garage'.

He paused and held his breath. To his enormous relief Dodi was delighted with the idea - gripping him warmly by the shoulders and giving orders that the decoy plan was to be put into effect immediately.

Downstairs the bodyguards were very unhappy. They did not want to run the gauntlet of the paparazzi again that night and much preferred to have their charges safely tucked up inside the hotel where they could keep an eye on them. But Dodi's decision was final. The only concession was that Trevor Rees-Jones would ride shotgun with the couple in Henri's car.

And so, at five past midnight, Henri Paul pulled the hotel's spare Mercedes limousine away from the kerb at the back of The Ritz. Trevor Rees-Jones sat primly wearing his seat-belt beside him and in the rear the two lovers giggled and held hands like teenagers on a first date. There were no photographers to be seen. Henri looked at his watch and smiled. He was going to make his appointment in plenty of time.

At the bottom of the Rue Cambon he turned right into the Rue de Rivoli. Traffic was light for a Saturday evening. Ahead of him the traffic lights at the Rue Royale had just turned red. He slowed and looked in his rear view mirror. Several motorcycles were approaching fast. The decoy plan had failed. The press were on to them. *No matter*, thought Henri.

He could easily out run them if he needed to. At least he was out of the hotel. He would soon be off duty and on his way to meet his handler.

By now the car was hemmed in by motorcycles – a popping, buzzing, revving, whining, throng. Henri glanced across at them. The same familiar faces were still there. It had been a long tiring day. Didn't these guys ever give up and go home?

One of the riders seemed taller than the rest. His bike looked more powerful than the rest and his light grey leathers gave him a sinister appearance. Unlike most of the others in the pack he kept the visor on his helmet down. The darkened glass masked his features but a street light beyond him picked out his profile in silhouette.

It seemed vaguely familiar to Henri – the Roman nose was large and distinctive – but he couldn't quite place it. The man turned his head lazily towards the Mercedes, apparently confident that his identity was secure. But, just as he did so, one of the paparazzi fired a flashgun at the occupants of the car. Momentarily the stranger's face was illuminated through his visor.

Instantly Henri Paul recognised him. He had met the man some years earlier while undertaking a particularly tricky surveillance job for "David". He was a DST agent. And a nasty one. At the time he had pushed Henri to the limit in pursuit of the information he wanted. His whole persona was aggressive and Henri remembered thinking at the time that if the rumours about spies being trained killers were true then this man was just the sort to be a paid assassin.

Henri's mind was racing. *What was this man doing trailing him at this time of night on a motorbike? Why did he not want Henri to know he was there?* David's words came rushing back. ...matter of life and death...my life is in danger...yours may be too.

Panic seized him. The light was still red but he hit the accelerator and surged away from the junction. Left around the Place de la Concorde. The tyres squealing. He should have carried on round and driven up the Champs Elysee – the most direct route to Dodi's apartment – but his thoughts were in turmoil. He had to get away.

He turned right on to the Seine Expressway at the Cours la Reine. That road would be relatively clear after midnight. The carriageway was straight ahead of him. Henri gunned the engine and let the throttle full out. He saw the lights of the motorbikes begin to recede behind him. He could swing right at the Rue Francois 1er and take the back route to the Rue Arsene-Houssaye. With any luck he would have opened up enough space so that the chasing pack would not see him leave the main drag.

As he approached the exit at speed he cursed under his breath. A motorcyclist sat astride his machine in the middle of the carriageway effectively blocking the road. He would have to carry on to the Chaillot Palace at the Place de Trocadero and double back.

The car rocked a little as the road swung down into the tunnel under the Pont Alexandre and the Pont des Invalides. He was going too fast but he had to get away. He could handle it.

Up again on to the straight. Only one light behind him now. He wasn't thinking straight. It must be the assassin. He knew it.

The motorbike drew alongside. His breathing had stopped. He was suffocating. The bike was past him. Two people on it. Pulling away. Danger averted – for now.

A big swing left. The car was airborne over a hump in the road then plunging down into the Pont d'Alma tunnel. Suddenly there was a car in front of him. A white car. A small car. A slow car. Too late to brake.

Henri twitched the wheel to the left. He was going to miss the car on the outside. Just. There was a metallic crunch. He had clipped the rear of the other car. A blinding flash directly in front of him. Now he was fighting for control. He swerved to the right. He was standing on the brakes. Nothing. Then the spin. Now he was skidding. The steering was not responding. Neither right nor left. He spun the wheel. Futile. He saw the pillar coming up. He braced himself.

He was going to crash......

Chapter Twenty

Champs Elysee, Paris, 30th August 1997, midnight

Maurice de Champvieux allowed himself an indulgent smirk.

The ruse had worked to perfection.

Someone inside his own organisation had been a very naughty boy. Now he knew who that someone was. And the punishment would be severe. Terminal in fact.

He'd had his suspicions for weeks but confirmation had come within the past hour through a piece of simple trickery. A red herring skilfully drawn across the path of the culprit.

No need to rush. Wait and see if the bad boy was acting alone or in concert with others. Then move in for the kill.

The stakes were high. The good name and deserved place in history of his lifelong friend and mentor, the late President Mitterrand, was under threat. Worse. The secret cabal, which had profited from clandestine dealings with the Iraqi tyrant Saddam Hussein, and was still doing so, was about to be exposed. His own part in the scandal would also emerge unless the whistleblower's mouth could be stopped.

One or two politicians had been making a nuisance of themselves of late. Worrying the subject like a dog with a bone. They seemed convinced that they were on to something. Demanding a police inquiry.

The noises they had been making for months suggested that they knew some of Mitterrand's closest allies were corrupt and just needed the evidence to nail the guilty parties. There were even rumours circulating in Paris that the former Prime

Minister Pierre Beregovoy had been murdered to stop him telling what he knew.

Some investigative journalists were hinting that a big political scandal was about to break but no one could crack it.

For Maurice de Champvieux all of this might have been shrugged off as meaningless tittle tattle but for the fact that it was true and the blame lay very close to home. It was clear to him that the campaigning politicians were being fed information straight from the files of the DST – his own intelligence.

For the first time in his long career in espionage he was facing a renegade agent. And that was dangerous.

As a matter of routine the DST kept tabs on Saddam's main armaments procurer whenever he was in France, which was frequently. Maurice, of course, knew all about who this man met, when and where and usually what was discussed. He turned a blind eye to most of the intelligence emerging from this surveillance and did what he could to destroy it or cover it up when it began to point towards the unpalatable truth.

To feed a false piece of information about this man and his French contacts into the internal intelligence gathering system was simple for de Champvieux. He had done it many times before. Once more and he knew he could flush the renegade out into the open. An anonymous tip, suggesting that Saddam's man was about to have a private meeting with a top official in the government, would be planted apparently innocently in the files. Surely such a juicy titbit would prove too tantalising for his bad boy not to react.

And so it was that a trace on his main suspect's mobile phone had yielded dividends. At eleven thirty-seven that very evening, listeners in the DST telephone intercept monitoring unit had overheard their own contact at The Ritz hotel – the head of security, Henri Paul – reporting that the fictional private meeting was not taking place.

Pierre Charron was the renegade.

Hearing the news he wanted to hear de Champvieux was quick to order further instructions. The Ritz was to be covered front and back. Henri Paul was to be followed wherever he went. He might lead them to Charron or he might lead them to another whistleblower. Maurice could not be sure that Pierre Charron was acting alone. He had to be sure.

Maurice was standing on the pavement outside his favourite nightclub, Le Queen, in the Champs Elysee. The noise inside would be too loud for him to conduct a telephone conversation and there was just one more thing he had to do before he immersed himself in the gyrating hedonistic world beyond the big black doors. He dialled a number and put the phone to his ear.

While it was ringing he blew a kiss to two scantily clad transvestites, as they tottered past on impossibly high heels, and wiggled his chubby fingers in an effeminate wave at a pretty young man in skin-tight leather hotpants and a pink Lurex singlet.

When the call was eventually picked up at the other end de Champvieux was brisk and businesslike. His instructions to The Decoy were simple. Take the first available flight in the morning to Corsica and await further instructions. The DST travel department would make all the arrangements as usual.

The Decoy assured him that would not be necessary and rang off.

Maurice slipped his mobile phone beneath his grey kaftan and turned towards the nightclub. In the distance he heard the wailing of sirens. The information about Balaam Abu Shafiq's plans to visit Corsica was news to him. That had not been part of his entrapment plan. Perhaps Charron would go there too. He could be eliminated much more easily on the island. But who was Saddam's man going to meet? He had to know. Surely no one in the cabal was acting behind his back.

'Denis, Denis', he heard his alter ego being hailed. A shaven-headed man with a diamond stud earring and a toothy grin was waving.

Maurice linked arms with him and instantly became Denis the Pornographer for the night.

If only he had known that he was the second caller to make contact with The Decoy that evening. Pierre Charron had already spoken to L'Appeau. And his instructions were much more explicit.

Funny. The Decoy had omitted to mention that.

* * * * * *

Montmartre, Paris, 31st August 1997, 1am

Le Sancerre on the Rue des Abbesses had been packed but now it was beginning to thin out a little.

It was a warm late summer evening. Authentic Paris nightlife was beginning to kick in. Most of the best people-watching tables on the terrace outside were still occupied. The dark wood interior was half full and had taken on a distinct late night cosiness.

Christopher cradled a whisky tumbler between the palms of both hands. As ever he was seated with his back to the wall and facing the entrance.

Meeting contacts in busy public places was a deliberate strategy of his. In his view the general hubbub in places like this made electronic spying virtually impossible and physical eavesdropping a hit-and–miss affair. Besides, if you were seen openly chatting to someone in public, you would not be drawing as much attention to yourselves as if you were found skulking away in some dark and dingy dive. A drink in Le Sancerre would look like an innocent meeting between two friends and could easily be passed off as such.

But where was his friend?

Christopher checked his watch for the third time. Henri Paul was late. Very late.

It was only a few hours since Pierre Charron had called him in an agitated state. He had bought an untraceable pay-as-you-go mobile phone and wanted Christopher to have the number. Saddam Hussein's chief security adviser was staying at The Ritz and was due to have an important meeting that very evening with a mystery contact, he said. Charron was convinced that this contact would prove to be the missing link between Iraq's hostile weapons programme and the top Frenchmen who were making money out of secretly re-arming Saddam. The shadowy group who would stop at nothing, not even murder, to cover up their corruption.

Christopher thought that Charron was paranoid. Nonetheless, if his opposite number was right, the British government would also be very interested to know what the French were getting up to behind the backs of the rest of the world.

He guessed that Charron would use Henri Paul to spy on the Ritz meeting. He also knew that Paul would not be able to resist the opportunity to double his money without having to double his effort.

So he had called the Ritz security man suggesting a meeting at Le Sancerre and offering a substantial payment for the identity of Balaam Abu Shafiq's mystery visitor. He set the appointment for forty-five minutes past midnight giving Paul plenty of time to finish off at the hotel, report to Pierre Charron and travel to the meeting point.

The thought of the Ritz brought to mind something that had been puzzling Christopher for several hours. He had always taken pride in his photographic memory. He never forgot a face. But as he got older he was finding it increasingly difficult to connect faces with times, places and, especially, names.

Some hours earlier, while sitting in his flat watching the early evening news, he had been startled by the sight of a face he recognised instantly but simply could not place. The news item concerned the arrival in Paris that day of Princess Diana and her latest boyfriend Dodi Fayed. Their presence in the city was causing quite a stir and the Canal+ TV cameras had captured the scenes outside the Ritz where large crowds were gathering hoping to glimpse the happy couple. While an American tourist was being interviewed the face of a man wearing a baseball cap swam briefly into view in the background. Instantly Christopher knew that he had met the man. But where? When?

He took another sip of whisky. Suddenly it came to him. Belfast. When? Eighty-two? Eighty-three? It didn't matter. Long time ago. The man was a squaddie. SAS. What was the job? It was one of his earliest assignments. That's right. The 'elimination' of the young IRA Commander. What was the squaddie's name? He'd heard it. They'd all been introduced during the briefing session at Lisburn barracks. Keith? Clive? Kevin? Kevin. *That's it*, thought Christopher. *But what the hell is he doing in Paris hanging around outside the Ritz?*

For the fourth time he checked his watch. It was twenty-five past one and the little Frenchman was nowhere to be seen.

Christopher pulled his mobile phone from his pocket and dialled Henri's number. He had the number because Paul was one of his paid informants. As the handler, he had not given Henri his number. He had to protect his own security.

The number rang out for fully three minutes before Christopher gave up. The bar would be closing soon.

He paid his bill and left.

Three miles away outside The Ritz all was quiet.

All the photographers had gone. The crowd of onlookers, which had been quite substantial earlier in the evening, had gradually drifted away. Only a handful of hardy celebrity-watchers remained. The Place Vendome, which had been a hubbub of noise and activity just two hours earlier, was largely deserted save for the occasional courting couple strolling past hand-in-hand at the end of some romantic Parisian summer interlude.

But Kevin Donne and Danny McCormick were still there.

There was a crackle in their earpieces. Both men simultaneously put their fingers to their left ears.

'All units, all units'. It was the voice of their team leader Gordon Frame once more.

'Stand down, repeat, stand down. Target Alpha remains in the hotel and he's not coming out tonight, by the looks of it.

'Report oh four thirty hours. Agreed Rendezvous point. Copy?'

One by one the Feathermen repeated the single word 'Copy'. There was weariness in their voices. They would get a maximum of two hours sleep.

Kevin and Danny were the last to respond. When they did so Frame came back with: 'I'm shutting down your observation point. I'll need you on the main plot. We'll pick up the target there. Do you read?'

Both men replied: 'Affirmative'.

'Where the fuck can we get a beer in Paris at this time of night? asked Danny as they turned away from the position they had not left for more than eleven hours.

Three hours later they were back on duty. Like the remainder of their colleagues they had not bothered to return to their accommodation. They had found a small bar in which to drink and pass the time. These were men accustomed to going without sleep.

Now they were lying together in the dark alongside the perimeter fence of Le Bourget airport adjacent to the area reserved for VIP arrivals and departures.

They were not alone. Spread out at intervals of about one hundred and fifty metres were three other two-man units each with a different vantage point.

To Kevin the area seemed a little busier than he would have anticipated at five o'clock on a Sunday morning. A Gulfstream executive jet appeared to be being prepared for departure. Through his night vision binoculars Kevin could see two men – the crew – checking instruments in the cockpit. As he watched several cars came and went and further away he could see two other aircraft with their navigation lights flashing as though they, too, were preparing for flight.

Next to him Danny fingered the M72 LAW rocket launcher which lay by his side in the grass. One of the other four units was also equipped with the same squat-barrelled American anti-tank weapon.

They had been briefed on a simple strategy.

Once they had identified which aircraft their target was going to use and once they knew he was safely on board, whichever of the two units had the clearest line of fire would unleash a rocket into the fully loaded fuel tanks. Nobody on board would survive the resultant fireball.

If, by some mischance, neither unit had a clear line of sight to the aircraft, the other two units carried shoulder-launched heat-seeking Stinger missiles which they would discharge once the jet was on the runway or actually airborne. The results would be equally catastrophic.

The only imponderable now was: which jet would he use?

'Target on plot, repeat, target on plot', came the radio message from the forward observation team. 'Moving in your direction'.

Kevin propped himself up on his elbows and adjusted the focus on his binoculars. Two floodlights came on unexpectedly, bathing the apron where the aircraft were parked in bright light. *How considerate*, thought Kevin. *That should make things much easier.*

'All units standby', it was the voice of Gordon Frame, almost whispering into their earpieces.

'Vehicles approaching', reported the observation team.

Kevin was suddenly aware of a familiar sound. He had been concentrating so hard that he had blotted out all noise except the radio messages. Now he heard the unmistakeable engine drone of a helicopter clattering overhead. Danny nudged him and pointed upwards. The aircraft was coming in to land.

As it descended they felt the downdraught but they were well outside the scope of its landing lights so their concealed position was not compromised.

The helicopter touched down no more than a hundred metres from their hiding place…completely obscuring their line of sight to the three executive jets they had been watching. The pilot switched off the engine and the rotor blades began freewheeling to a stop.

'Standby', came Frame's voice again, this time more urgently. And then: 'Wait one, wait one'.

A convoy of four vehicles came racing into view. At the front and rear of the column were squat grey police vans with flashing blue lights rotating wildly on their roofs. In between were two gleaming black cars – a Mercedes limousine and a Range Rover. They came to a halt in front of the helicopter.

'Oh shit', came Gordon Frame's voice, no longer attempting to whisper. 'Abort, abort, abort. All units abort. Copy?...'

Kevin took a closer look at the helicopter, which had so unexpectedly, and apparently innocently, terminated their operation.

It was a Sikorsky S-76. Kevin knew his aircraft. The bottom of the helicopter was painted olive green with two gold stripes running the length of the body from nose to tail rotor. The upper part of the cabin was white and just below the main rotor, in distinctive bold script, were two words also in olive green – "Air Harrods".

Huh, thought Kevin, *Mohamed Al Fayed is in town. I wonder what brings him here at this time of the morning?*

The telephone rang in James Sutherland's room at The Ritz. He was not asleep.

'Yes', he said.

It was Gordon Frame.

'Had to abort the operation, sir', he said, 'for reasons I will explain later.

'Target has decamped to the location as previously advised. Do you want us to re-base and proceed with option three?'

'No, no', said Sutherland. 'Too complicated. Shut down and pull out. We'll debrief in London. There will be another opportunity…very soon.

'Make sure the boys are looked after. Thank you, Gordon'.

Chapter Twenty-One

Figari, Corsica, 31ˢᵗ August 1997

Early morning sunlight streamed through the windows creating orange ovoid shapes which rolled languidly across the cabin ceiling as the aircraft turned towards the terminal building.

The Decoy was relaxed. As they landed he had spotted a Gulfstream private jet parked on the VIP apron and mentally ticked off the tail plane registration number against the briefing he'd been given a few hours earlier. So far, so good. His target was in town.

He pulled his shoulder bag down from the overhead locker and, when the aircraft door opened, was first down the steps and marching purposefully across the tarmac before the stewardess could wish him a pleasant stay and thank him for his custom.

It was still the holiday season in the Mediterranean and despite being the first flight out of Paris on a Sunday morning the plane had been uncomfortably full. The cramped arrival hall in Figari International airport was also bustling with people.

The Decoy had a heavy bag crammed with the tools of his trade, which he had checked in as hold luggage. He paused momentarily to study the overhead screens and then set off towards the carousel where his baggage would be deposited.

'Well, well, well. Fancy seeing you here'.

The voice was familiar. The Decoy turned.

The speaker was Martin Casson. A junior minister in the Finance Ministry, he was the rising star of French politics and had reputedly been a particular favourite with the late

President Mitterrand. He had once been unflatteringly lampooned in a newspaper cartoon, which poked fun at "Mitterrand's Boys" by depicting the President as a schoolmaster and Casson as the goody-goody pupil presenting him with an apple.

The volatile nature of the French electoral system, which saw power transferring rapidly from right to left and back again, had kept Casson from fulfilling his potential, however. But the recent general election had forced the conservative President Chirac to appoint a socialist prime minister in Lionel Jospin and he, in turn, had given Casson his chance to shine by appointing him a junior Finance Minister – a post in which he had served twice before.

An expensive pair of sunglasses was pushed back on to the top of the minister's head. He was casually dressed in jeans and a tangerine-coloured polo shirt that showed off his immaculate tan to perfection.

'Ah, Martin. Still on holiday I see', said The Decoy.

'Yes, just until tomorrow then back to work. It has been a lovely break with the family, though', replied Casson. 'But what brings you? I must say I'm surprised to see you here after the goings on in Paris'.

The Decoy feigned ignorance.

'What do you mean? What's been happening in Paris?'

The minister looked quizzically at him.

'Your favourite lady?', he asked. Then, after a silence, 'Diana? The Princess? She's dead'.

The Decoy smiled. 'You're kidding me', he chuckled.

'No, no. In a car crash in the Pont d'Alma tunnel last night,' said Casson. 'There's great symbolism there, don't you think,

299

because Al-Mah in Arabic means moon goddess and in Roman paganism the al-mahs served as maidens of Diana the lunar virgin'. He sounded nervous. He was rambling and he knew it.

With an exaggerated show of gravity he added: 'I'm amazed that you, of all people, shouldn't know because she was being chased by the paparazzi at the time'.

A frown spread across The Decoy's face. He appeared genuinely shocked. 'Oh my God this is terrible', he stammered. 'I must call the office. Excuse me'.

He dashed off towards a bank of telephones in the corner of the arrivals hall.

As he turned away the minister noticed a tiny blinking green light on the mobile telephone clipped to his belt but thought no more of it.

At the Hertz Car Hire desk the smiling assistant, Charles, greeted The Decoy like a long-lost friend.

'Bonjour Monsieur. I have something for you', he said. 'The guy you telephoned about? I think I have him'.

They had done business together before. There was a tacit understanding. Charles knew this particular client's needs only too well. He turned the customer contracts pad around and slid it across the counter.

The Decoy looked at the carbon copy facing him.

"Customer: Balaam Abu Sharif. Address in Corsica: Grand Hotel Miramar, Propriano".

The car allocated to this customer was a metallic silver Lexus LS400 sedan. Top of the range luxury. That would figure.

The Decoy memorized the license number and turned the pad back to face Charles. As he did so he placed a folded wad of 5,000 francs on the counter beneath his left palm and slid it towards the eager assistant.

'Your usual vehicle is ready, monsieur', said Charles. 'Bay E45. Here is the key'.

The Decoy was familiar with Figari airport. He had been here many times. He turned right out of the car park into the one-way system and followed the service road until it linked up with the D859 from Figari to the coast.

His first port of call was a tiny whitewashed church tucked away on the wooded slopes behind the exclusive resort of Saint-Julien. A single bell was tolling from the belfry as the car turned into a walled courtyard just behind it. One side of the yard comprised the outer wall of a squat stone-built building with green-painted iron grilles across the windows. The door, which was badly in need of a fresh coat of paint, stood ajar. The Decoy tapped lightly on it.

'Come on in, it's open', called a man's voice.

The Decoy entered.

A short, dark, passage led into a larger workshop area. He had been in this room several times but its chaotic state always amazed him.

The grimy, cobweb-festooned ceiling was cracked and pockmarked. A single, bare, light bulb, dangling from a dangerously frayed flex, illuminated a scene of apparent confusion. It seemed as though not one square inch of floor or wall space was unoccupied. A large workbench ran the full length of the longest wall. In one corner a jumble of electrical cables nestled against a cluster of power points. The cables in turn led to a regiment of strange-looking devices – some large, some small – which variously displayed illuminated dials, screens, or simply flashing lights. Mounted on the walls were several locked cabinets and a number of racks, which contained firearms, mostly rifles. There was a lathe and a bubbling coffee percolator but for the rest, the room was packed with tools of every description, boxes of ironmongery, paint tins, spools of cable and wire, and rolls of fabric.

'George'. said The Decoy as the two men embraced. That was all. Just the one word of salutation. This was a relationship based on few words.

George Kastrinakis was a wiry little fellow. He wore faded denim shorts and a grey T-shirt, which bore the legend "Chicago Bears" beneath a picture of a fearsome-looking grizzly. His feet were bare. He wore his spiky grey hair in an American college boy brush cut style. His skin was wrinkled with a texture somewhere between leather and parchment and his complexion was the pallid beige colour of someone who has spent a lifetime outdoors but is no longer exposed to the sun's rays. On his right forearm was a giveaway tattoo depicting a skull wearing a paratrooper's beret with the words 'Le Diable Marche Avec Nous' – The Devil marches with us. George was, or at least had been, a Legionnaire.

Now in his late seventies George ran a one-man freelance operation providing specialist services for a number of clients – some governmental, some inhabiting the twilight world at the fringes of legality – whose needs were out of the ordinary, urgent, and always clandestine.

He bent down and pulled a small blue canvas bag from beneath the workbench.

'You've used one of these before', he said to The Decoy. 'I assume you want the plug-in one not battery'.

The Decoy nodded.

Kastrinakis reached up and lifted a rifle from one of the wall-racks.

'I know you've seen this before, too', he said. 'Kalashnikov. AK-47. Probably best for the range you have in mind.' He fished in a drawer and pulled out a telescopic sight which he deftly fixed to its mounting with expert fingers.

The Decoy seemed almost reluctant. He frowned and opened his mouth to speak. Apparently thinking better of it he simply said, 'thank you'. Turning to leave he added, 'I'll return these later'.

'A moment', said George, rummaging in an army surplus holdall at his feet. 'Just in case', he said, slipping a Beretta pistol into The Decoy's pocket. 'The stack is up. Don't forget the safety catch if you need to use it'.

The drive to Propriano took three quarters of an hour but, when he reached the Grand Hotel Miramar, The Decoy knew his luck was in.

In the car park he spotted the silver Lexus sedan immediately and to his relief and delight noticed that there was a parking space right next to it. He drew in nose first so that his own door was next to his target vehicle and checked in the rearview mirror to see that he was not directly overlooked from the hotel building.

He put his hand inside the canvas bag that George Kastrinakis had given him and withdrew a black disc about the size of a small bathroom basin plug. The disc firmly in his right hand, he opened his car door and, muttering a curse, ostentatiously dropped his wallet on the ground allowing his credit cards to spill under the adjacent sedan. As he knelt to retrieve them he slid the disc under the doorsill of the Lexus and moved it around until its powerful magnet found a recess into which it would comfortably sit. With a tweak of his fingers The Decoy checked that the disc was firmly in place and could not easily be shifted. Then he stood up, dusted himself down, and strode towards the entrance of the hotel.

303

Once inside he asked the desk clerk for a list of tariffs and used the men's toilet so that a casual observer might assume he had a reason for parking in the car park. Then he left, drove out of the hotel grounds, and found a spot under a tree a hundred yards away where he could watch the car park entrance without drawing attention to himself.

Once more he began to delve inside George's canvas bag. He drew out a flat oblong about the size of a paperback book. On one side it had a small opaque screen like a computer "tablet" notebook beneath which was a set of buttons and lights. There were two small suction pads on the back of the box and a small rigid aerial protruded from one corner.

The Decoy attached the device to the car dashboard with the suckers and plugged it in to a short cable, which he then connected to the car's cigar lighter.

He punched one of the buttons and a green light appeared on the bottom row. The screen flickered and slowly lit up. The Decoy pressed another button and the screen filled with a series of mazy lines and disconnected squiggles. He swore under his breath and worked his way in sequence through the buttons with one hand as he bent and adjusted the aerial with the other. Suddenly the screen cleared and a crude diagrammatic map appeared. In the centre of the map a red light pulsed intermittently. He pressed another button and a high-pitched whine began. It was almost a whistling sound. He adjusted the volume to a bearable level.

The Decoy sighed and slumped back in his seat. Good. George's neat little tracker was working. Now it was just a question of waiting and The Decoy was good at that. Waiting was the staple diet of his profession.

The sun was just beginning to ease towards its westerly resting place before he saw any action. The whistling sound, which had merged into his subconscious as the hours passed, suddenly gave way to a beeping note. He glanced at the screen. The red light was moving. Almost imperceptibly, but it was moving. Each beep coincided with a pulse of the light.

From his semi-prone position with the seat tilted back he could just see between the top of the dashboard and the steering wheel. The Lexus pulled out of the hotel car park and turned away from him. There was one man behind the wheel, alone in the car. He looked at his watch. It was ten past five in the afternoon.

The Decoy counted to ten, then started his engine and set off in the direction which the red light was taking across the primitive little map on his dashboard.

They were heading out of town.

From time to time he spotted the Lexus in the distance but there was no need to follow too closely. The crude little tracker was working perfectly well.

First it was the D19a through the village of Santa Julia. Then, at the roundabout, on to the motorway N196 heading south the way he had come from Bonifacio. They passed the turn-off to Campomoro but just beyond the town of Sartene the Lexus took a right on to a minor road, which hit a sharp hairpin bend almost immediately. The Decoy eased up as they began to climb through rugged, rocky, terrain for fear of catching his quarry too soon. He was watching for road signs. Abu Shafiq could not possibly know this remote part of Corsica so he must be following detailed instructions, he reasoned.

On and on they drove. Past the turning for Foce di Bilia. Heading for Bergerie. Branching right towards Tizzano. Passing a disused quarry roughly hewn from the unforgiving rock face. All the while the beeping sound accompanied the pulsing red light as it traversed the map on the screen.

They branched right towards somewhere called Tivia. Looking at the horizon between the folds in the mountains, The Decoy could tell that they were heading towards the sea.

He saw it as they descended through a lushly forested valley. There was a fork in the road. He went left. He glanced at the screen. The red light had left the road.

The Decoy hit the brakes. He had noticed a track branching off the road about half-a-mile back. He turned round and retraced his route until he reached the track and turned on to it. The red light still flashed and the beeping sound continued. After about ten minutes the beeping suddenly returned to the single high-pitched tone and the red light stopped moving across the surface of the screen.

The Lexus had stopped somewhere up ahead. The Decoy would soon know the answer to an intriguing question.

His hire car of choice – the one that Charles, the Hertz man, had so carefully set aside for him – was a Toyota jeep. It was the perfect vehicle for his normal assignments, being a four-wheel drive, which could handle almost any kind of rough terrain relatively easily.

He turned off the track and bumped over the low scrubland towards a small copse of trees. He skirted around them until, looking back, he was satisfied that the jeep would be obscured from the view of anyone passing along the track. He parked, collected his equipment, and set off on foot in the direction of the sea. He could see the horizon and hear the distant rumble of waves but he could not see the water. He must be high up.

Within a few hundred yards he realised that he was on a cliff top. He dropped to his haunches and shuffled towards the edge. Below him was a tiny secluded cove where two men stood talking. They were almost a quarter of a mile away. To the naked eye the figures were small but his first glance answered the riddle he had come to Corsica to solve. One of the men was wearing a tangerine-coloured polo shirt.

The Decoy flopped on to his belly and propped himself up on his elbows. His left eye screwed shut and his right pressed lightly against the rubber rim of the sight. He adjusted the focus and Martin Casson's handsome face came sharply into view. Head and shoulders. The minister's temple was neatly positioned in the cross hairs.

The Decoy's aim was true. His hand was steady. He was good at this. This was his profession. He was on autopilot. Everything was happening automatically. His right index finger, the trigger finger, squeezed involuntarily backwards.

The motor drive on the camera whirred and the shutter clattered out a staccato tattoo as a dozen or more frames were captured in an instant. The evidence. For The Decoy's paymasters.

The two men below were too far away to hear anything. Balaam Abu Sharif was animated. His body language suggested agitation. He was gesturing aggressively. The minister stood impassively listening.

The Decoy was using a doubler lens to ensure the best quality of his images despite his distance from the subjects. He shifted his position and fired off several dozen shots of the pair, together and singly. There would be no doubt. Saddam Hussein's head of security was having a clandestine meeting with one of France's most trusted and highly placed ministers and both men had gone to considerable lengths to keep their meeting secret.

The late afternoon sun came darting from behind a cloud and glanced across the lens momentarily sending a flash of light into the cove below. The strength of the unexpected rays directly into his path of vision blinded The Decoy for an instant so that he didn't notice Martin Casson glance up in his direction.

The conversation between the two men continued for almost twenty minutes. Eventually they shook hands and parted.

The Decoy stayed where he lay. He had the evidence he had come for. He would give his two targets plenty of time to clear the area.

While he waited he occupied himself by photographing the birdlife. Various species of terns, gulls and cormorants were nesting on the cliff face opposite, perching on the rocks below, and diving for fish in the sea. The light was good and they made excellent subjects. He became so engrossed that he failed to notice stealthy footsteps approaching.

'I guessed it might be you...'

The Decoy leapt to his feet and spun round. Martin Casson stood, hands on hips, confronting him.

'I should have n-n-known. You. Of all people. Here. Today. When you should have been in P-P-Paris. I n-n-knew there was something wrong at the airport but I c-c-couldn't put my f-f-finger on it. I should have realised when you didn't use your m-m-mobile phone to call your office. You weren't going to c-c-call the office at all'.

There was a pause as the two men glared at one another.

The Decoy realised that he had never heard Casson stammer before. He'd been around the inner circles of French politics long enough to know most of the ministers' nicknames. He'd heard Casson called 'Le Begue' occasionally but could never understand why. Now he could recognise the origins of the soubriquet. The stutter must only come through in moments of stress.

'And n-n-now here you are, s-s-spying on me', said Casson. He spat the words out. 'How dare you? You d-d-don't understand the situation. Who sent you? Who are you working for?

There was a moment of realisation, of recognition. Something had dawned on the minister.

'Just a minute' he said. 'I have just realised who you really are. Y-y-you are a legend. "L'Appeau", right?'

The Decoy's mind was in turmoil. This was not supposed to happen. He had been identified. His operation was compromised. His role had always been simply to lure out the prey for others to deal with. They had never survived, not one of them, to recount his part in their demise.

'I suppose you're going to g-g-give me some bullshit about being on an assignment', scoffed Casson. 'A summer feature about p-p-politician's at play, perhaps? You were going to have me p-p-pose with the f-f-family for a nice portfolio of snaps depicting me with the wife and k-k-kids on holiday?'

The minister was smiling. With his mouth. Not with his eyes.

'Well, if you wanted to sh-sh-shoot me, you only had to ask'.

The Decoy felt the weight of the Beretta against his thigh. He reached in his pocket and slipped the safety catch off with his thumb.

The gun seemed to come out of his pocket in slow motion. He pulled the slide back with his left hand and pointed it unsteadily at the target. He squeezed the trigger with his right index finger. The trigger finger. There was nothing involuntary about the motion this time. His mind blotted out the sound.

The expression on the minister's face froze. He slumped on to his knees. His right arm stretched out as if appealing for alms. He toppled forward on to his face. He was grunting in short, sharp bursts of pathetic sound.

The Decoy stepped forward. Once more he drew the slide back with his left hand and held the muzzle of the pistol against the back of the minister's head.

The action seemed to trigger a reflex deep in the recesses of his subconscious. His unarmed combat training kicked in automatically. No need to waste a bullet.

He bent forward and, from behind the stricken man, hauled his torso upright by the shirt. In one swift motion his right arm lashed around Casson's neck placing his elbow beneath the chin while his left hand pressed against the back of the minister's head. Then a violent twist and an upward jerk. There was a sickening noise like the sound of a man breaking a raw cabbage in half with his bare hands. The grunting stopped.

There was silence. The waves were still crashing against the rocks below. A seagull mewed above.

The Decoy reached inside his camera bag and pulled out the chamois leather he used to clean his lenses. Carefully he wiped his fingerprints from the gun. He rolled the corpse over with his foot. A dark red stain was spreading across the tangerine-coloured polo shirt. He lifted the dead man's right arm, placed the pistol in his palm and closed his lifeless fingers around it.

He stepped back. Suicide? No. Not this time. Not with a hole in the middle of his chest and a broken neck.

It had been different with Beregovoy. Then his role was simply to lure the victim to the killing ground. Wait for the sniper to do his work then fire the dead man's gun once so that one slug was missing and place it in his lifeless hand to suggest that he had taken his own life.

This time he had a corpse to dispose of.

He dragged the body, feet first, to the edge of the cliff and looked over. He guessed he was about four hundred feet up. Some fifty feet to his right there seemed to be an inlet where the sea lapped tight against the cliff face. The water looked deep.

He dragged the body along the cliff top until he was in line with the inlet. He bent down to retrieve the gun. It was missing. He looked back towards his camera bag and spotted the pistol where it had slipped from the minister's hand.

He rolled the body to the edge. He was about to push it over when he was seized by a reality check. *What would happen if the minister's body were washed ashore?* He needed to make sure it did not float. At least not until the fish had been given time to destroy all the incriminating evidence.

He knelt down and began scrabbling in the dirt trying to gather enough handfuls of small stones and pebbles. When he thought he had enough he stuffed them into Casson's trouser pockets. But that would not be sufficient to do the job. He knew that. He looked around for a more substantial weight. There was a small rock half buried in the earth. It looked about the size of a man's head. That would do. It took several minutes of energetic rocking backwards and forwards before he could loosen the stone from its position. When it broke free The Decoy stood upright for a minute or two to get his breath back. He was sweating profusely.

He pulled the tangerine polo shirt over Casson's head and removed it from his body. Then he tied a firm knot at the neck and, treating the shirt like a makeshift sack, he rolled the rock inside and tied the waist end of the shirt in a double knot. Then he wrapped the shirt around the dead man's waist and tied the arms together in a double knot. Finally he looped the minister's belt, still attached to his trousers, through the loop in the sleeves of the shirt and re-buckled it. He tugged hard at the rock to make sure it was secure. It was.

Once more he dragged the body to the edge of the cliff and pushed it over. It rotated slowly three times in the air, like a springboard diver, before disappearing with a splash which The Decoy could see, but not hear, from his lofty vantage point.

311

He walked back to his camera bag, picked up the Beretta, wiped it once more, and bowled it over arm as far out towards the sea as he could. He looked over the edge. There was no sign of the minister's body. Just a cluster of green bubbles where it had entered the water.

He looked at his hands. They were bloodstained. Instinctively he went to wipe them on his trousers but stopped himself just in time. The sea was too far below and there was no time to wash them. He bent and wiped them on the grass and then rubbed them in the dirt.

He thought about Casson's car. It must be parked nearby. Perhaps he should drive it to the edge and push it over the cliff to destroy all evidence that the minister had even been there. Then it struck him that the keys would almost certainly have been in Casson's trouser pocket. Too late. The keys were in the sea.

He dusted the dirt from the knees of his jeans and picked up his camera. He looked around at the remoteness of the location. It was clumsy. He knew he had botched the job. But with any luck he had bought himself enough time to get back to Paris before the body was discovered.

Jean-Jacques Iversen had crossed the line.

The Decoy had become the hunter.

Chapter Twenty-Two

Charenton-du-Cher, France, 4th June 2000

Jean-Jacques Iversen was feeling restive. He paced back and forth across the kitchen clutching a mug of steaming coffee.

He had read the letter a dozen times. He picked it up again.

The printed heading announced that it came from the headquarters of the DCRG –the *Direction Centrale des Renseignements-Generaux* – France's equivalent of the British Special Branch. The political police.

The same phrases leapt out of the page at him. *"Strictly Private and Confidential", "Your client is required to submit himself for interview", "matters of national security", "relations between government of the Fifth Republic and a foreign power", "death of former Prime Minister...".*

He glanced at the covering letter from his lawyer. It told him that a new inquiry had been launched into alleged malpractice by the late President, Francois Mitterrand. The investigators had been given a wide-ranging brief to look into the suspicious deaths of several individuals involved in scandals associated with the former President including the alleged suicide of Pierre Beregovoy. Possible corruption relating to France's support for the Iraqi tyrant Saddam Hussein was also on the agenda.

Iversen sighed and looked out of the window. The Union flag fluttered proudly from a mast on the front lawn – a constant reminder of his Anglophile tendencies. *The British would not treat me this way,* he mused. *They would understand. They do understand.*

He looked around the spacious kitchen. Le Manoir de la Foret was his pride and joy. A large farmhouse built ten years earlier with the profits from chasing stars and Royals all over Europe.

He was normally an ebullient character but suddenly Jean-Jacques Iversen felt weary. *I could lose all of this*, he thought. *What can I tell them that they don't already know? What do I want to tell them that will not incriminate me?*

Lost in thought, he wandered through to his study. On his desk a copy of the newspaper *Le Figaro* lay open, as he had left it. He looked down almost wistfully at a picture of a blonde woman with scarlet trout-like pouting lips and unfeasibly large breasts, and began to read:

"Police investigating the death, two months ago, of Lolo Ferrari, the surgically enhanced singer, actress and television presenter best known as the woman with the biggest breasts in the world, are to formally question her husband Eric Vigne.

Ferrari, a former porn star, was found dead at the couple's home in Grasse on March 5th. An initial post mortem examination indicated that she had died of a drugs overdose but a new report by police scientists suggests that she may have been suffocated".

The article was accompanied by a series of glamour photographs with a caption, which read: *"The Final pose. Society photographer Jean-Jacques Iversen captured these stunning images of Lolo Ferrari just hours before her death when he visited her luxury Riviera home".*

'They must surely work out, and quickly, that it is no coincidence – the death of so many prominent people on the same day that I photographed them', he said out loud, not realising that he was talking to himself. 'I can't go through with this. I need protection. I have earned it'.

The killing of Martin Casson, which still haunted him, came rushing back to mind. A vivid image of the look on the dying man's face swam before his eyes. They couldn't pin that one on him, surely. But if they checked they must wonder why he was in Corsica on the same day that the politician disappeared.

As a photographer Iversen had always possessed the perfect cover for any activity he undertook on behalf of *Le Sanglier* and his boys. Actually de Champvieux had offered him the services of the DST's deep cover unit on more than one occasion. At the drop of a hat they could have concocted what the British would have called "legend" for him – an alibi to explain his presence in any given place at any given time. But he preferred to rely on a network of close friends to produce an alibi for him should the need arise. Being French they all assumed they were being asked to cover for some extra-marital sexual activity and imagined that, if they were ever called upon to swear that Jean-Jacques Iversen was with them when he was not, it would be to his wife that they were lying.

On Corsica, Iversen's resident false witness was his old friend Gilbert Becaud. On the fateful Sunday when Casson died, he had realised, once his breathing and heart-rate had returned to normal, that he was within an hour's drive of the legendary French singer's luxurious home at Calalonga just eight kilometres south-east of Bonifacio. A quick telephone call had secured Becaud's company for the evening and after shooting a set of relaxed pictures of the star in his home surroundings, the pair were soon sipping chilled drinks on the verandah and gazing across the Strait of Bonifacio at the twinkling lights of Sardinia.

Iversen had an alibi should he ever be asked about his movements at the time of Casson's disappearance. He'd even had time the following morning to return what he called 'the toys' to George Kastrinakis before flying back to Paris from Bastia in the north of the island. His tracks were well and truly covered.

In the event the police had come nowhere near him – or Becaud. Casson's car had been found, of course, but there had never been a body. The missing man's wife didn't seem overly concerned at his disappearance. She spoke bitterly about another woman and financial difficulties. It looked very much like a deliberate attempt to escape from domestic strife.

Besides, the newspapers had been full of the death of Princess Diana for weeks. The disappearance of a junior minister warranted very little coverage by comparison so there was no impetus for the police to pursue the case with the same vigour as they might have done had there been a public hue and cry over the matter. But he knew the file was still open. The authorities were still investigating.

The telephone rang. Iversen jumped.

The voice on the other end was familiar. Calm. Unhurried. Assertive. They spoke in code. There would be another phone call in precisely half an hour. Jean-Jacques Iversen felt reassured.

His wife, Marguerite, an elegant woman in her forties put her head around the door. 'Will you be in for dinner tonight?', she asked.

'What?', replied her husband absently, 'oh, no, I've got to go away on a job for a couple of days. I'll call you'.

Marguerite shrugged and withdrew. She had learned over the years not to ask questions and to keep her own counsel.

Iversen began busying himself by collecting together a number of digital discs containing specific photographs, which his earlier caller had requested.

When the appointed time came he was ready for the second call. This time there were specific instructions. He made a mental note. Everything made perfect sense to him except for the order to purchase a can of petrol.

But Jean-Jacques Iversen had been a military man. He was used to obeying orders without question.

Then it came to him. Perhaps the petrol was needed to destroy something. Set fire to it. Incriminating discs perhaps? Yes. That would be it.

He picked up the discs and his camera bag, made a show of calling a cheery farewell to his wife, and left the house, pausing only to glance admiringly at the Union Jack as he sped away in his powerful Mercedes.

Epilogue

CIA Headquarters, Langley, Virginia 6th September 2000

The metal toecaps on Greg's highly-polished shoes clicked and clacked in military rhythm on the black and white marble of the Central Intelligence Agency seal inlaid into the floor as he strode across the lobby to meet his guest.

Hand warmly outstretched he was all smiles and bonhomie but Christopher sensed there was an extra agenda beneath what he had come to recognise as a thin veneer of friendship.

'Hey, Chris, good to see you. How ya doin? You're looking great. I hope you're hungry. We got some fantastic steaks and the chef char grills them just the way you like 'em'. The greeting came pouring out in an uninterrupted stream of charm.

Christopher had not intended to mix business with pleasure on this trip but CIA hospitality was legendary and the cafeteria at their headquarters eight miles outside Washington DC had a reputation as something of a gastronomic Mecca. So when his old sparring partner called and invited him to lunch he accepted readily enough, though he had a strong premonition that he would be expected to sing for his supper.

'Say, if you gotta second before we eat I got something to show you that I figure you'll be real interested in', said Greg.

'Sure, why not', said Christopher. 'Lead on'.

His companion chattered aimlessly about the weather and the 1950's architecture of the headquarters building as they

318

strolled across the gardens to the New Headquarters building. Passing through the impressive glass-encased atrium they took the lift to the fifth floor then along an anonymous corridor and into a small conference room.

Christopher realised immediately that the room had been set up in anticipation of his arrival. The windows were blacked out, the lighting was low – ultra violet he assumed – and a small electronic screen at the end of the long table bore a coloured version of the CIA seal which was flickering and distorting as though the equipment had been switched on too long and was over heating.

'Take a seat', said Greg, gesturing towards a leather-upholstered armchair at the head of the table. Christopher sat and his host drew up a chair alongside him. He leant forward and began to tap at the keyboard of a laptop computer, which showed the same flickering image of the seal on its screen.

'Tell me what you make of this', said Greg as the picture on the screen cross-faded to an aerial photograph. It was a picture of the Mediterranean taken from space. The outline of Spain and Italy were unmistakeable.

Two more taps of the keyboard, two more cross-fades and the southern coast of France began to emerge as the focus of attention. Christopher shifted in his seat. He had an inkling of what might be coming next. Neither man spoke.

Christopher was familiar with satellite photography and had always admired the sophistication of the American spy satellites. For years the United States Geological Survey had been releasing, on the Internet, so-called declassified intelligence pictures taken by orbiting NASA space stations for the enjoyment of geeks and espionage freaks the world over. But these pictures showed buildings, roads and rivers at best.

Christopher knew the spy satellites were better than that. He had seen an American Drugs Enforcement Agency picture, taken from space, which showed members of a South American drug cartel transferring a consignment of cocaine from a truck to a car on a remote Colombian road. He had even heard a rumour that car index numbers could be read from space.

The slow zoom continued. As the Mediterranean Sea disappeared from view and the camera began to focus on the land the cross fade gave way to a series of jerky freeze-frame pictures. The digital equipment was loading the zoom frame by frame.

Christopher noticed a date in the bottom right-hand corner of the screen. "06-04-00" it read. Still neither man spoke.

Eventually the screen was filled with an aerial shot of farmland. The tones were predominantly greys, mauves, and blues. There were no shadows. It was after sunset. Dusk was setting in but the detail was remarkably clear.

Much of the frame was taken up with a field through which some sort of track seemed to traverse from the bottom left to top right of the frame. The right half of the picture showed a forested area. The legend at the bottom of the screen now read: "Millau, France -20.48 – 06-04-00".

At the next zoom Christopher could make out two vehicles in the field just off the track and close to the edge of the forested area. Greg tapped his keyboard. The definition in the picture, which took shape on the screen, was a little fuzzy in parts. But the vehicles could be clearly seen. One was a saloon of some kind. The other was a larger, dark-coloured four-wheeled drive. There were four indistinct figures in the picture. One stood at the rear of the four-wheeled drive facing away from the vehicles and apparently looking across the field out of the frame to the left. The other three stood close together between the vehicles. One figure appeared to be being held by the other two, one of whom held one hand up to the side of the captive's head, while the other seemed to be holding the arms of the captive.

Christopher did not need a commentary. He noticed that the index numbers on the vehicles were not legible.

Greg tapped again. The vehicles and the figures were gone. It was now after dark. The field had taken on a steel-grey hue and the forested area was a solid mass of indigo but near the edge of it there was an intense red, white, and yellow splash – like the spark from an arc-welders torch. Christopher could tell it was a fire. The legend read: "Millau, France – 21.19 – 06-04-00".

'It took me a long time to figure out who would need to eliminate "The Decoy"', said Greg after a long silence. 'Still longer to figure out why'.

Christopher said nothing.

'I guess the French would be the most obvious, but he was their asset'.

'And yours', snapped Christopher.

'And yours, too, I believe', went on Greg. He paused and looked Christopher in the eye.

'Iversen was compromised in Corsica, right?'

No response.

'But why wait almost three years to terminate him?

'Then I remembered that the *Direction Centrale des Renseignements Generaux* – the French FBI if you will – had just begun to take another close look at our friend on a number of issues. So who would need to shut his mouth before he became indiscreet?

'Then I worked it out.

'We know that Iversen was in the frame for the elimination of Beregovoy – at least he was carrying out his decoy role on the day and would certainly know which side paid him for the job. It was always assumed that poor old Bere was removed to save Mitterrand's skin over France's secret involvement in Saddam's ballistic missile programme.

'But what if a foreign power – lets say the Brits - who knew of Mitterrand's culpability, was putting the squeeze on Monsieur le President - blackmailing him if you will – to dance to their tune in Europe? Having got rid of Beregovoy so that he didn't blurt out the truth and ruin their nice little plan, they would have to make sure that the deal wasn't made public years later by Mr Iversen'.

Christopher had listened impassively but was showing signs of impatience. 'Look old man I fail to see what any of this has got to do with…'

He was cut short by a gesture from Greg who tossed a sheaf of paper across the table at him. He recognised it instantly. It was a printout of mobile telephone messages. Christopher was familiar with these documents. Sometimes they were obtained under court order from the mobile telephone service providers. More usually they had been provided to his department by the division responsible for electronic intercepts. Either way he knew that the fruits of this kind of eavesdropping usually meant many hours of painstaking reading – sifting through a mass of trivial, banal telephone conversations searching for evidence of terrorist conspiracy or anti-British political activity.

In this case the work had been done for him. Halfway down the page an entry had been circled with a pink highlighter pen.

The date and time read: "June 4 2000, 21.21". Christopher did not recognise the telephone number of the sending mobile but he knew the number of the receiving mobile. It was his own. It was the one he had been using on operations in mainland Europe for several years. He did not need to read the

322

transcript message. He knew it would consist of just one word.

'Nemesis, huh?', said Greg. Christopher looked at him blankly.

Greg winked. 'Lunch?', he asked.

CHESTER STERN has been a writer and broadcaster on crime and police matters for more than forty-five years. A former head of the Press Bureau at Scotland Yard, he has lectured extensively on terrorism and the media in Britain, Europe and the USA.

He was Chief Crime Correspondent for *The Mail on Sunday* for nineteen years and is past President of the Crime Reporters' Association.

In 2001 he became Corporate Affairs Director for Fulham Football Club and Controller of Public Affairs for Harrods, acting as media adviser to Mohamed Al Fayed and advising on the investigation into the death of Diana, Princess of Wales.

He has published two true crime books: *Dr Iain West's Casebook* – the investigations of Britain's leading forensic pathologist, and *The Black Widow* – the story of Linda Calvey, the UK's most notorious female gangster, (written in collaboration with Kate Kray, widow of Ronnie Kray). He has also written two other works of fiction – a terrorism thriller based in South Africa called *Code Zulu,* and a murder mystery detective novel based in the newspaper world of Fleet Street called *The Green-Inker*.

Since the early seventies, he has been a sportswriter and broadcaster on football, rugby and golf for the *BBC, The Sunday Telegraph, The Mail on Sunday* and the *Sunday Mirror*.

Acknowledgements:

Cover design: David Naylor

Legal advice: Tom Crone

By the same author: ***Code Zulu***

The Green-Inker